"*Worse Than Death* is a sexy, supernatural whodunit; Gottlieb's vampires are compellingly original, with compellingly human problems. One wild, fast-paced ride . . . "
—Jeanne Kalogridis

"Gottlieb is at her best when she chronicles Jace and Risha's vampirism and the intersection of their domain with the human world. . . . Insatiable fans of fanged creatures will likely appreciate the tale." —*Publishers Weekly*

"Sherry Gottlieb's *Worse Than Death* is one hell of a sexy, funny, exciting read. Miss this wonderful novel and you'll be kicking yourself into the next life." —Pat LoBrutto

"A sex-heavy vampire thriller with an L.A.-noir detective-story framework and a triple dose of cunnilingus, fellatio, and nipple pinching that actually drives the plot."—*Kirkus*

ALSO BY SHERRY GOTTLIEB

Hell No, We Won't Go!
Resisting the Draft During the Vietnam War
(1991)

Love Bite
(1994)

WORSE
Than Death

SHERRY GOTTLIEB

TOR®

A TOM DOHERTY ASSOCIATES BOOK
NEW YORK

This is a work of fiction. All characters and events portrayed in this book are either products of the author's imagination or are used fictitiously.

WORSE THAN DEATH

Copyright © 2000 by Sherry Gottlieb

Edited by David G. Hartwell

A Tor Book
Published by Tom Doherty Associates, LLC
175 Fifth Avenue
New York, NY 10010

www.tor.com

Tor® is a registered trademark of Tom Doherty Associates, LLC.

ISBN: 0-812-58963-7

First edition: January 2000
First mass market edition: June 2001

Printed in the United States of America

0 9 8 7 6 5 4 3 2 1

ACKNOWLEDGMENTS

The writing of this novel required a more-than-passing acquaintance with several subjects not in my experience. To the experts who helped me to understand, I am grateful:

Leslie Gates
Jeanne Kalogridis
Dr. Sol Kaplan
Elliott Ireland Moorhead
Dr. Michael Perry
Lee Troxler
Joseph Valentinetti
Janice Van Bever
Dennis Whitlow

Thank you, also, to David Hartwell and Tom Doherty, my editor and my publisher; and, as always, love and thanks to my guardian agent, Sandra Watt.

1

Lieutenant Schrank picked up the gun and took a step toward the corpse in the middle of the playground.

"Don't you touch him," Maria screamed as she protected her lover's body.

The cop froze, pity playing across his grizzled face, then he stepped back.

Maria looked entreatingly at the group closest to her, silently asking them to help her. The Sharks looked everywhere but at Maria; no one moved. She swiveled to look at the Jets, Tony's friends. Finally, Action took a step toward Tony's prone body; two others followed.

"Te adoro, Anton," whispered Maria.

As the three Jets struggled to lift Tony, one arm slid off his chest; two Sharks jumped in to be additional pallbearers.

As the star-crossed lover was carried away by members of both gangs, Jace heard Risha sniffling. He'd never seen her cry before. He put his arm around her and smiled.

"Don't tell me you've never seen *West Side Story* before?"

"Only about a dozen times." Risha laughed. "And it makes me cry every time. You think this is bad, wait 'til you watch *Camille* with me."

The end credits began. Jace hit the remote and the TV screen went blank. "Let's go out. I could kill for a hot pastrami and a couple beers." He pulled Risha up off the couch.

"I could do with a bite myself. I'll get the raincoats."

They'd returned to Los Angeles two weeks earlier, and it had been raining ever since, quite a contrast to the drought-stricken city they'd left nearly a year before. The saturated landscape was not the only change—after Jace and Risha left for Europe, much of L.A. had burned in the spring riots; Jace's former boss, L.A. Police Chief Darryl Gates, had finally been ousted; and a Democrat had been elected president for only the second time since Jace was old enough to vote.

The streets were nearly empty, even though it was before midnight on a Friday; people in L.A. didn't like to go out in the rain, perhaps unsure of what it was, which was just as well, because Angelenos were notorious for driving poorly on wet streets.

Jace braked the BMW to a stop as a light changed to red. Risha took out a Grateful Dead CD and was about to slide it into the player when they were jarred by the impact of another car rear-ending theirs.

Jace leapt out of the car, yelling, "You stupid ass—" even before he'd looked at who rammed them.

They were already out of their car, a beat-up puce Oldsmobuick on its third 100,000 miles: two young black punks. One pointed a shotgun through the passenger window at Risha, the other shoved the barrel of his handgun against Jace's head.

"Chill, motherfucker, and mebbe we'll let you live," Handgun snarled at Jace as he stole his wallet and watch.

"Keys in the car, my man, let's go," Shotgun yelled to his partner as he got in next to Risha.

Handgun swung his pistol hard and Jace felt his head explode. The last thing he saw was Risha's face in the passenger window as the carjackers sped off with both vehicles.

Even though she was looking back at Jace in concern, she was smiling.

Lamar floored the gas pedal and the BMW slid across all four wet lanes of the Santa Monica Freeway to the Overland exit in Culver City, while his partner's car continued east.

He turned at a driveway and parked the BMW in the lot behind a closed warehouse; when he turned off the ignition, the windows were immediately obscured by the pounding rain of a fresh cloudburst. He pulled out his blade and held it at the left side of the bitch's neck, daring her to attempt escape. The drop-off point was a mile away, but he planned to tear off some snatch before he deserted his hostage.

"Get your clothes off!"

She quickly obeyed and pulled off her sweater, revealing snow-white breasts unhampered by lingerie. Her nipples were erect; Lamar wondered if it was from the chill of the air . . . or because she was excited. Maybe this white cunt always dreamed of having a hung black stud fuck her. With the blade, he drew her auburn hair aside to see her face. She was smiling. Don't that beat all!

"You don't need a knife with me, sweetie," she crooned softly. Her full lips parted as she leaned toward him.

This was going to be easy as shit. Lamar squeezed her breast, the nipple hard as a bullet against his palm, as she trailed her tongue passionately around his ear. The switchblade forgotten in his right hand, he had only a second to wonder why her mouth was so cool when he felt a sharp stabbing at his neck. The pain immediately turned to pleasure as her venom rushed through his bloodstream, the best drug he'd ever had. Multicolor mandalas rotated in front of his eyes, and the very air vibrated with a hum that changed in intensity with his pounding pulse. The visual, auditory, and tactile hallucinations floated him from consciousness without his being aware of it. His spontaneous orgasm was the last thing Lamar ever felt.

Jace was grateful that the bus bench was enclosed. He had a splitting headache, centered under the painful lump on the left side of his head, but at least he wasn't getting any wetter. Of course, he'd gotten pretty well soaked lying by the side of the road for however long he'd been out, and he was getting really cold. All he needed was a concussion *and* pneumonia.

He looked at his watch—or where the watch used to be. His left wrist was bare, reminding him he'd been robbed before he was hit. His left hand was jerking to its own beat; Jace put it in his pocket, preferring to believe the shaking was a side effect of the blow he'd suffered than another confirming sign of his looming mortality.

He checked the bank clock across the street—one-thirty. He decided to catch the next bus home—if they hadn't stopped running. He had just patted his jeans pockets to check for change—the RTD was strict about exact change—when Risha drove up in the Beamer.

"You look like a man with a headache," she said sympathetically. She handed him a bag containing a bottle of Advil and a Perrier as he got in. "Are you OK, honey?"

"As well as can be expected after you go gallivanting off with carjackers, leaving me lying pistol-whipped on the street in the rain." He kissed her, then pried open the bottle and shook out four tablets. "Did you get them?"

"Just one. The one with your wallet took another route, sorry." She made a U-turn. "Should I take you to an emergency room?"

Although Jace knew that explanations to outsiders would be risky, he was touched that she was worried enough about him to put that aside.

"No, thanks—I've got The Mother of All Headaches, but I'll live. Where did you leave him?"

"Some parking lot in Culver City. No one saw me. I slashed his neck with his knife before I left. His shotgun's in the trunk. So, should we go straight home?"

"Hey, just because you got to eat doesn't mean I'm not still hungry." He looked down at his wet blood- and mud-spattered clothes. "I can't go anywhere like this. Let's swing by Zucky's and you can get me pastrami and beer to go." He grinned, even though it caused his head to throb. "Then we can go home and you can atone for abandoning me."

"Fuck you," Risha said fondly.

"Exactly what I had in mind, my love."

Jace Levy had no more intention of returning to detective work than he had of falling in love with a vampire, but his life seemed never to work out quite the way he'd planned.

Of course, his retirement at forty-two hadn't been completely voluntary; he'd really had no other choice. Even as one of the LAPD's top homicide detectives, he would have been put out to pasture the moment he said he'd solved the serial murders he'd been investigating—no one would think twice about committing him if he'd announced that the killer was a real vampire. Just as Risha probably wouldn't give a second thought to murdering him if he betrayed her. Love was dangerous, Jace reflected, possibly one of the reasons he'd avoided it so long.

Avoidance was one of Jace's strongest traits. He ignored all the signs that he had inherited Huntington's chorea, his mother's fatal genetic disease—in fact, he hadn't mentioned it yet to Risha, though they'd been living together for over a year. If she thought anything about his occasional memory lapses, or the periodic weakness in his knees and shaking hands, she never mentioned it. The only person he'd ever told was his ex-partner, Liz Robinson, in a moment of vulnerability he only half regretted. He'd eventually cited the disease as the reason for his retirement from the force; Liz understood his reluctance to discuss it, and had accepted the excuse without question.

Jace hadn't expected to return to L.A. so soon, but Risha's photo-essays in *City of Angels* magazine had gained her a modicum of fame, generating the show she was about to open at the Moss-Erlich Gallery in Beverly Hills, and a commission from the magazine to do an additional series. Risha's excitement over the accolades was infectious, so he'd agreed to a six-month stay in L.A., but he was already climbing the walls with boredom. Two weeks of rain hadn't helped.

So when the balding movie producer pulled him aside at a *City of Angels* cocktail party, Jace was more than willing to listen to whatever he had to say—no small concession, since Robert Brandon had just been holding forth on the immorality of Hollywood cinema, pompously proclaiming that his production company was the last family-film bastion, now that Disney had ventured into sin.

"I hear that you're a detective. That right?" Brandon whispered, though there was no one in earshot. His right eye twitched behind horn-rimmed glasses.

"I used to be," Jace answered in a normal tone of voice. He might be willing to listen to this guy, but he wasn't going to play games with him. "I retired from the LAPD a little over a year ago. You wanna do a movie about my experiences? I can't guarantee a G-rating . . ."

Brandon looked about nervously. He whispered, "I need to hire a detective . . . a little private investigation. I can't talk about it here." He pulled an ivory-linen business card out of his tweed jacket's pocket and handed it to Jace. "Come see me at my office on Monday, will you?" He squeezed his eyes shut twice and the twitching stopped.

Jace looked at the card. Brandon's production company was called Right Path Films, located on Second Street in downtown Santa Monica.

Jace began to demur, "Look, Mr. Brandon, I don't—"

"Please! It's very important to me; I'll pay you twice your usual fee! I need—"

Brandon's face fell as a plain woman broke from the crowd and headed toward them with a smile. "Anytime Monday," he added in a rushed whisper to Jace before turning toward the woman.

"Robbie, it's after ten—the baby-sitter has to be home by eleven," the woman told her husband. "Hello, I don't think we've met," she said to Jace, putting out a plump hand, "I'm Diane Brandon."

"Jace Levy."

"Mr. Levine was just telling me how much he and his family enjoyed *Little Cabin on Sugar Ridge*, dear," Brandon said as he took his wife's arm. "It's good Christians like you who keep us making movies, sir. Good talking to you."

He moved his wife rapidly toward the door, turning back with a brief glance of entreaty at the Jewish ex-cop before they left.

"I think you ought to check it out," Risha said that night. "It'll give you something to do when I'm out shooting or feeding. Maybe it'll even be an interesting case."

She reached over him to the bedside table for a joint and a lighter, trailing her nipples softly across his bare chest on the way. He slid down and caught one nipple between his lips as she drew back to her side of the bed, tonguing it quickly before it escaped his mouth.

"I've got an interesting case right here," he grinned, grabbing his cock.

"Don't you ever get tired?" Risha lit up the joint, inhaled deeply, and handed it to him. Holding her hit, she said, "So what do you think?"

Jace took a drag and shrugged, miming an inability to talk.

Risha finally exhaled when he did—no one can hold a hit as long as a vampire; they have to breathe only once or twice an hour—then repeated, "What do you think?"

"I think you're a swell broad, and I love you very much," he responded. "Now, will you put out before I get blue balls?"

Risha laughed, her pale eyes sparkling in the golden lamplight. "Not your color, huh? OK, stud, once more into the breach, but don't complain to me if your knees are weak tomorrow."

The lobby of Right Path Films was a study in browns. The Early American furniture was upholstered in beige corduroy; the walls alternated wood paneling with tan pebbled wall fabric displaying wood-framed one-sheets of several Right Path releases. Jace recognized *Little Cabin on Sugar Ridge* as the movie Brandon had mentioned Friday night, but none of the other titles was even faintly familiar to him. Of course, Jace hadn't seen any G-rated movies in decades, except for *Beauty and the Beast*, but he suspected that Right Path wasn't the mover and shaker in the industry that Robert Brandon wanted it to be.

"Mr. Brandon can see you now, Mr. Levy," the brown-haired, brown-clad receptionist announced, getting up. "Please follow me."

Brandon's office carried on with the Early American decor, but with more color . . . red, white, and blue. Jace looked in vain for the American eagle he was sure must be there. The wood credenza behind Brandon's desk held framed family photographs—his wife, Diane, with two boys about five or six years old; a more recent photo that showed the Brandons and a little girl about two, with the same boys at nine and ten, and a Labrador; another of a man and woman in their early sixties on a tropical beach somewhere—Brandon's parents, Jace guessed. Above the credenza were two larger framed pictures—George Bush and Billy Graham. Jace wondered if Brandon would change Bush's photo to one of Bill Clinton after the inauguration on Wednesday. Somehow, he doubted the Democrat would secure the same adulation here as his predecessor.

"No interruptions, Kathy," Brandon dismissed the brown lady before offering Jace a chair.

"Jake Levy, is it?"

"Jace, Mr. Brandon, with a soft C, short for Jacob." For some reason, Jace, a lifelong atheist, felt very Jewish in this office—and proud of it.

"Before I tell you the problem, Jace, I need your solemn word that what we discuss here goes no further. You will talk only to me about this, and only when there is no one else around. Understood?"

Jace crossed his heart, then raised his right hand in the Boy Scout salute. Robert Brandon didn't look amused. He stared through his glasses at Jace, apparently trying to read the ex-detective's mind to see if he were really trustworthy. Eventually, he heaved a deep sigh and came to a decision.

"I'm having a little difficulty"—Brandon's right eye began to twitch—"with blackmailers. It's cost me ten thousand dollars so far, and it doesn't look like they're going to stop at that."

"Not as long as the hen's laying eggs." Jace shrugged. "What have they got on you?"

Brandon's tic increased in frequency. "A videotape. I don't think it's necessary for you to know the contents, but obviously they can easily make copies, so getting it back wouldn't necessarily stop them." He squeezed his eyes shut twice, and the twitch disappeared.

Jace pushed out the flood of mental images: the balding Brandon with a male hooker, an underage girl, Mary's Little Lamb. "What do you want me to do, Mr. Brandon?"

"That's up to you, Lehman; I just want it stopped." He took off his glasses and polished them with a cloth from his desk. "Do whatever's necessary, but don't get me involved." He put his glasses back on. "It's very important that I not be involved," he reiterated.

"I'm not a hit man, but I might be able to persuade them that their best interests will not be served by continuing to press you. Do you know them?"

"Not exactly." The twitch started up again. "It may be actors I've met."

"Actors? Could you be more specific?" Jace watched the tic keep beat with unheard music; he thought it might be a Strauss march.

"I . . . no. It's just that the limited number of people who had an opportunity to get the tape were all . . . actresses. But it was a man who contacted me."

"I see." Jace didn't, but it seemed the right thing to say. He decided to try another track. "Why don't you start with the original contact—how did that occur?"

"I received a call about three months ago, on my private line, here at the office. A man told me he had a video that he would make public if I didn't pay. He described the contents of the tape accurately enough for me to know it was real."

"Who has your private number?" Jace asked.

"Half the film industry, Jack," Brandon smiled ruefully.

"OK, go on."

"He told me to get five thousand dollars in cash, and to bring it to the pay phone at the McDonald's down the street at two-thirty two days later, and answer the phone when it rang. When I did that, I was told to go to the Odeon around the corner"—Brandon gestured vaguely in the direction of the Third Street Promenade a block east—"and watch a movie until I was contacted."

"So you saw the man then?"

Brandon shook his head. "No. He said to give the money to anyone who said 'movie magic' to me. After I'd been there maybe five minutes, a woman said 'movie magic,' so I gave her the envelope." The tic had changed to rap tempo; Brandon did his squeezing trick to stop it.

"Did you recognize her?"

"No. She was a Negro—old, short, and fat, looked like someone's nanny. After I paid her, she told me to go into the men's room and count to two hundred—when I came out, she was gone."

"Earlier you said ten thousand dollars. How did the other five come in?"

"The same man called again a month later. He wanted more money. This time, I was to go to the Pier."

The Santa Monica Pier was a block in the other direction. Brandon's extortionists were keeping it in his neighborhood.

"And did the same woman pick up the cash?"

"That time it was a Mexican boy, about fourteen. I tried to grab him, but the little beaner ran like molasses in July."

"This isn't much to go on, Mr. Brandon," Jace pointed out. "How about giving me a list of people who had access to the video?"

"I'd rather not."

Jace stood up. "I'm sorry, but I don't know what I can do with the little information you gave me. If you call the police, they might arrange for a tap on your phone in case the blackmailer—"

"Wait. I have a way." Brandon motioned Jace back into his chair, waiting until he sat before continuing. "It's been almost a month since the last contact. If he plans more blackmail, he'll probably contact me again any day now. You can follow me, see who makes the pickup, and tail them to the blackmailer."

Jace must have looked dubious, because the producer reached into his desk and passed over an envelope.

"Here's two thousand dollars retainer. You can bill me for double your usual fee and any expenses. If you stop the problem, there'll be another eight grand. Not bad for maybe a week's work."

Jace opened the envelope; it contained a stack of crisp hundred-dollar bills.

"The next blackmail payment comes out of your bonus, Levine—if you don't catch the blackmailer until after the money disappears, you'll only get three thousand more. Call it incentive."

"OK, Mr. Brandon, we'll play it your way until the next contact. I'll need to get a beeper or a mobile phone—I'll call you with the number tonight."

"No need. Kathy will give you one when you leave. Is there anything else?"

Jace shrugged. "I guess not." He got up and went to the door, then turned back. "One thing: My name's Jace Levy, Jacob Simon Levy. If you can't remember any of it correctly, just use Jew-Boy."

2

It was just after dark when Jace got in, his arms filled. He dumped the bag of novels on the living-room couch and went into the kitchen in search of a vase for the cymbidiums he'd bought for Risha.

Elliott was making a tuna-fish sandwich—as far as Jace could tell, it was all he ever ate. A short, bespectacled man with a fringe of gray hair, Elliott was Risha's darkroom assistant and loyal factotum; he'd been taking care of her for over twenty years.

"Good evening, Detective."

Elliott seldom used Jace's name, preferring his former title; Jace expected it was a holdover from Gregor's reign—Risha's late ex had always been addressed as "Baron."

"Hey, Elliott—*que pasa?*" Jace opened a cabinet.

"I was at the gallery all day, setting up Risha's exhibit. It's a very nice space. Can I help you find something?"

Jace closed the cabinet and opened the next one. "Do we have any vases?"

"Certainly."

Elliott put down his spatula and went into the study, returning with a graceful thin, black, vase. "Will this do?"

"Perfect." Jace ran water in the vase and removed the orchid spray from its water-filled test tube. "Is Risha up yet?"

"I think she's still in the bath; she hasn't called me to do her makeup yet." Another of Elliott's many skills—Risha found it difficult to put on makeup as she cast no reflection in mirrors. "She's due at the gallery at eight to check placement," he added.

"I'll remind her."

Jace got a Harp lager out of the refrigerator, opened it, and took it upstairs with the flowers.

He found Risha soaking in a bubble bath, working on a crossword puzzle. He leaned in to kiss her. "Hi, beautiful."

"Hi, handsome. What's a six-letter word for 'subordinate ruler'?"

"What have you got so far?" He leaned over her shoulder to look, inhaling the delicate scent of Ombre Rose.

"Starts with *S* and ends with *P*—and the second letter might be an *A*."

"Try S-A-T-R-A-P," Jace suggested.

Risha added the missing letters. "Right! You're soooo literate!" She turned on an exaggeratedly fawning smile and batted her lashes.

"Why shucks, ma'am—t'wernt nothin'." Jace scuffed one foot and looked down bashfully. "These are for you."

"Oh, Jace, they're exquisite! What's the occasion?"

"I got a down payment on the job for Robert Brandon."

He put the vase down on the sink, then perched on the side of the tub. He offered her his beer, but she shook her head.

"So you took it?"

Risha pulled the plug. When she stood up, Jace handed her a towel, admiring the way the light played against her wet ivory skin.

"Before I get too distracted, I told Elliott I'd remind you you're due at the gallery at eight."

"I didn't forget. It shouldn't take more than an hour—you want to come?"

"Why not?" He followed Risha back into the bedroom, and told her about his meeting with Brandon while she dressed.

"So you can't do anything until the blackmailer contacts him again?" She put on a jade cashmere sweater over matching slacks.

Jace shrugged. "That's the way he wants to play it." He pulled the compact cell phone out of his pocket. "I carry this at all times, and when he calls, I drop everything and try to save his money. Pays well if it works, though."

Risha held up two pairs of earrings at Jace. He pointed to the black pearls. They contrasted well with her nearly colorless eyes. She put them on, and they promptly disappeared under her dark auburn hair.

"I'll have Elliott braid my hair back before we go." She pulled Jace up off the bed and they headed downstairs. "What do you think Brandon's being blackmailed over?"

At the bottom of the stairs, Jace turned right, toward the kitchen, for another beer, while Risha turned left into the living room to put a CD in the player. They met in the study, less than a minute later, as the Jefferson Airplane's *Surrealistic Pillow* began playing. Ninety percent of their CDs were music from the hippie era; most of the more recent ones were Jace's.

"I've been thinking about that," he said as if there had been no interruption. "It's probably some sexual pecadillo. He's too straight to be involved in serious drugs, and gambling debts don't usually lead to extortion. If he's involved with anything violent like homicide, he wouldn't use me to get someone off his back."

"It'd have to be pretty kinky sex to be blackmailable in this town," Risha observed with a smile.

"Not if you're the only God-fearing family movie producer in the industry. Look what just playing around with bimbos did to Jim Bakker and Jimmy Swaggart.

What is it with these superrighteous types? 'Do as I say, not as I do'?"

"People's morals bend to fit their desires. You smoked grass when you were a cop," she pointed out. "Look at me. If you'd told me twenty-five years ago that I'd be killing people for food two or three times a week, I'd have died first! Well, actually, I did die first . . ." She laughed. "Anyway, it doesn't surprise me that Brandon is involved in—what did you call it? Sexual pecadillos?"

Elliott came in with two photographic prints to show Risha. One was the first of her photos to run in *City of Angels*, under the heading "After Midnight in the City of Angels"; it showed burly men loading sides of beef into a refrigerated truck at a meatpacking plant. The other was the photograph that had originally led Jace to meet Risha in the course of a murder investigation: she'd taken a picture of Teece Cabot at a cowboy bar, hours before he was killed. Jace had already fallen in love with her when he discovered that she had been Cabot's killer.

"There's room left for only one of these," Elliott said. "If you'll choose now, I can get it framed before you leave tonight so you can take it with you."

"That one," Jace and Risha said simultaneously, pointing to the meat picture. They laughed, having agreed there was no reason to call public attention to their connection with an unsolved murder, even though it was nearly eighteen months cold.

Elliott left with the photographs.

"Do you regret leaving the force for me?" Risha asked suddenly.

"Sure—that's why I brought you flowers. Expensive, out-of-season flowers, I might add."

She smiled. "I'm serious, Jace. I mean, you gave up your whole career . . ."

"Yeah, but for eternal life with the woman I love. Not a bad trade, from where I sit." He kissed her. "Why suddenly so insecure, Rish?"

"I guess it was those carjackers the other night." She sighed. "They could have killed you. Once you cross over, I don't have to worry about losing you . . . to murder, at least," she added, in subtle reference to her ex's death. "So I was wondering if you hadn't done it yet because—"

Jace put a finger on her lips. "Not because of you, Rish. It's me. It's a big commitment, the biggest I'll ever make, and I'm just not ready yet. But that doesn't mean I don't love you, or that I'm sorry I'm with you. I promise I won't let anyone kill me but you, okay?"

"But—" She stopped, seeing the futility of continuing the discussion. She stood. "I'm going to get Elliott to do my hair and paint my face." She headed for the door, then turned back to face him. "I don't want to pressure you, Jace—I just don't want to lose you." She left without waiting for a response.

Two mornings later, Robert Brandon called while Jace was watching the inauguration with Elliott.

"Can you talk?"

Jace got up and carried the phone into the study. "Sure, go ahead."

"He just called—"

"During the inauguration? How rude."

Brandon ignored the comment. "He told me to bring five grand at two this afternoon."

"Where?"

"I'm supposed to wait at the same pay phone for further instructions."

Jace scratched his stubbled cheek. "You got the cash?"

"I'll get it out of my bank—it's just down the street."

"Okay, get the bread, make the drop like he tells you. I'll be there."

"How will you know where to go? I'll probably have to go straight from the pay phone, and he might be watching—he'll see if you approach me."

"Take a matchbook and a pencil to the phone booth

with you. Write down the drop locale on the inside of the matchbook while you're on the phone and drop it on the ground before you walk away. I'll get it after you've left. If it's nearby again, walk slowly, stall a bit so I can get there before they make contact. Otherwise, take a few moments to warm up your car before you drive; I'll have my car ready. You might not see me, but I'll be there; if you do see me, don't make eye contact."

"How will you know who to follow?"

"You'll give me a sign as soon as you make the pass." Jace thought for a second, discarding the Burnett earlobe tug as being too obvious. "You wearing a suit?"

"Navy blazer and gray slacks."

"Good enough. Wear the blazer open. As soon as you hand over the cash, button it. Then don't wait around. Go back to your office, or whatever you'd normally do then. I'll report to you as soon as I can."

Jace broke the connection and went back into the living room. George and Barbara Bush were waving goodbye from the steps of a helicopter. *Good riddance*, Jace thought.

"Hey, Elliott, want to help me with a surveillance this afternoon?"

"Me? Really?" Elliott smiled, a rare sight. "What do I have to do?"

"Hopefully not much. I may need quick access to the car in downtown Santa Monica, and I don't want to waste time getting out of one of the lots. I need you to be strategically placed in a loading zone with the engine running, so we can tail a suspect."

"We're going to follow someone? Then we should take the BMW instead of my Honda."

"OK with me, but this isn't going to be a high-speed chase. If the suspect makes our tail, the game's over."

The drop-off instructions read, "Walk 2nd floor S.M. Place." Santa Monica Place was the three-story indoor mall at the foot of the Third Street Promenade, the three-block outdoor mall. Downtown Santa Monica had undergone urban renewal a few years earlier, and was now lousy with stores and people. Jace positioned Elliott in the BMW near the Place's parking structure exit on Colorado Avenue, one of the few two-way streets in the neighborhood, before he trotted upstairs.

It didn't take him long to locate Brandon walking stiffly past the Mad Hatter, even though the mall was fairly heavily trafficked with January sale shoppers. Jace kept an eye on him from across the way. He saw a teenage girl bump into Brandon and say something, but when she moved on, the producer's jacket was still unbuttoned.

Brandon reached the Broadway, at the eastern end of the mall; he had turned and started back the way he'd come when a bearded man in jeans and a gray sweatshirt spoke to him. Jace saw Brandon hand an envelope to the man, then button his jacket as he walked away.

Jace kept the sweatshirt in sight until the courier disappeared momentarily into a crowd of teenagers coming in from the parking structure. Jace pushed through the noisy group, then realized the man must have turned off down the hallway to the garage. He stepped out and looked both ways before seeing a gray sweatshirt and jeans heading down the ramp toward a tan VW bug.

Jace was planning to read the license plate as he headed on toward the exit where Elliott was waiting, but as he glanced toward the VW, he stopped short. The driver turning the key in the lock was wearing a gray sweatshirt and jeans, but the beard was gone, the hair had lengthened . . . and tits had appeared under the sweatshirt.

Jace scanned the structure in both directions—there was no one else in sight.

Well, at least the rain had stopped.

Robert Brandon was very agitated, his tic going full speed.

"Look, Mr. Brandon, I searched the whole mall before I left. There was nothing else I could do. The courier just got away."

"That was your five grand," Brandon reminded him with a snarl. He squeezed his eyes shut twice. "What are you going to do about it, Levy?"

Well, at least he got my name right. "We did it your way this time and it didn't work out, so how about letting me try mine? I work a lot more efficiently when I plan my own investigations."

Brandon took off his glasses and polished them. He held them up to the light, peering, then rubbed one lens again before putting them back on.

"What can you do?" he asked Jace with resignation.

"Let me talk this through a little. Basically, an extortion victim has three choices. One: pay. That's what you've been doing, and it's kept your secret, but is it worth sixty grand a year—or even more? Trust me, an extortionist doesn't stop while the mark is still paying.

"Two: You can refuse to pay. Calling his bluff will probably result in exposure of your secret. You ought to think rationally about worst-case scenarios in that event—legal, professional, and personal. If the legal risk isn't overwhelming, you can call in the police, who might be able to catch him; your secret would still come out, but you'd have the satisfaction of taking your extortionist down with you. You should also consider how much the repercussions might be lessened if you yourself reveal the secret before the blackmailer does—for instance, a wife might be more apt to forgive an infidelity if she hears of it through her husband's apology, rather than from an outsider."

Jace kept his eyes on Brandon's face, but the producer's grim expression didn't change . . . on the other hand, it couldn't get much more grim.

"Three: You can buy him off, offer a big lump sum for the evidence and perpetual silence. But, as you've pointed out, videos can be easily copied. You pretty much have to take his word that he's going away; you could find the extortion renewed at some later date, and you'd be in the same position you are now, albeit poorer. However, it may be possible to get something on your adversary that will ensure silence—"

"You're talking about blackmailing the blackmailer," Brandon interrupted.

"Exactly. And if his fear of exposure is strong enough, you might even be able to get off the hook without buying him off. However, this would entail continuing to pay until I find out exactly who is involved and get something on him—and I mean paying both the extortion and my fees and expenses.

"OK, those are your general options. The only one that comes close to a guarantee of keeping your secret is to continue paying, possibly for the rest of your life."

"If I was willing to do that, I wouldn't have hired you."

"That's what I figured. But the other two options require you to be open about your secret—to the world at large, or to me. I can't investigate this without some leads."

"How much do you need to know?" Brandon's tic started again.

Jace didn't blame him for being nervous, but it was time to stop holding his hand and get moving on this. "Everything you can tell me—what they have on you, who had access to it, the whole enchilada."

Brandon clasped his hands on the desk in front of him and sat in contemplative silence as he decided—or prayed for divine guidance. But in the end, he really had no choice.

"I love my wife—" he began.

Jace put up a hand. "Mr. Brandon, I'm sure you do, and I'm sure you didn't intend to get yourself in this mess, but I'm not the one you have to explain to. What do they have on you?"

"I videotaped some . . . screen tests. Some actors doing . . . roles . . . with me. Apparently, one of them stole a tape when I wasn't looking."

"What was involved in these screen tests?" Jace prodded.

"Uh . . . some love scenes from classic movies. I like to think how they could have been done differently, so I occasionally get an actress to . . . play one out with me."

"This video—you made it yourself?"

Brandon nodded miserably.

"Then you know who is on the tape?" Jace asked hopefully.

"Well, not exactly. Each tape had a few screen tests."

"There's more than one?"

"I had a total of maybe ten actresses on three tapes."

"All different actresses?" Jace wished Brandon would just open up; he felt like he was picking up a haystack straw by straw.

"I . . . don't remember. I might have used one or two more than once."

"Let's get down to the nitty-gritty here, Brandon. These actresses were taped in sex acts, right?"

Brandon kept his eyes glued to his desk, but he nodded.

"OK, now we're getting somewhere. How did you find them?"

"Some I met at Hollywood parties. There are so many women who want to break into the movies. . . . Others, I found through talent agents."

Plus ça change . . . "Alright, so they do what you want to get a part in a movie. That means you have some way of contacting them, right? I mean, just in case you decide to actually give them a role?"

Brandon muttered something.

"What was that?"

"I said, I've got their headshots and résumés."

"Who are these—old girlfriends?" Risha looked at the seven beautiful women whose eight-by-ten glossy headshots were on the desk in front of Jace. In the other room, Janis Joplin was singing about Bobby McGee.

"You're the oldest girlfriend I have," he retorted with a grin.

"Talk about 'old'! Where'd you get that line— grammar school?" she laughed. "So, not that I'm jealous or anything, but who are they?"

"Possible extortion suspects."

"Professional portraits of your suspects? How did you manage that?" Leaning over his chair from behind, Risha ran both her hands down his chest under his polo shirt, pinching his nipples lightly.

"Mmmm . . ." Jace turned to bury his face in her chest, over her Grateful Dead T-shirt. "I've got résumés, too. They're actresses who want parts in Right Path Films."

He reached under her T-shirt to fondle a breast.

"So it was sex—I mean, Brandon's blackmail," Risha said, pulling Jace up out of his chair. When he was standing, she began to unbuckle his belt.

"He called the missing videos 'screen tests.'" Jace pulled her T-shirt over her head and she unzipped his fly. "I'll start checking them out tomorrow." He slid his hand under her waistband to cup her ass. "Since I'm not in the Job anymore, I'll have to see if Liz will run them through NCIC."

Risha pulled Jace's jeans down as she knelt on the rug in front of him. "Just don't forget my opening tomorrow night."

"I never forget your opening," he laughed, dropping down next to her. "Hey, baby, want a screen test?"

3

The homicide detective was turned away from the door when Jace entered the squad room, but the white silk shirt, mauve slacks with knife-edge creases and matching Charles Jourdan pumps could belong to only the Yuppie Princess. Jace waited until Liz Robinson was off the phone before he stepped into her line of vision.

"Jace!" Her eyes lit up as she threw her arms around him. "When did you get back in town?"

He hugged his former partner and grinned. "A couple of weeks ago. How the hell are you, Liz?"

He held her at arm's length. She looked great. Her light brown hair had been permed and had grown to shoulder length since he'd last seen her, but otherwise she hadn't changed.

"What do you care?" she laughed. "You're too busy to even call your old friends. All I get are postcards from London and Paris . . ."

"I was on the move too much to send you an address, but we're back in L.A. for six months—"

"We?"

"Let's catch up over lunch. Can I talk you into going to Phillipe's for french dip? You can't get a decent french dip in France, you know. My treat."

"Only you would make a big deal about treating me to a two-dollar lunch. I want potato salad, too," she warned.

"You trying to break me?"

Phillipe's, downtown on North Alameda, was an L.A. institution, virtually unchanged for sixty years. Jace and Liz took their sandwiches to one of the long picnic-bench tables, where Jace added a generous dose of Phillipe's lethally hot mustard to his.

"I see you still have a cast-iron stomach," Liz observed, peering suspiciously at her pork dip. "So you're feeling all right?"

He knew she was referring to Huntington's disease. "Sure. Maybe a few more symptoms—just enough to confirm that I've got it—but no paralysis or dementia yet, thank God. What's happening with you and Sandy? Or would you rather not talk about it?"

Sandy was Liz's attorney husband; they'd been having marital difficulties when Jace left. He took a big bite out of his sandwich; meat juices sluiced over his palm and down his arm. Liz passed him a stack of napkins, then nibbled at her own sandwich daintily before speaking.

"We're still together—and still seeing the marriage counselor. Things aren't perfect, but they're a lot better than they were. We're trying to schedule a trip to Hawaii; get away from work for some quality time together, and all that. Sandy's in trial, so we're hoping for sometime next month. So what's this 'we' you mentioned in the squad room? Has The Man Who Can't Commit finally been tamed?"

"Captured, maybe, but never tamed. Her name's Risha Cadigan; she's a photojournalist."

"So you're supporting the arts now?"

Jace laughed. "On my pension? Not likely. Anyway, Risha has all the money."

"A rich artiste? Well, you certainly lucked out, didn't you? Is this serious?"

Serious? Jace thought about it. He loved Risha, he was sure of that. He'd betrayed and abandoned his career for her, he'd even helped her dispose of her feeders' bodies . . . and his only hope for avoiding a horrible death from Huntington's was to let her make him a vampire.

"Yeah, it's serious. Hell, she'd kill me if I tried to back out now," he grinned, knowing it was literal truth . . . and knowing Risha would also kill him when he committed. "But don't start planning our wedding yet; I'm not rushing into anything here."

"When do I get to meet her?"

"Tonight, if you want. She has a one-woman show opening at the Moss-Erlich Gallery in BevHills. I brought you an invitation." He pulled the card out of his pocket and handed it to Liz. "Whoops—sorry about that."

Liz wiped the mustard off the card with a napkin, then read it. "Cocktails and hors d'oeuvres. Eight o'-clock. Great—can I bring Sandy?"

"Sure, the more the merrier. How's the Job?"

"Same old same old. Of course, we had to drop everything when the riots hit last spring—canceled all vacations and leaves and added about ten hours to each day. I must have spent the next six months doing riot-related investigations to the exclusion of everything else. The only good thing is that Willie Williams is a sweetheart to work for, and department morale has improved since he came aboard. That pattern killer we were tracking before you retired apparently moved on— we haven't found any vics in about a year—which is just as well, since no one could have been spared to work on it anyway."

Jace was relieved to hear that the investigation into the deaths of Risha's feeders had been shelved. He'd have to make sure she was efficient about disposing of her garbage so the cases wouldn't be reopened while they were back in town.

"Who's your new partner?" Jace licked mustard off his fingers and started on his other sandwich.

"Pat Fujikawa—she transferred from Foothill after you left. Did you ever meet her?"

"Wasn't she the one who filed sexual harassment charges against a deputy DA?"

"That's Pat. Barr threatened to get her demoted to meter maid if she didn't come across. The scumbag eventually resigned and the city bent over backwards to prove they didn't penalize whistle-blowers, so Pat got a transfer to the big time."

Jace whistled. "Boy, she's lucky Gates wasn't still in charge. She'd have been kicked off the force."

"Williams doesn't have Gates' prejudices about women or minorities, fortunately. There are still some Neanderthals left—none of the men were willing to team with her, and not everyone can accept two female detectives partnering, so we've had to work twice as hard as the other teams to prove ourselves." She shrugged, then forked some potato salad. "Pat's good— a little green, but learning fast. She hasn't got your instincts, but then, who has? We just cleared a multiple homicide that looked like a dead end. Do you miss the Job?"

"Naw. Traveling around the world with a beautiful woman beats fourteen-hour days delving into man's darker side hands down. I am doing some investigation now, though."

Liz put down her plastic fork and stared at Jace in surprise. "Really? Private work?"

"Yeah—I was hired by an extortion victim. I was actually hoping you could help me." He finished his sandwich.

"Jeez, Jace, I don't have time to moonlight. What do you need?"

"Just run NCIC on some suspects for now. Maybe I'll need more later, but . . ." He let the sentence hang as he looked hopefully at Liz.

"You're expecting a lot in exchange for a french dip, Levy," she smiled. "OK—it's been pretty quiet lately; give me the names, and I'll run them when I can."

"You're just about acesh with me, Lizsh," Jace said in an exaggerated Bogart voice. "So I'll even throw in cocktails and hors d'oeuvres for two tonight."

Even though it was four in the afternoon, Jace had to turn on the bedroom light, the only way he could see in the permanently dark room. He didn't worry about waking Risha; it was virtually impossible to stir her once she'd gone to sleep for the day. Although sunlight wouldn't be fatal to her as it would be to a much older vampire, it would suddenly propel her from her apparent age of thirty to her actual age of fifty-one—something she was understandably loath to do unnecessarily. The few times she'd stayed awake past dawn, she'd been careful to be completely shielded from the sun; however, as the sun rose, she became so lethargic she might as well have slept. Jace's daily schedule didn't coincide much with Risha's, although that would change when he crossed over. He usually awoke about ten in the morning, a luxury after a lifetime of early rising, and dropped off about 3:00 A.M. Risha took advantage of her solitary three or four hours to work in her darkroom, to cruise the city shooting photographs, or to feed.

Looking at his sleeping lover, her dark auburn hair spread across the pillow, Jace realized she must have gone out to feed the previous night after he went to sleep; there was a tiny fleck of dried blood at the corner of her sensuous mouth. Although he'd never watched her feed, he'd seen several of her victims afterward. None of them had resisted, and some had died with smiles on their faces. She'd told him it wasn't unusual for male feeders to have spontaneous ejaculations when they felt the rush of her hallucinogenic venom enter their bloodstreams.

Most of her feeders were better dead, anyway—she preyed on society's dregs. Before they'd left L.A., Jace had even directed her toward several career criminals who'd slipped through the system, and the city was probably a safer place for it. Fortunately, her feeders wouldn't be coming back from the dead as invincible criminals. It took repeated exposure to her venom to make the transition, so immortality was a deliberate honor seldom bestowed. In fact, as far as Risha knew, she was the only vampire left . . . at least until Jace was ready to join her.

He dropped his clothes on the carpet and went in to run the shower. He looked in the mirror which Risha had installed for him, and thought it'd be a good idea to shave again for tonight. He ran his fingers through his straight black hair, frowning at the silver strands which seemed to multiply overnight. It occurred to him that he ought to cross over before he became completely gray.

He stepped into the shower to let the hot water pound his upper back, but his knees suddenly gave way under him and he fell, unable to get up. His head jerked uncontrollably, banging against the tile side of the stall until he managed to twist his body into a fetal position, protecting his head with twitching arms. The spasms seemed to last forever, but eventually stopped as suddenly as they had begun.

Jace huddled on the floor of the shower, now shaking from fear, as the water streamed over him. It took several minutes before he was conscious of where he was. He got up cautiously, holding on to the walls as he tested his legs. This was the worst episode he'd ever had. There was no doubt about it, the Huntington's was progressing past the ignorable. He knew that the inevitable death came anywhere from five to thirty years after onset, but the paralysis and dementia that preceded death scared him more. He'd watched his mother deteriorate, unable to control her bodily functions or her mind, and he'd spent much of his adult life terrified that the same thing would happen to him, praying that his fifty-fifty chance of inheriting the disease would fall on the right side. Before he met Risha, he'd had frequent nightmares, but the knowledge that vampirism was a way out had calmed his subconscious, and the dreams came only infrequently now.

As he toweled dry, Jace finally faced the question of crossing over. For the last year, he'd shelved the idea as something he had plenty of time to consider later; there seemed to be no need to rush voluntarily into death. On the other hand, he realized, it wouldn't be the same as mortal death; he would still be able to function, enjoy life, and would gain in strength, health, and longevity. No matter what vampirism would mean to him, it could never be as horrible as what waited for him without that omnipotent healer. What was he waiting for?

The turnout for Risha's gallery opening was much larger than Jace had expected. David A. South, the editor in chief at *City of Angels* magazine, had taken a proprietary interest in Risha's career, since he felt he had "discovered" her; his additions to the mailing list had brought heavy response from the film and literary communities. Jace recognized Bruce Willis and Demi Moore, Meryl Streep, Ray Bradbury. Even in the silk Armani suit Risha had given him for his birthday, he felt like a poor relative amongst the elite.

Risha looked spectacular. She was wearing a layered Laize Adzer creation that set off her hair and eyes to great effect. As she walked through the room, men's eyes followed her. Jace grinned. *Eat your hearts out, fuckers—she's with me.*

The show featured twenty-five of Risha's prints, most of which had been printed sixteen-by-twenty, half of which had run in *City of Angels* under the caption "After Midnight." All her pictures, for obvious reasons, were night shots. After the next batch for the magazine was done, she hoped to have enough good prints for a book.

Her agent, Michael Tesman, had flown in from New York for the opening, bringing good news.

"*Aperture* has already made an offer on the book," he told Risha. "Ten thousand. It's pretty low, but Pantheon and Warner Books are also interested. I think we ought to wait 'til you have some new prints, then we'll put the book up for auction. What would really help is if we could get an introduction or text by someone famous. Madonna wouldn't hurt your sales one bit, and Warner published her book."

Risha frowned. "I'm not sure I want my photographs associated with hers."

"There are some famous people here," Jace pointed out. "Maybe one of them would do it."

Tesman looked around the room. "Maybe," he said dubiously. "Offhand, I don't see anyone who'd fit naturally. Who else do you know?"

"Look," Risha said, "David South is over there. He knows everybody; let's talk to him about it."

South was speaking with two well-dressed men in front of a picture Risha had taken at the Hollywood Ranch Market. As soon as they'd headed over, he stopped to embrace Risha and shake Jace's hand. He introduced the two men, Jeffrey Roth and Roger Craigh. Risha introduced Michael Tesman. Everyone shook each other's hands, and Roth and Craigh complimented Risha on her work.

"I've nearly convinced Jeffrey that we need this print for our living room," Roger said.

"That's a major compliment. Roger's an artist too, a sculptor," South told her.

"Only one of my hats," Roger laughed. "Another one is as an art reviewer for the *Advocate*, which is why we happened to come tonight. You can expect a rave in the next issue."

"That's wonderful! I'm delighted you're covering the show." Risha smiled.

"Unfortunately, Roger doesn't understand that we

can't buy a piece from every show he likes; we haven't got the wall space," Jeffrey said. "However, this time I just think the picture should go in my office and not the house."

"What kind of office?" Jace asked. The print in question showed a pimp and a bag lady; there weren't a lot of businesses that could exhibit such a photo.

"I'm a literary agent." He reached into his pocket and handed Jace his card. "What do you do, Jace?"

"I'm . . . retired. No card."

Jace saw Liz and Sandy come in. "Excuse me, there are some people I need to greet." He turned to Risha. "Rish, Liz Robinson and her husband just arrived. When you can, come over to meet them."

"The show doesn't even open to the public until tomorrow, and they've already sold three prints!" Risha gushed on the way home. "And a good review in the *Advocate,* too!"

"So how much did you make tonight?"

"Let's see: three-fifty for the Hollywood Ranch picture Roger Craigh and his lover bought, two-ninety-five for the Westwood picture from the white-haired man with the comb-over, and I think the meat print was two-eighty; that's nine hundred and twenty-five, less the gallery commission. And that woman in the black-leather jumpsuit said she was going to bring her husband to look at the kissing punks photo next week. And I thought the prices were set too high!"

"They're worth every penny, sweetheart." Jace turned into the driveway and switched off the ignition.

Risha was beaming from ear to ear, her excitement endearing. "Do you think Michael will really make the book happen, too?"

"It sounds like it, Rish. You've already got one offer, and you haven't even taken all the photographs yet."

They got out of the car and entered the house through the kitchen. The sound of Elliott's snoring came through his door; they tiptoed up the stairs so they wouldn't wake him.

"I don't think he's feeling well," Risha whispered. "Did you notice the circles under his eyes at the party? And it's only—" she checked her watch "—midnight. He's usually still up now." She turned on their bedroom light and closed the door.

Jace shrugged. "Maybe he's got a cold. He's not a youngster, and he's been putting in a lot of time on the show. I'm not surprised he's wiped out."

Elliott wasn't the only one who was feeling weak. Jace hadn't quite bounced back from his episode in the shower earlier. He hadn't mentioned it to Risha, not wanting to worry her, but he wasn't as calm about it as he wanted to be, either. He took off his suit and hung it in the closet, while she went to remove her makeup.

When she came back in, Jace was lying on the bed, trying to read the new Jonathan Kellerman novel. The problem wasn't the writing—Kellerman was always good—but rather, Jace's inability to distance himself from the question of his future.

"You want to read or make mad, passionate love?" Risha asked with a comic leer. She wore a crimson lace teddy and a black velvet choker.

Jace tossed the book on the nightstand. "I can read anytime." He patted the bed next to him. "Let's smoke a joint first. Is there one up here?"

"What a good idea—I've got one in my purse."

She got the joint and climbed into bed with him. Jace put his arm around her, and she snuggled against his chest as they smoked. He was glad her show had gone over so well; she was so elated, she glowed. Jace realized, at this moment, he would be happy to spend the rest of his life with this woman . . . but how would he feel twenty years from now—or two hundred?

"How long does it take?"

"How long does what take?" she responded.

He hadn't even been aware he'd spoken out loud, but

now the question was out, he might as well follow through.

"To change into a vampire."

He'd surprised her. Risha sat up and looked at him. He'd never really broached the subject after they began living together, and she'd seemed content to let him set their pace.

"It depends. I took six weeks, but that's because Gregor was ultracautious about how much blood he drank. He told me that he crossed over in three weeks, but he nearly died permanently when he was drained because his venom sacs hadn't developed sufficiently yet. You can sort of tell when you're ready—your fangs become extensible and you stop getting so high from the venom." She paused for a moment. "Why do you ask?" she added pseudocasually.

Jace laughed. "Why do you think? I'm doing a thesis on the last vampire." He passed her the joint, but she shook her head. "So we could take our time with it?"

"Somewhat, but your venom sacs develop at their own rate, so you won't have a lot of control over the timing. You've probably got at least a month from first exposure, I guess."

A month. And he'd still be able to run around in the daylight for a while afterward, though he wouldn't be at his sharpest then.

"What happens if I get partway there, then stop?" *Always keep an eye on the back door, old man.*

Risha shrugged. "I'm not sure. Maybe you'd just metabolize the venom and it would dilute into ineffectiveness; maybe it would catalyze the change eventually anyway, even without more venom. For all I know, you could build up an immunity to the venom and then wouldn't be able to cross over. Gregor never told me, and all of our feeders have been killed after the first feeding. Either way, I think it would be risky to stop the change before it's complete."

All or nothing. Jace took a long, thoughtful drag on

the joint and passed it to Risha. This time she took it. He thought about telling her about the Huntington's, but he didn't want her to think it was the reason he was with her. Hell, it wasn't even the only major reason, but Huntington's was a certainty . . . and love was not.

He traced a finger along the bottom of her lace teddy, then insinuated it under the hem to lie against her vagina. She moaned a little, turning her head to close her lips over his nipple. Jace felt his cock surge as her cool tongue teased him. He took the grass out of her hand and put it in the ashtray next to the bed. When he turned back, she was lying on her side with eyes half-closed; one strap had slipped off her shoulder and her ivory breast was trying to escape its crimson lace prison. He helped it get out, marveling at how luscious she looked sprawled there for him, and bent to take her nipple lightly between his teeth while his hand probed her wetness.

He pushed her flat, unsnapping the bottom of her teddy and rotating to replace his fingers with his tongue, whipping her easily into a frenzy as blood hardened his cock into steel.

"OhgodJace—yes! Mmmm . . . oh, right there . . ." And the more she moaned, the hotter he got, the more urgent his need to plunge into her as deeply as he could go, to fill her.

He trailed hot wet kisses up her belly, stopping to nibble one erect-hard nipple before he thrust his cock into her. Her vaginal muscles grabbed him like a hand and squeezed him so hard he nearly came, but he began to stroke shallowly in and out, dropping his urgency a notch while increasing hers. He lowered his chest onto her, feeling her breasts against him, the nipples hidden in his chest hair. She stifled a shriek of ecstasy in his neck as he suddenly plunged all the way into her.

"Bite me now, Risha," he urged in a growl, "bite me hard."

She gasped, "Yes!", then Jace felt her fangs enter his

neck. He felt a rush of warmth and became aware that his saliva suddenly tasted very sweet. He exploded in a paroxysm of ecstasy that surged throughout his entire body; brightly colored lights swirled in front of his eyes, the air hummed, and it felt like every nerve in his body was firing on all cylinders; his orgasm shot out with more force than he'd thought possible, even as his blood pulsed into Risha's mouth.

Then he lost consciousness.

4

Jace scratched absently at the two small scars on his neck as he studied the computer readouts Liz had dropped off on her way home from work. Two of Brandon's seven actresses had been in minor trouble with the law—Suze Daly had been busted twice for prostitution in Overland Park, Kansas, and Crysse Tanner had shoplifted a dress in Bakersfield, California—but no one had been charged with extortion anywhere.

Most of them had spiced up or simplified their names for their careers—Sandra Mason had become Candra Mason, while Maria Ajowleczni had become Marya Ashley—but one of the actresses had remained a complete cipher. Liz had drawn a blank on the computer checks of Tinah Powers: no driver's license, no credit history, no police record. It was entirely possible that Tinah Powers had made a name change too recently—or too casually—to show up, so the lack of info wasn't that unusual, but Jace flagged her résumé. Anything out of the ordinary was worth checking.

Neither Candra Mason nor Felice Sullivan had an agent; Marya Ashley was a client of Kathleen Bester; Tinah Powers, Suze Daly, and Crysse Tanner all shared the same agent, CineArts—and Joy Bonner had crossed out the name and phone number for Marvin Roth and had substituted an answering service, apparently having lost her representation for some reason.

Jace picked up the phone.

SCREEN TEST—CANDRA MASON

Charlie climbs back on board the African Queen and drops his armload of firewood next to the boiler. He limps over to Rosie.

"Picked up a thorn in my foot," he explains. "It's gone right through the rubber sole." He begins to remove his shoe.

"Here, let me," Rosie says, kneeling at his feet. She takes off his shoe, then carefully removes the thorn with her fingernails.

"Oh, thank you, Miss," Charlie smiles.

Rosie looks shyly away, then quickly back at Charlie before she turns away again; she finally finds her voice. "Do you . . . recognize these flowers, Mr. Allnutt?"

"Huh?"

"I've never seen them before."

"Why, I can't say as I have either," Charlie says, amazed that they are talking about flowers.

"Perhaps no one has. I don't suppose they even have a name."

"Well, whether they have or not, they sure are pretty," Charlie says, obviously not talking about flowers. He puts his hand on Rosie's shoulder.

All too aware of the contact, Rosie looks down. Still not looking at him, she covers his hand with her own. Charlie looks at her tenderly, but she still cannot meet his eyes.

He leans close to her, takes her in his arms, and kisses her. Rosie responds eagerly, and Charlie begins to unbutton her pale blue dress at its high neck. She buries her face in his shoulder, but doesn't stop him.

He gently pushes the dress off her shoulders, and helps Rosie to stand; the dress drops, forgotten, at her feet, revealing the cotton camisole and bloomers underneath. Embarrassed, Rosie turns her back to Charlie and finishes removing her undergarments herself before turning back to him.

Charlie has removed his striped shirt and tan pants, but still wears his stained red neckerchief. The sight makes Rosie smile, even in her nervousness, and she unties the cloth. They fall into each other's arms, naked as the other denizens of the Ulanga River.

Charlie is very tender with Rosie, very patient and gentle. She stifles a little cry when he breaks through her hymen, but quickly gives in to her first sexual experience with an abandon uncharacteristic of her missionary demeanor.

Afterward, Rosie's face is alight with pleasure. "I never dreamed that any mere physical experience could be so stimulating. I've only known such excitement a few times before. . . . I must say, I'm filled with admiration for your skill, Mr. Allnutt."

"Do you think she pronounces Candra with a K or an S?" Risha asked, looking at the actress's résumé.

"She said Kandra on the phone," Jace said, amazed that Risha could read in a car at night with no light. "Although Liz's report said her name was Sandra before she moved to Hollywood from . . . shit! I can't remember where she's from."

"Des Moines."

"Did I tell you that?" Jace hadn't shown the report to Risha, but his memory had been unreliable since the Huntington's began to manifest.

"I guessed. She has twelve plays listed under regional theater, and the first ten were in Des Moines."

Jace grinned. "You're a natural detective, my love. If you get a chance to snoop in her bedroom while we're talking, see if you can find any hidden videos, but don't get caught. And remember that you're here as a photographer, and let me ask the questions."

He parked the Honda in front of a thirty-year-old stucco apartment building in North Hollywood called the Sunset Palms.

Candra Mason looked to be in her early thirties, about ten years older than her headshot. She was attractive, not drop-dead gorgeous, but with great cheekbones and full chestnut brown hair, high, small breasts, and long legs. She was obviously excited about being interviewed. She'd prepared a plate of salami and jack cheese cubes, each speared with its own colored toothpick. She had placed the plate in the exact center of the freshly dusted but rickety coffee table in front of the cat-shredded plaid couch where they sat.

The orange cat had fled as soon as Risha had entered the room, and stood hissing, back arched, at the bedroom door.

"Gosh, I'm sorry about Pumpkin—she usually loves people," Candra apologized, putting the cat in the bedroom and closing the door, effectively cutting off any chance of a surreptitious search there by Risha.

"Can I get you something to drink?" Candra offered when she returned to the living room. "I have Viennese Chocolate Cafe and caffeine-free Diet Coke and white wine."

Amused that wine was the only generic offering, they both declined.

"Just ignore the photographer while we talk, Ms. Mason," Jace suggested, turning on his pocket tape recorder and placing it on the table.

"Call me Candra," the actress told Jace. She turned to Risha. "Is what I'm wearing okay? I could change if the colors are wrong."

"What you have on is fine; I'm shooting black-and-white anyway," Risha told her, taking a reading from her light meter.

Jace glanced at Candra's clothing—far from being an indication of a recent fifteen-grand windfall, it had obviously just been made; a loose thread hung from a wobbly sleeve seam. Candra's hair hung down over her thin shoulders, but had been moussed and sprayed so much, it hardly moved when she turned her head.

Jace spent nearly an hour interviewing the actress about her career, the highlight of which was a production of *Man of La Mancha* in Des Moines in which she'd played Dulcinea. She showed Jace the reviews (there were two, both enthusiastic) and the award she'd won at the Lions Club Theater Festival for Best Actress in a Musical.

"I won this trip to Hollywood," she bubbled, "so I quit my job and moved here two years ago—lock, stock, and Pumpkin!"

"How do you support yourself between acting jobs?" Jace asked.

"Oh, I'm a parking valet for this company that's hired to work, like, Hollywood parties, and I also work for this messenger service. I get to go to I.C.M. a lot, but I never get past the front desk," she smiled with a shrug.

"So, no luck getting an agent yet?"

Candra's permanent smile faltered almost imperceptably. "Oh, you know—it's hard getting into the industry. I've taken really good acting workshops and been in some showcases, and I've gotten callbacks on two commercials, but I'm still waiting for my big break." As Risha aimed her camera, Candra turned her smile back on full force. "I know that after this article appears in *City of Angels,* I'll be getting a lot of calls from agents."

"I'm sure you will, but I'm writing on spec—there's no guarantee that it'll be run." Jace felt a little guilty leading Candra on; his instincts told him she was too guileless to be the extortionist, but he had to investigate more. "One angle that they're interested in is the casting couch. Are actresses still encouraged to . . ." he groped for a journalistically objective phrase and failed, ". . . come across sexually for a role?"

Candra looked startled. "Oh, you hear stories, you know . . ."

"Then you haven't been approached that way yourself?" Jace asked, beginning to shift as if the interview were coming to an unsatisfactory close.

"Well, sort of," Candra allowed uncomfortably. "But I wouldn't want to tell you any names or anything." When Jace began to stand, she quickly added, "I'll talk about it, but I have my career to think of, you know, so I can't offend anyone."

Jace sat down again, looked interested. "Of course, Candra. No names. What happened?"

Risha excused herself to go into the bathroom. As she passed the bedroom door, Pumpkin screeched.

"Wouldn't you like some cold cuts?" Candra picked up the platter and offered it to Jace.

"Not just yet, thank you."

He waited, and her reluctance hung in the air a moment before she put the plate back down on the table with a tiny sigh.

"Okay. About a year ago, I met this producer at a party who said he might be doing a remake of *The African Queen*; he said I looked like the perfect Rosie Sayer."

"Uh-huh," said Jace. "The Katharine Hepburn role. What happened?"

"He said he needed a video audition, a screen test, but he had to do it on the sly, because he didn't want word to get out that he was negotiating for the rights. He told me he'd shoot the video himself. He sent me the sides and a costume and I met him at his office in Santa Monica. There's this, like, apartment in the back. I thought he'd have an actor there to play Charlie, but he said he was too worried about leaks, so he'd do Charlie's lines himself."

Risha came back into the room, heralded by another

muffled screech from the bedroom, and Candra turned from the subject to offer the plate to Risha, who declined. She picked up her camera again, and crouched on the floor to snap another picture of Candra, who turned on an instantly radiant smile.

"The office apartment," Jace prompted.

"Oh, right. So anyway, we did a dry run of this scene—it was the one where Charlie and Rosie kiss for the first time?—and then Mr.—the producer set up the camera and we did it again. After the kiss, he started to take off my clothes. I didn't remember that from the original movie, but he said there was no sense remaking a movie if you're going to do it exactly the same way; besides, they would have shown the sex if it hadn't been made so long ago."

"So you went along, but you still didn't get the part?"

"I didn't go along with it," Candra corrected, the shift of her eyes denying her claim. "I told him I'd do the nudity only when I got the role. I left right away, and mailed the costume back to him."

"And did you hear from the producer again?" Jace asked.

Candra shook her head. "I don't think he got the rights to the movie anyway, because I haven't heard anything about a remake, and it's been a year." She paused, then added in a small voice, "It would have been horrible to do it with him and then not even get cast. At least I kept my dignity."

She tossed her head and flashed an awkwardly big smile for Risha's camera. It wasn't until Risha printed the film later that they saw the sparkle of a tear in Candra's eye.

Had she been unhappy enough to get revenge?

Jace barely woke when Risha climbed into bed with him, but he mumbled a greeting and embraced her naked body with an arm and leg.

"Staying asleep?" she whispered.

"Not if you've got a better offer," he said thickly as he ran a hand down her cool flank. He opened his eyes and kissed her hello. "Get some good pictures?"

"Probably nothing worth printing. I went to an all-night coffee shop, but it was almost deserted; then I spent an hour or two at the Greyhound Depot downtown. I might have gotten a good shot of a counterman nodding off, but it depends how a reflection on his window turns out. Brassaï was great with reflections, but I never seem to get them the way I want."

"Maybe it's 'cause you don't have any of your own. Did you feed?"

"Yeah. Some drunk. I left his shell in an abandoned building downtown." She stroked Jace's cock. "I'm not quite full, though . . ."

"Oh?" Jace trailed his hand up the inside of her thigh. "Fill 'er up, lady?"

It was the third time Risha had fed on him, and the first time he hadn't passed out when the rush overwhelmed his senses. As they lay in each other's arms, the afterglow from the sex and the venom made Jace feel at peace, happy, and . . . safe, he realized, for the first time in his adult life.

"That's some drug you've got there," he told her in sincere admiration.

She laughed. "Enjoy it while you can."

What did that mean? "You going someplace?"

"Not without you. I just meant that the venom won't get you high for long. Does it still taste sweet?"

"Like an intangible sugar cube. Why?"

"As your own venom gland develops, mine will stop affecting you so much. As the high lessens, so will the sweetness." She rubbed her belly. "Mmmm, I'm full . . . and sleepy. Must be dawn." She snuggled in and put her head on his shoulder. "What are you going to do today?"

"Depends on what calls get returned. I left messages for the agents and the other girls without agents. I also

want to check with the utility companies to see if I can
find any record of Tinah Powers . . . you know, the one
Liz didn't find anything on?"

But Risha was already asleep. Jace kissed her fore-
head tenderly, then turned to spoon against her. His fingers went to the fang marks on his neck; as before,
they'd closed as soon as she'd stopped feeding. Once
he'd crossed over, they'd disappear entirely; he once
saw a bullet hole in Risha's back heal to invisibility
within a week.

No wonder he felt safe.

While his coffee cooled, Jace rummaged around in the
refrigerator, looking for something to eat. It was hard to
choose amongst the riches: mayonnaise, mustard, green
olives with pimentos, beer, and salsa. He fished out an
olive and closed the door.

Elliott appeared in the kitchen doorway, still wearing
his rubber gloves from the darkroom. "I can make you a
tuna-fish sandwich if you like, Detective."

"No thanks. I'll grab something while I'm out.
Maybe a pizza," he ruminated. "I won't be eating it
much longer."

"Risha told me you were crossing over," Elliott said
as he removed his gloves. "Congratulations."

Jace grinned. Where else, but in the house of a vampire, would one be congratulated on one's imminent
death? "Thanks. Did I get any messages?"

"A Miss Joy Bonner called and said she'd be working
at the Hard Rock Cafe until three today and asked if you
could meet her when her shift is over. Here's the number
if you can't make it."

Two hours. He'd have time to stop at the California
Pizza Kitchen on La Cienega for Caribbean shrimp
pizza before he met the actress, but it would mean de-
laying the utility company check on Tinah Powers. It
could wait 'til Monday; he was famished.

He took his coffee into the study to take another look

at the rundown on Joy Bonner. The stunning brunette had been represented by a Marvin Roth, but was now apparently without an agent. She looked a little familiar; her résumé solved that—she'd been in *Stiletto and Lace*, a boring direct-to-video thriller he and Risha had rented once. She hadn't had the lead role, that of a Mafia hit woman, but had played the girlfriend of the drug-dealing police commissioner, Jace remembered. She'd had a phony Southern accent that had sometimes lapsed into Brooklynese.

When he got up to go shave, the phone rang.

"Jace Levy? This is Kathleen Bester returning your call about Marya Ashley." Her voice was hoarse. "I'm sorry I can't speak up—I have laryngitis."

"I hear that's been going around," Jace sympathized.

"It's really going to put a crimp in my yelling on Sunday," she laughed.

"I'm sorry?"

"I've got Super Bowl tickets—I'm a big Cowboys fan. Are you going?"

Jace forgot the Super Bowl was going to be held in Pasadena, but he didn't much care, not being a football fan. "No such luck—I'll be watching it on TV, like the rest of the country."

"At least you'll have a good view of the field." She coughed, holding the receiver away from her mouth until the paroxysm had passed. "Excuse me. I really shouldn't be talking at all. What can I do for you, Mr. Levy?"

"I wanted to get in touch with Marya Ashley to interview her for an article I'm writing on some of the problems faced by actresses in Hollywood."

"Marya Ashley hasn't done any professional film or TV work yet—although she's done three student films at USC and has a good shot at being one of Murphy Brown's secretaries. If you need to talk with experienced screen actresses, I have several other clients who might be closer to what you want. How did you hear about Marya?"

"A couple of producers told me she was a promising talent and when I looked her up in the Academy Players Directory, I saw she had the look my photographer wants to balance the other actresses we're interviewing."

"Who did you say you write for?"

"*City of Angels* magazine. I'm doing it on spec, but David South, the editor, can vouch for Risha Cadigan, the photographer I work with; they've run quite a lot of her work. A Cadigan photograph alone could bring your client a fair amount of attention."

"I'm sure you're legitimate, Mr. Levy, but I'm afraid I can't give out my clients' numbers; you understand. But perhaps I can set up a meeting after Ms. Ashley gets back in town."

"Is she out of L.A. for long?"

"Only a week; a play in Aspen. She should be back Monday or Tuesday, unless she stays over to ski."

"Next week will be fine. My schedule is flexible, but my photographer is only available evenings."

"Would she want to shoot the same time you do the interview?"

"We'd prefer it that way, but if necessary, I can have her arrange a session later. Why? Do you have some objection to photographing the interview?"

"No, no. I just thought it advisable to meet for the interview in my office, but it might not be the setting you want for photographs."

Jace didn't really want Marya Ashley's agent motherhenning her while he was delving, but offhand he couldn't think of a way out of it that wouldn't sound suspicious.

"Let's play that by ear, shall we? I'll discuss it with Risha and maybe we can come up with an acceptable location by the time the appointment is set up."

"Good. I'll talk with you sometime next week then."

"I'll be looking forward to it, Ms. Bester. Enjoy the Super Bowl."

As he headed upstairs, it occurred to Jace that maybe he ought to take Elliott with him to play photographer with Joy Bonner, but then decided against it. If he didn't have a camera with him, it would give him a handy excuse for another visit if necessary. Besides, Elliott just didn't have the right look for a professional photographer . . . Jace laughed. The contact with the film industry was already warping his views; he was thinking in terms of casting a role.

5

Scarlett has heard enough.

"If you weren't so drunk and insulting, I'd explain everything. As it is, though . . ." She rises to leave.

Rhett stands to tower over her. "You get out of that chair once more . . ." She drops back into her chair. "Of course, the comic figure in all this is the long-suffering Mr. Wilkes." He pours another drink. "Mr. Wilkes, who can't be mentally faithful to his wife and won't be unfaithful to her technically." He drinks. "Why doesn't he make up his mind?"

Scarlett stands. "Rhett, you—"

Rhett slams her back down into her chair, then circles around behind her, enveloping her. Scarlett is scared.

"Observe my hands, my dear." He holds them in front of her face. "I could tear you to pieces with them. And I'd do it if it'd take Ashley out of your mind forever—but it wouldn't. So I'll remove him from your mind forever this way. I'll put my hands so—one on each side of your head—and I'll smash your skull between them like a walnut. And that'll block him out." He begins to push his hands against her head.

Scarlett is terrified, but she shows characteristic bravado. "Take your hands off me! You drunken fool," she snaps.

Rhett chuckles and removes his hands, stepping back.

"You know, I've always admired your spirit, my dear. Never more than now, when you're cornered."

She stands and faces him. "I'm not cornered. You'll never corner me, Rhett Butler—or frighten me. You've lived in dirt so long, you can't understand anything else—and you're jealous of something you can't understand. Good night." She turns and walks deliberately to the door.

He laughs. "Jealous, am I?" He strides over to her and takes her by the shoulders, leaning his face in close to hers. "Yes, I suppose I am, even though I know you've been faithful to me all along. How do I know? Because I know Ashley Wilkes and his honorable breed—they're gentlemen." He sneers the word. "Which is more than I can say for you, or for me. We're not gentlemen, and we have no honor—have we?"

Scarlett pushes her drunk husband away and walks out.

Rhett turns back toward his drink, then reverses and comes after her. He grabs her arm roughly and spins her to face him. "It's not that easy, Scarlett."

He kisses her hard; she fights him, but not terribly convincingly.

"You turned me out while you chased Ashley Wilkes, while you dreamed of Ashley Wilkes. This is one night you're not turning me out!"

She gasps as he picks her up and carries her to bed.

Rhett is violent; he tears open her red velvet dressing gown and savages her without foreplay. But Scarlett doesn't fight him; caught up in the excitement and the passion, she responds avidly to a rape she hadn't expected to welcome.

Joy Bonner had already changed from her white uniform to a red jumpsuit when Jace walked into the Hard

Rock Cafe. He had no trouble recognizing her; the actress would turn heads in any crowd. She was mid-twenties, tall, with long, shiny brunette hair, and an olive complexion that screamed Mediterranean heritage. Her full lips and dark eyes promised thrills to any man who braved their taunt. When Jace introduced himself, her smile was simultaneously warm and enigmatic, as if she knew his secrets.

"Do you mind if we get out of here?" she shouted over the musical din. "I've had enough of this for one day."

"Sure. Where would you like to go?"

"There's a nice lounge in the hotel across the street," Joy said, gesturing through the glass to Ma Maison Sofitel.

The rain had stopped, but the drivers didn't. It took them ten minutes to cross Beverly Boulevard and enter the plush hotel.

When their drinks arrived, Jace began to explain about the "article for *City of Angels*," but he stopped because of the strangely knowing nature of Joy's smile.

"Did I say something weird?" he asked.

"No, it was a great reading . . . for a cop. Finish, if you want," she laughed.

Jace tried to look confused. "Jesus, what makes you think I'm a cop?"

She shook her head, still smiling. "The delivery on that line didn't play at all. Look, I can make a cop a block away. My family's lousy with them: my father, my uncle, my oldest brother—they're all with the NYPD. I practically grew up in a station house. So why don't you drop the shit about the magazine article and tell me what you're investigating? I'll be a lot more willing to cooperate if you're straight with me." She sipped her Chardonnay, watching Jace over the rim.

"OK, OK," Jace conceded with a grin, "but I've retired from the force; I'm working privately."

"Retired voluntarily or kicked out?"

"Voluntary. Health. LAPD Robbery-Homicide until about a year ago," he told her. "My partner's still there if you want to check with her." Joy nodded that she was still open, so he continued. "There's a producer who's rumored to be sexually harassing actresses during auditions."

She threw back her head and laughed, a deep throaty sound of true amusement. "You're going to have to narrow that down a little."

Jace grinned. "I guess that was a pretty broad statement. But I don't want to be the one who brings his name into this discussion. I have reason to believe you've run into him; he would have videotaped a screen test with you, maybe a scene from a classic movie?"

Comprehension dawned on the actress's face, followed by an unexpected blush. "Robert Brandon, right?" she whispered. "Has the video gotten out?" she added in a genuinely worried tone.

"Not that I know of. I haven't seen it, if that's what you're asking. Will you tell me about your experience?"

"Would there be something in it for me?"

Jace nodded. "Fifty bucks."

Joy compressed her lips into a line as she thought, rotating her wineglass in her hand to catch the light.

"I wouldn't be willing to testify," she said finally. "Among other things, it could really harm my career. In fact, you've got to swear that anything I say doesn't go any further. Otherwise, find someone else to talk to." She took a swallow of her wine, then put it down.

"Fair enough. You have my word."

"I need a different drink. Cutty on the rocks."

After Jace had ordered her drink and another beer for himself, she began.

"I met Brandon last spring sometime—April, maybe. My agent then was Marvin Roth—you heard of him?"

Jace shrugged noncommittally.

"Anyway, he called me in and said that a big producer had seen me in *Stiletto and Lace* and was interested in auditioning me. Marvin asked me if I was willing to 'go along to get along'—he said this producer could do big things for my career, and if I wanted a role, I'd have to cooperate."

"Cooperate," Jace echoed.

"Yeah. Agentese for 'fuck.' He told me he could get the guy to pay fifteen hundred bucks for one evening; Marvin wanted forty percent, but I'd get my cut in cash."

She stopped when the waitress arrived with their drinks, and took a belt before continuing.

"I wasn't doing too good then—the bills were really piling up, and I don't like to call home for money; I want to make it on my own, you know?—and he was talking about a month's rent." She shrugged. "So I said yes—but I told Marvin this was a one-time thing. I mean, I'm not a whore, you know. I just wanted a part—and I really needed the money. The next morning, there was a costume delivered for the audition, a beautiful red velvet dressing gown, and FedEx brought me the sides for that night."

"FedEx brought you what?" Jace asked.

"The sides. The scene. The script pages."

He nodded.

"I recognized the dialogue right away. It was from *Gone With the Wind*—I've seen that movie about a jillion times. So I called Marvin back, and said, 'What's this?' I mean, the sides are s'posed to be from the role they're casting, but this was the Scarlett O'Hara part in a movie that was made, what, fifty years ago?"

"What did Marvin say?"

"That if I did whatever the guy wanted, I'd be in a great position to get cast in their next movie before the breakdowns came out. 'Don't ask questions,' that's what Marvin said."

"Marvin seems like a real sweetie."

"Yeah—" she laughed ruefully "—that's why I don't have an agent anymore."

Jace was fascinated. This was classic Hollywood sleaze.

"I didn't know it was Right Path Films until I got there. The office was closed, but Robert Brandon unlocked the door when I arrived. He's got this extra room off his office—you know, a bed and a bathroom?—and that's where we went. He told me to change in the bathroom. He's a bald guy with glasses, but when I came out, he had taken off his glasses and he was wearing a rug." She smiled at the memory. "He probably thought he looked like Clark Gable, but I had a hard time not laughing."

Jace grinned, imagining Brandon doing Gable with a twitch. "That must have been some sight," he agreed.

"Do you have a cigarette? I quit three years ago, but . . ."

"No, sorry. I can get you a pack from the waitress."

"Forget it." Joy sighed. "Where was I? Oh yeah, so he wants to run through the scene a couple times first, so he can block it and check out my Georgia Peach accent. You've seen the movie, right?"

He nodded.

"Okay. You remember the scene where Scarlett comes downstairs and finds Rhett Butler getting drunk in the dining room and they have this big argument? and he carries her off upstairs, like he's going to rape her?"

Jace remembered it. "Not PC," he commented. Joy looked blank at the acronym. "Politically correct," he clarified.

"Yeah," she said, obviously unfamiliar with the term. "So we do the scene from the top a couple times, right up to the point where he's s'posed to pick her up." She laughed. "I figured he didn't want to strain his back. Pretty dumb, huh?"

"Logical assumption," he smiled. "So what happened?"

"He said we were ready; I could see *he* was. He must've pressed a button on a remote, but I didn't see him do it then, just later, when he turned it off. So I went

all-out, Southern belle accent and all, and he did Rhett
Butler. It was kind of fun, once I got into it—I mean, it's
a role you'd kill for, you know?—but then we got to the
end. Instead of breaking, he swept me up and carried me
over to the bed. He whispered, 'Stay in character,' but
that's when it stopped being fun." She paused. "He tore
open my robe and raped me."

She stopped to drain her scotch. "Well, I guess he
technically raped Scarlett, because Joy was getting paid
for it; I mean, I wasn't really fighting hard or anything,
but . . ." She took a deep breath, sat up straighter. "Anyway, afterward, I went into the bathroom to wash up,
and when I came out, he'd opened this big cabinet and
turned on the TV. I looked to see what he was watching—and it was us! The *caffon'* had taped it!"

Her indignation seemed real to Jace. If she had stolen
the tape, why had she asked if he'd seen it? And would
she risk her career by making it public if Brandon de-
faulted on blackmail?

"When it was over, he said, 'Perfect take. That's a
wrap.' So I say, 'Fine. Can we talk about the part you
have for me?' But he'd gotten hard again, so he says,
'I'll tell you about it while you blow me.' "

Jace tried not to imagine Joy performing fellatio, but
erotic images of her full lips wrapped around his erect
cock kept intruding. He yanked himself back to her
story.

". . . schoolteacher in the Old West or something like
that. Nothing ever came of it. When I asked Marvin later
about it, he said Brandon told him the guy with the
money wanted someone else, but he'd cast me in the
next one. Then he tells me Brandon was really hot for
me and wanted to see me again, same deal. I told Marvin, 'No way: fool me once, shame on you; fool me
twice, shame on me.' He dropped his commission to
twenty-five percent, but I still said no. Then he tells me
to put out or get out—I fuck Brandon or I can find another agent." She shrugged. "I walked. I got *Stiletto and*

Lace without an agent, I don't need a *caffon'* like that helping me. So I guess if anyone sexually harassed me, it was Marvin Roth, not Robert Brandon, but I'm not going public with it—I can't, without complicating myself."

She lifted her glass, was surprised to find it empty.

"You want a refill?"

"No, I should get going. Did you get what you wanted?"

"I think so. I appreciate your honesty. Thanks." He took two fifties out of his wallet and slid them across the table to her.

She took one. "You said fifty."

"Carfare," he said.

She pushed the other bill back. "Buy me dinner sometime," she smiled.

Jace put the note back in his wallet, dropped a twenty on the table for the waitress, and stood.

"Thanks, Joy. One thing: Did you see any other videos?"

"I didn't watch any others, but there were a bunch of 'em in the cabinet."

She opened her purse as she stood and handed him a card. "Here's my home number if you think of anything else. Or even if you don't." Her smile was encouraging. "Why don't you give me your card, too?"

Being without business cards in L.A. was proving to be a handicap. "I don't have a card, but—" he pulled a page out of his notebook and scribbled his number "—you can leave a message for me here."

Jace watched Joy Bonner walk out, admiring the way her ass moved. Risha should be waking up soon. If he hurried, he could get there before she got dressed.

"So what did you think of the movie?" Risha asked him as they left the theater.

"It sure wasn't what I expected—I thought it was going to be about the IRA—you know, political stuff. But I guessed Dil was a man the first time we saw her."

"Boy, I sure didn't. How'd you know?"

She ignored the homeless man panhandling at the edge of the parking lot. Jace gave him the change in his pocket, for which he received a "God bless."

"Her hands were too square. It didn't spoil the rest of the movie for me, though. Did you like it?"

"Definitely. In fact, I'd like to see it again, now that I know. It was really touching how he loved her." They'd reached the car. "You wanna drive?" she asked.

"Sure." Jace beeped off the alarm and unlocked the car. "Loved her? He wouldn't touch her after he found out," he continued after they got in.

"Sex had nothing to do with it. He still loved her. Why else would he have taken the rap for her?"

Jace pulled out of the parking lot and turned south. "I don't know; I'd have to see it again. How can you say that sex had nothing to do with it?"

"Where are you going?" Risha asked.

"I just meant that sex always has something to do with love," Jace explained.

"I didn't mean the conversation; I meant, where are you driving us?"

Jace had thought he was heading back to their house, but he suddenly realized he couldn't remember where they lived. He muttered something about being "on automatic pilot" as he frantically searched his memory for some clue, even a general direction. He turned right, a fifty-fifty chance it was the correct choice.

He lost.

"Jace? Are you all right?"

No, I'm not all right, he wanted to scream. *I'm fucking dying from Huntington's and it's eating my mind, piece by piece, and it's going to keep chomping until . . .*

He pulled over to the curb. "It's just a headache, Rish. Maybe you'd better drive."

They switched seats. Risha made a U-turn. "You've had a lot of those since the carjacking," she said. "Maybe you ought to get it checked out."

Jace ignored her and closed his eyes.

Elliott was up when they got in and wanted to know how *The Crying Game* was. While Risha told him, Jace went upstairs and lay down on the bed. By the time they'd reached Pico Boulevard, he'd remembered the route home, but the lapse had him shaking—or was the shaking its own symptom? Was the Huntington's even going to give him enough time to cross over, or would it delight in snatching him from right under the nose of his salvation?

Risha sat down on the bed next to him. "Feeling better?" she asked solicitously.

"Sort of," he muttered. He reached for her. "Bite me, Risha. Your venom will get rid of it for me."

She frowned. "That's not a good idea, Jace. I just fed on you last night. I don't want to overexpose you to venom—plus there's the blood loss—"

"Bite me!" he interrupted. "I want to cross over as soon as I can!" He tilted his head to the side, exposing his carotid.

Risha could tell there was no sense arguing with him. She planted her fangs just long enough to inject Jace with her venom, pulling away with a mere mouthful of his spurting blood before the punctures sealed themselves.

The rush was much less than Jace wanted—not enough for oblivion, nor even for distraction. Either he was already adapting to her venom or she hadn't given him enough.

"Again," he insisted. "More!" He pulled her head to his neck and held it there while she fed.

When she stopped, Jace was comatose.

6

Elliott brought his tuna-fish sandwich upstairs and resumed his watch from the chair he'd pulled up to the bed. It was midafternoon and although Risha was dead to the world, she slept with one hand protectively on Jace's shoulder, though she wouldn't know until dark if he moved or spoke. Elliott checked Jace again; although his temperature seemed normal, his pulse was slow and his face was still pretty ashen. He tried to wake him, shaking him and calling his name, but there was still no reaction.

Risha hadn't left Jace's side for three days, not even to go out and feed, and Elliott was beginning to worry about her, too. If she didn't eat soon, she might drop into a coma, remaining that way until force-fed human blood. Elliott decided that if she still refused to go out when she awoke that evening, he would insist she feed off him, even if it were to cause his death. With the chance that he might lose an appreciable amount of blood that night, he thought it wise to build up his strength. The sandwich was his second, even though he'd had little appetite for the first. There seemed to be nothing else he could do, and he wanted so badly to help. Risha would be devastated, perhaps suicidal, if she lost Jace, and Elliott would rather die than lose Risha. After all, she was his reason for living.

He picked up part of his sandwich and took an unenthusiastic bite. He always cut his sandwiches on the diagonal, just like his mother had done for him in his dimly remembered childhood, and he always took his first bite from the exact center.

"Can I have the other half of that?"

He looked at the bed, startled at the voice. Jace's eyes were open. Elliott was so surprised, he couldn't speak; he quickly handed Jace the sandwich, then stood to help him sit up.

"Thanks, Elliott. I'd like a Harp, too, if there are any in the fridge." Jace swallowed the sandwich in two bites, then looked longingly at the partly eaten half still on Elliott's plate. Elliott handed that to him, too.

"Maybe some juice would be better than beer," he told Jace. "You haven't had any food for quite a while."

He checked Jace's pulse. It was still on the slow side, but more steady than it was—and a hell of a lot faster than Risha's one to two beats per hour. Jace seemed to have more color in his face, too, now that he was awake.

"How long's quite a while?" Jace asked, running a hand over his stubbled cheek.

"Three and a half days; this is Tuesday," Elliott said over his shoulder as he left the room.

Three days! Jace remembered going to the movie Friday night, but not much after. He didn't think it was another Huntington's symptom; they'd probably overdone the sex-and-drugs-and-venom. He looked at Risha and smiled. She must have told Elliott to watch him during the day. He brushed an errant hair off her face, but of course she didn't stir. Jace licked the last of the tuna fish off his fingers and swung his feet to the floor. When he stood, he felt a rush of dizziness and sat down again quickly on the bed, leaning back against the headboard as he regained his equilibrium. *Take it slow, old man.*

By the time Jace had made it to the bathroom and

back, Elliott had returned, a tray in his hand. He cleared off the end table and pushed Jace into the chair. The tray held a large tumbler of orange juice, a mug of coffee with milk and sugar (even though Jace drank his coffee black), four pieces of toast neatly sliced on the diagonal, and a soft-boiled egg in a cup. He watched approvingly as Jace consumed everything.

"I'm fine, Elliott," Jace assured him between bites, "honest. So what's been happening the last few days?"

"Risha and I have been taking turns watching you. Did you see her note?"

Jace shook his head, and Elliott looked around the bed until he'd found the paper where it had fallen and handed it to him.

Welcome back, my love, it read. *If it's daytime when you wake up, don't you dare leave the house. I love you.*

Jace grinned and put the note on the tray.

"She hasn't fed since you became unconscious," Elliott added. "You have to make her eat tonight," he insisted.

Jace nodded. "Don't worry, she'll get a nice fat scumbag with lots of nourishing blood, I promise. Did I have any calls?"

"Nothing that can't wait. Risha said I wasn't to let you leave the house . . ."

"I won't leave. Just give me my messages." Jace pushed back from the food, scratching his chin. "Jesus, I need a shave."

He stood up, slowly, and went into the bathroom, leaving the door open.

Elliott stood at the jamb and recited, "Robert Brandon called yesterday morning. I told him you were out working and that it would be a while before you were back in contact. He said you weren't answering your cellular phone, and I told him you were probably out of range. Kathleen Bester called and said Marya Ashley was staying in Colorado at least another week, and she'll call when Ms. Ashley is back in town. Someone from CineArts called and said that they're 'no longer handling talent.' Felice Sullivan returned your call and left a number."

Jace finished shaving and turned on the shower. "Is that it?" he asked Elliott.

"Yes. It's all written down on the desk in the study. Can I get you anything else?"

"No, I'm just going to shower and get dressed. What time is it? Is Risha due to get up soon?"

"About two more hours," Elliott said, checking his watch. "She'll be very upset if you leave."

"I'm not leaving! Guard the door if you want. I'll just catch up on the news and mail and phone calls downstairs, and I'll be right here when she wakes up. You look like you could use a nap yourself, Elliott. Go."

Robert Brandon was out of the office, and Jace left a message that he would call back the next day. Felice Sullivan, one of the actresses without an agent, had left a number with a New York City area code. Jace dialed it.

"What is it now?" The woman answering the phone was obviously annoyed.

"Felice Sullivan?" Jace ventured.

Her voice immediately softened as she realized the caller was not whomever she'd expected. "I'm sorry, yes. Who's calling, please?"

"This is Jace Levy, from—"

"*City of Angels* magazine," she finished for him. "I remember. I'm sorry it took me so long to return your call, Mr. Levy; I really should have just put a referral on my L.A. number to New York, but instead I depended on . . . well, never mind, it's not important; it just goes to show you that if you want something done right, you have to pay someone to do it."

In spite of her "never mind," Felice went on a long-winded explanation of how her ex-roommate was apparently too involved with her new boyfriend to fulfill her agreement to forward Felice's messages to New York.

"How long have you been there?" Jace asked when he had an opportunity to speak.

"Since late August. New York seemed like such a nice place in the fall, and then winter hit—God! I miss Southern California—how's the weather been? Sunny and warm, I bet. You don't know how lucky you are . . ." and on and on and on.

When she stopped for a breath, Jace jumped in. "Are you coming back into town anytime in the near future? I was interested in interviewing you—"

"God! I wish I was! I'd love to be in *City of Angels*—in fact, just to warm up for a change would be great, but I have performances every day but Monday; the only reason you caught me home tonight is because I did a special matinee—did I tell you I'm in *Fata Morgana*? You know, the off-Broadway musical?—it's great being on Broadway, sort of, but after nearly six months, I'm having a hard time making my lines sound fresh every day. Can you imagine how terrible it would be to say, 'Even if you're a liar, Fanjoy, I don't care. Come back to bed with me' the way you'd say it after hundreds of times? At least in film and TV, once you've said a line right, you don't have to do it again. On the other hand, if I stay here, I could get cast in a movie version—"

"You haven't been back to L.A. since the show opened then?" Jace ventured, afraid her answer would continue for hours.

"No, I told you I've been—"

"Of course. Then you haven't had any recent contact with Robert Brandon?"

The first silence since Felice had answered the phone hung in the air for a good five seconds before she spoke again, almost in a whisper.

"Who?"

"Robert Brandon, Right Path Films," Jace said. "I understand you did a screen test for him—"

The tone of her curt interruption was icy. "You're wrong. Don't ever call me again."

The dial tone informed Jace that their conversation had ended. He replaced the receiver with a shrug as Elliott stuck his head in the room.

"I'm going up to run Risha's bath now. She'll be awake in fifteen minutes," he informed Jace.

"Okay—one more call and I'll come up."

He dialed the number for Marvin Roth that had been on Joy Bonner's résumé, but it had been disconnected. He pulled the phone book out of the desk drawer and looked up the agent. The listed number, a West Hollywood exchange, was different than the one he had just dialed.

The phone was answered after the first ring. "CineArts Agency, please hold."

CineArts. The same agency that Suze Daly, Crysse Tanner, and Tinah Powers used. The same one that had left a message that they "no longer handled talent."

The male receptionist came back on the line. "May I help you?"

"My name is Jace Levy. I'd like to make an appointment with Marvin Roth."

After a brief pause, the receptionist responded, "I'm afraid Marvin Roth has passed away."

Jace stepped into Risha's line of vision as soon as she awoke and was rewarded with an enthusiastic embrace appropriate for a returning prisoner of war. As a matter of fact, she clutched him to her so tightly, he was having some difficulty breathing.

"Jace! Thank God! Are you okay? I thought I had killed you!"

"If you don't relax your grip a little, you still might." He laughed. "I'm not only okay, I feel great. But what about you? Elliott said you haven't fed since last week."

He tilted his head to expose his neck. "Want a snack before your bath?"

"Not on your life," she said, pushing him away. "I'll get a disposable feeder later." She got out of bed and stood, scrutinizing him. "You know, I may never take your blood again after what happened. I was sure I hadn't drunk more than a pint or two, at the most . . . You scared the hell out of me, Jace!"

"Hey, I'm fine, honey—really. I probably just OD'd on your venom—my fault."

He stood to kiss her in reassurance, but the kiss became sensual. The extent of Risha's concern enchanted Jace; his tongue filled her mouth as his blood rushed into his cock. He slid both hands down to cup her cool buttocks, pulling her up against him, transferring heat and sexual electricity.

Risha responded avidly, pulling at his clothes while simultaneously twining her body around him. She gasped when his fingers pinched her pebble-hard nipple. She stopped trying to unbutton his shirt and ripped it open; the last three buttons flew, and she dropped her lips to his chest, her tongue searching, as she pulled ineffectively at his belt buckle. Jace laid her back on the bed and took off his jeans, inflamed by the sight of her writhing body into a full erection which somewhat hampered the process.

Their lovemaking was intense and urgent, and orgasms quickly overwhelmed them both. Risha stifled an ecstatic scream at the base of Jace's neck. He could feel her fangs lengthen and he wanted to feel them sink into his skin, pumping hallucinogenic venom into his bloodstream as he came; the memory of the sensation pushed him past the brink and he released explosively, even as Risha pulled her head back.

"OhgodJace—I'm so afraid to lose you . . . I love you so much!"

Their spasms ebbed, and Jace kissed Risha, then rolled off to one side. He propped himself on an elbow, touching her cheek as he looked seriously into her pale eyes.

"We can't stop partway, Risha, you've said so yourself. Once I've crossed over, you can stop worrying about me all the time; nothing can affect me then. But if we don't go through with it, you will lose me one day."

She closed her eyes for a moment, then nodded.

"Your bath is getting cold," he said. "Get dressed and we'll go find you a feeder." He got up and pulled gently on her hand. "But save a little room for some of my blood."

Jace maneuvered the Honda around a sightseeing bus and turned south, off busy Hollywood Boulevard. Nearby Selma Avenue had fewer people on the street than the boulevard, and few of the pedestrians were tourists.

"How about a nice hooker?" he suggested to Risha.

"Too big a chance of AIDS."

Jace was startled. "You can get AIDS? But I thought—"

"Vampirism made me immune? It does . . . but feeders with AIDS can upset my stomach, and I'd rather not have one for breakfast after not feeding for so long. Let's find a healthy-looking homeless person."

Jace continued to cruise the dark Hollywood streets, saying nothing, but he was slightly disturbed. He knew that Risha had fed on the homeless before—he became aware of several such victims during his original investigation—but he thought she'd since limited her feeders to those who preyed on others. He realized he was probably being naive; she'd been feeding over a hundred times a year for more than two decades—it was unrealistic to expect that she would confine her hunt to such a tiny percentage of the human population. He'd sort of assumed that, together, they would become secret assets to the city, quietly removing the less desirable elements as they fed, but perhaps he should face up to the inevitability that he would soon be murdering innocent people.

"Pull over," she commanded as she stared through the passenger window.

A man in a scruffy camouflage jacket sat against a brick wall near an alley, a bottle in a paper bag gripped in his fist. His clothes and long hair were dirty, his stubble two weeks old, but his skin and eyes were clear.

Risha got out of the car and went over to talk to the man. Jace saw her reach into her pocket and hand him a twenty, then gesture at the idling Honda with Jace at the wheel. The man nodded and got up, screwing a cap onto his bottle before jamming it into his pocket. He got into the backseat with a "hey, man" to Jace as Risha followed him in.

Jace said nothing as he pulled away from the curb. He had no idea what story Risha had told the man. An unwashed miasma from their passenger filtered throughout the car. Jace glanced into the rearview mirror. Risha was already feeding, her fangs planted in the bum's neck. His face was ecstatic—eyes closed, he hummed tunelessly, grinning as Risha swallowed pint after pint of his blood. As Jace drove quickly out of the neighborhood, the humming from the backseat quieted, and the sounds of sucking rose over the traffic noise. Jace was uncomfortably aware that he was jealous, almost as if his woman were giving head to another man while he drove them around.

"I'm done," she announced, wiping her lips.

Jace pulled over again, and Risha moved into the front seat. He looked into the back before continuing toward the hills; the man lying on the seat was still smiling, as if he'd just gotten the best blowjob of his life. Jace put a possessive hand on Risha's thigh. He suddenly remembered an old line—"Suck it, baby; 'blow' is just a term"—and chuckled to himself.

"So, is he dead?" he asked.

"Not quite, but he will be soon. He hasn't got much blood left; I was hungry. Let's dump him; he stinks."

"Leftovers'll do that."

Jace drove through the canyon until he saw an overgrown vacant lot. He switched off the headlights and pulled the car off the road, behind some thorny bushes. He got the shovel out of the Honda's trunk and dug a shallow grave while Risha disguised the fang marks on the feeder's neck with a knife, just in case the body was discovered before it had decomposed sufficiently.

They finished burying the body and left without having been seen, but a block away, Jace pulled the car to a stop again. He got out and looked around, then picked up a fallen branch still holding its dying leaves and trotted back up the road with it. When he got to where they had parked, he could see their tire tracks in the damp earth next to the bushes. Swinging the branch back and forth over the ground as he backed up, Jace obliterated the tracks, both the car's and his own, before returning to Risha.

"No sense making it any easier for Homicide than necessary," he said when he got back in. "Where to, Vampira?"

"Wherever you want, but let's swing by home first. My clothes are dirty and smell of feeder."

Jace was quiet during the drive back to Beverlywood, trying to control a sense of irritation with Risha. He'd never watched her feed before, hadn't really even imagined it. From his own experiences with her venom, he knew how happily the man had died, but he still felt somehow betrayed. Some unreasoning part of his psyche was demanding that she atone . . . for what, he didn't know.

When Risha got out of the shower, Jace was standing right there, nude under his open robe. Instead of handing her a towel, he pushed down on her wet shoulders until she knelt in front of him. He began to stroke his cock, holding a mass of her wet hair to position her face at his groin. She took him into her mouth and he grew harder, pistoning in and out between her pale lips without regard to her comfort as he watched her swallow him to his root.

When he neared climax, he yanked her hair hard. "Use your fangs now!"

Risha bit him. Jace roared and his semen and blood erupted into her mouth simultaneously. He actually had time to feel a twinge of guilt before the venom reached his brain, but it didn't interfere with his second magnificent orgasm of the night.

She was forgiven.

7

CineArts Agency was located in an attractive mock-Tudor building just off Melrose in West Hollywood, where it occupied half of the second floor. The oak door bore two highly polished brass plates; the larger one had the agency's name, the smaller read PLEASE ENTER.

The modern reception room somehow still managed to maintain the anachronistic feel of the building. Perhaps it was all the oak furniture, the most prominent of which was a large desk, currently unoccupied, facing the door. An artistic arrangement of exotic flowers graced a corner of the desk. Jace glanced about the room, but he was the only one there. The walls boasted framed movie posters and blowups of book jackets, apparently by agency clients, several of whose names Jace recognized. Two of the inner doors were closed, the third stood ajar.

Jace looked at the receptionist's desktop. The computer monitor showed a blank WordPerfect page. A telephone-system light informed him that one of three lines was in use. Three buttons for intercom use were marked "J.R.," "M.R.," and "Conf.Rm." A pink message slip next to the phone was unaddressed, but noted that Douglas Milburn was sending contracts by FedEx; it had been dated and timed fifteen minutes earlier, so the receptionist had probably not gone far.

A chuckle came from the open door. Jace stepped over to the door and looked in. A handsome Asian in his early twenties was seated in a leather executive chair, his sneakered feet on the desk, reading a script. He had a stack of scripts on either side of him and an aluminum clipboard in his lap. He was alone in the office.

"Hello," Jace said cheerily from the door. "There was no one outside . . ."

"Sorry, I didn't hear you come in," the young man said, using the clipboard to mark his place in the script as he stood, revealing remarkably long legs in faded designer jeans.

"I go in there to read because the chair's more comfortable," he explained as he joined Jace in the reception area.

"You're the receptionist?"

The young man laughed. "Receptionist, reader, gofer. Can I help you?"

"Reader? You get paid to read?" Jace leaned casually against the desk, appearing to have no pressing business.

"Sure. Nobody could read all of everything that comes in, so I do the first pass." The receptionist sat behind his desk, glanced at the phone buttons; one line was still in use.

Jace made the observation that reading might possibly be the best job he'd ever heard of, and he meant it.

"It sounds better than it is. Most of the submissions are pretty poorly written. If they can write dialogue, they can't plot; if they can plot, their characters are unrealistic. Plus, they tend to be pretty much alike: college students writing about the Mafia, housewives blowing the cover off their dysfunctional families, lawyers writing legal thrillers with no action outside of the courtroom. It's a rarity to find something worth finishing, so that's where readers come in. Mr. Roth reads only the best of the submissions."

"Marvin Roth," Jace clarified. He noticed the light on the telephone had gone out.

"Jeffrey Roth," the receptionist corrected. "Marvin Roth was a talent agent. Did you—"

"Larry, has Douglas Milburn called yet?"

Jace turned toward the voice. He'd seen the man standing in the newly opened door before, but couldn't quite place where.

"Yes, Mr. Roth, he's FedExing the contracts . . ."

The man obviously recognized Jace too; he ignored Larry's response as he searched for a name to go with the face. "Mr. Cadigan?"

The penny dropped. Jeffery Roth and his lover had bought one of Risha's photographs; Jace suddenly remembered he'd said he was a literary agent.

"Right person, wrong name. Jace Levy." He stuck out his hand and Jeffrey shook it, simultaneously smiling and looking puzzled.

"That's right, sorry. Did we have an appointment, Jace?" He looked at Larry semi-accusingly, but Larry shrugged.

"No, I'm afraid I dropped in without one. Could you spare me a few minutes?"

"Certainly. Larry, buzz me when Raymond Dunaway shows up."

Jeffrey ushered Jace into his office, a stylish room in mixed grays with accents of muted greens. Risha's black-and-white photograph was in a black-lacquer frame with a wide sea-green mat, hung over the pearl gray leather sofa.

"Looks good there, doesn't it?" Jeffrey said, offering Jace a seat. "But I'm sure you didn't come by to check placement. Are you investigating me?"

"Investigating?" Jace was taken aback. He'd been prepared to give his line about an article for *City of Angels*, but obviously, he'd have to vamp. Jeffrey knew

David South, and might easily mention his visit to the editor.

"Risha said you were a detective, so I assumed—"

So much for his cover. "Actually, I was trying to locate certain actresses. Their résumés said they were clients of yours."

"They might have been my father's clients, but we haven't handled talent since he died."

"Marvin Roth was your father?"

"Believe me, I wouldn't have had him be my partner, much less my father, if I'd had any choice. But my mother had a stroke, so Roger and I moved from New York five years ago to be near her. Unfortunately, joining my father's agency was the most practical way to do it. Now that they're both gone, I can do what I want with the agency, so we're strictly literary. However, his Rolodex is still in the other office. Whom do you need to find?"

Jace gave him the names of the three actresses. Jeffrey instructed Larry over the intercom, then turned back to Jace. "Anything else?" he offered.

Well, as long as he's willing to talk . . .

"What do you know about your father's . . . business dealings?"

Jeffrey laughed. "Don't get me started! I'll go on for—" He stopped, his face becoming serious. "What's this all about?"

"I'm investigating a case of extortion. The names of several of your father's clients came up in connection with it. Frankly, I was beginning to think that he might have been involved, too, but I gather he passed away some time ago."

"Last September—but to tell you the truth, blackmail would be just Marvin's style. I'll be happy to help any way I can, but only if the agency isn't involved. I'm turning CineArts into a well-respected, legitimate agency, and I'm not about to let my father's bullshit ruin it now."

"No problem."

Larry knocked on the door as he entered. He handed a sheet of paper to Jeffrey. "I found Daly and Tanner in M.R.'s Rolodex, but there's no listing for Tinah Powers."

"See if you can find a file folder for her in the cabinet behind the desk," Jeffrey suggested.

Larry went to look.

Jeffrey passed the information to Jace, who glanced at it briefly before putting it in his pocket.

"Why did you say that blackmail was your father's style?"

Jeffrey sighed and ran a hand through his hair. "Have you heard any of the industry gossip about him? If you have, it's probably true. My father made a lot of money with a stable of talent who seldom got cast. He'd sign up these eager young things fresh from the hinterlands, then send out their photos to a select list of industry contacts who'd pay well for a gorgeous companion. There are a lot of them, Jace: producers, studio execs, Japanese businessmen, Arab backers . . . You can get anything you want in Hollywood if you pay enough— underage boys and girls, drugs, hit men, snuff films . . . you name it, someone can have it delivered to your door before you've hung up the phone. The bastard who sired me was one of those movers; no drugs, no violence, no jailbait that I'm aware of—just willing bodies of both sexes. He got a lot of money for them, over a thousand a day per person—and I know Marvin took a lot more than the standard ten percent. I didn't find out what was going on until about a year after I moved out here; when I confronted him about it, he laughed. He told me his 'bodies' had sent me through college. That's what he called his clients: bodies."

Larry stuck his head back in. "No file on Powers, and Mr. Dunaway is here."

"Tell him I'll just be a moment."

Jace stood, stuck out his hand. "Jeffrey, I appreciate your candor, and your time."

Jeffrey stood and shook. "You need anything more,

give me a call. Maybe you and Risha would come over for dinner one night? Roger is a fantastic cook." He walked Jace to the door.

"Thanks, I'll ask her. One more quick question: Was there anything . . . suspicious about your father's death?"

"Depends on what you'd consider suspicious," Jeffrey said, his hand on the doorknob. "He snorted too much cocaine and died of a massive coronary."

Jace parked in the Southern California Electric visitors' lot, but didn't get out of the car until he'd finished his calls on the cell phone. He set up an interview appointment with Crysse Tanner and left a message on Suze Daly's machine, then he called Robert Brandon and assured him the investigation was "moving along."

He strode past the reception desk as if he belonged there, and headed for the computer center without challenge. He passed through the room holding nearly a dozen techs working at terminals and knocked on the glass door of the office at the back.

Phil Bloom was on the phone; he looked up at the knock and his face lit up. He used his free hand to beckon Jace inside. Jace closed the door behind him and sat in the chair facing the desk. Although both men were the same age, no one would have guessed it. Phil had been nearly bald since his late twenties, and his generous belly helped to add years; only his ruddy and unlined face gave doubt to the illusion.

"Look," he was saying into the phone, his tone exasperated, "the beta test barfed. What are you guys doing down there? The bridgeware is crufty, Patterson—I can't even get a menu." He grinned at Jace, then turned back to his conversation. "Don't give me that RYFM shit! Get your ass in gear and unwedge it!" He slammed down the phone.

Phil opened a desk drawer and brought out a bottle of tequila and two shot glasses. He poured for them both without asking and passed one to Jace.

"Was that English? What's RYFM?" Jace asked.

" 'Read Your Fucking Manual'—it's computer slang; bears no relation to the English Kulp tried to teach us, that's for sure." Mr. Kulp had been Jace and Phil's high-school English teacher. "Well, Jacob, I haven't seen you since you lost fifty clams to me in poker. Take you this long to save up another stake?"

"That loss was intentional, and you know it. Your wife begged me to stop taking your paycheck . . . Phillip. Called it police brutality, as I remember, said I was taking advantage of your substandard intelligence. I stayed away to protect the harmony of your family."

"To family harmony," Phil toasted. They threw back the shots.

"How is Robyn?" Phil's second wife was a perky blond drug-company sales rep.

"Knocked up. I'm going to be a father at forty-three, Jace," Phil said, shaking his head with a grin. He poured refills.

"That's what you get for marrying a woman half your age. *Mazel tov, boychik!*"

They tossed off the tequila again. Jace declined a third, so Phil put the bottle and glasses back in the drawer.

"So, old pal, you here on business or pleasure?"

"Hey, business is always a pleasure with you, Bloom. But I do need you to run a name through the computer—unless it's down."

"It's fine—that call was about another system." Phil hit some keys and the computer screen changed. "You know the zip code?"

Jace shook his head. "All I've got is a name. Can you check by county?"

"I can check all of southern California if you've got a couple minutes. What's the name?"

Jace took a scratch pad from the desk and printed TINAH POWERS in block letters. He handed it to Phil. "The *h* at the end of Tinah could be a casual affectation. Try it with and without."

Phil hit keys and watched as the screen scrolled, finally punching a key to freeze it. "No Tina, with or without an *h*. I've got a Theodora, three—no, four—Thomases, a Timothy, a Titus, and a Todd. Jeez, who names a baby Titus?"

"Bet the kids in school called him Tight Ass."

Phil laughed. "We would have, Jack-off. You want these?" He indicated the screen.

"Naw. Her last name could be a ringer, too."

"I can get a friend at PG&E to check northern California, but it'll take a while. You want me to leave a message for you Downtown when I find out?"

Jace shook his head. "I'm not with the force any longer, Phil, retired last year."

"Retired? You trying to make me feel old?"

"How can you feel old with a baby on the way?"

Phil shook his head. "Wasn't my idea, it was Robyn's. So what do you do with your time?"

"Travel, do some private work. That's what this is."

Phil knew it was illegal to give information to a citizen, but neither of them mentioned it. They'd known each other too long.

"OK, if I find anything, I'll call you at home. Same number?"

"No, that's changed, too. I'm living with someone in Beverlywood." Jace wrote his number on the pad, realizing he was going to have to get some cards made one of these days.

Jace spent the rest of the afternoon checking the tax rolls only to discover that Tinah Powers wasn't on them.

Before he left for home, he stopped by Robbery-Homicide to see Liz, but she was out. He left a note for her to call him and was heading back to his car when he ran into her coming toward the building with her partner, a young Asian woman. Liz's usually flawless attire was filthy and bloodstained at the hem. Her partner was equally dirty and held a revolver in an evidence bag. Liz introduced him to Pat Fujikawa, who smiled, said something about signing in the gun, and left, leaving Liz alone on the sidewalk with Jace.

"What happened?" Jace asked, indicating Liz's clothes.

"Gang war in a mudhole. One fifteen-year-old kid shot another, and the kid's homies offed the shooter. Then all hell broke loose. We needed four ambulances just to haul them to the ER. It's Bloch and Disch's case; they're still there, counting Uzis and picking up corpses." She looked down at her skirt. "Ruined my Donna Karan." She shook her head. "How can you not miss the Job, Jace? All this excitement . . ."

"You've counteracted any nostalgia I might otherwise feel." He laughed. "At least extortion is clean."

"How's your case coming?" She brushed at her skirt, but only managed to smear the mess.

Jace shrugged. "Still plugging away. Can you run some shit for me?"

"Why not? I'm wearing enough of it. What do you need?"

"Tinah Powers. The one you didn't find anything on?" Liz nodded, distracted by the sight of her ruined shoes. "She's not on the tax rolls, hasn't got an account with SCE. The only contact I have for her is a dead end."

"And?"

Al Watt, one of the other Homicide detectives, emerged from the building, greeted Liz, and slugged Jace on the shoulder, then continued on to the parking lot.

"Her résumé said she worked for a year at the Tokyo Disneyland. How about checking the passport records for me?"

"If I can do it without a warrant. The Feds are kind of hinky about rules," she reminded him. "You might check with the Japanese Embassy—she'd need a work permit for Tokyo, wouldn't she?"

"Good idea. I'll do that. Her résumé has her social security number"—he circled it on a photocopy which he handed to her—"which might help you."

"I'll run the number through TRW, too, if I get time."

"Thanks, Liz; you're a rock."

She waved it off. "A rock is cleaner."

"Yeah, but nowhere near as solid."

"Just before I left, Jeffrey Roth suggested you and I come over for dinner one night," Jace told Risha.

She laughed. "I'm not about to feed on people who pay good money for my photos. Let's go hear some music with them instead."

She played four tiles and smirked as she counted her score. She'd played the X on a triple-letter score in both directions—forty-eight points for that letter alone. "Sixty-two," she announced.

Jace groaned and wrote down her score. "That puts you forty points in the lead and we're only five turns into the game. Gimme a break, Rish—I've been running my ass ragged all day; no need to add humiliation to it."

"If you can't stand to be beat, get out of the competition. God, the male ego is so fragile." She drew tiles to replace the ones she'd played. "So you think the elusive Tinah Powers is the blackmailer?"

"Right now, she's just suspicious because I can't locate her, but I wouldn't be surprised. Invisible people usually have a strong reason they don't want to be found. But the connection could just as well be one of the actresses I've already talked to—or the ones I have yet to meet. It's just too early in the investigation to tell. Whoever it is has an awfully big network to be invisible—Brandon was called by a man and the drops have been made to an elderly black woman, a teenage Mexican boy, and a thirtyish white man. What do they have in common and how does an unsuccessful actress get so many diverse people to cooperate with her scheme?"

He rearranged his letters. He had A-U-T-I-S-C-C. He

looked in vain for a *T-I* already on the board so he could play *autistic*.

"Money?"

"A payoff of five thousand doesn't spare a lot for financial incentive to cohorts," he pointed out. He wondered how low his chances were of trading in one of his *C*s for an *I;* playing all seven of his letters at once would net him a fifty-point bonus. "What keeps them from taking the whole five grand for themselves when they pick up the cash?"

He rearranged his tiles again, then grinned. He studied the board. The *S* would fit at the end of *axe*. He played his tiles.

Caustic. "Twenty-two, thirty-two, thirty-four, plus fifty—eighty-four," he said triumphantly, writing it down. "Forty-four points ahead. I am Man, hear me roar!"

Risha lowered her eyes, and simpered, "Mah goodness, Mr. Levy—y'all have jes' humbled this poor woman. Ah jes' doan know how Ah'm evah going to catch up to you, suh."

"No reason to try, my dear. Just bask in my glory." He drew seven new tiles. "I have an appointment to interview Crysse Tanner tomorrow. You want to come play photographer again?"

His new letters were shit: *O-U-I-I-T-V-A.* His best word, three letters, was worth a swift six points . . . if there were even a place to play it.

"Sure. As long as she hasn't got any cats. They don't seem to like me."

"No guarantees, Cadigan."

"No, I guess there never are." She played her letters. "*Quipped*—seventy-two for me, he-man."

8

SCREEN TEST—CRYSSE TANNER

"Richard, I'm sorry. I'm sorry, but you are our last hope. If you don't help us, Victor Lazlo will die in Casablanca," Ilsa Lund begs.

"What of it? I'm going to die in Casablanca; it's a good spot for it." Rick Blaine turns his back on her, lights a cigarette. "Now, if you'll—"

When he faces her again, she's holding a gun.

"Alright, I tried to reason with you; I tried everything. Now I want those letters. Get them for me," she demands.

"I don't have to. I've got 'em right here."

"Put them on the table."

Rick smiles, shakes his head. "No."

"For the last time, put them on the table."

"If Lazlo and the Cause mean so much to you, you won't stop at anything." He steps closer to her, so her gun is pointed right at his chest. "Alright, I'll make it easier for you." He glances down at the revolver. "Go ahead and shoot—you'll be doing me a favor."

Slowly, she lowers the gun, pain and tears in her eyes. "Richard, I tried to stay away. I thought I would never

see you again, that you were out of my life." Ilsa's tears
spill over; she turns away, turns her back on the man
she loves.

Rick goes to her.

She turns and falls into his arms, burying her face in
his shoulder with a sob. "The day you left Paris . . . if
you knew what I went through, if you knew how much I
loved you . . . how much I still love you."

They kiss, their arms tight around each other.

Rick tears off Ilsa's paisley blouse and her long dark
skirt drops to the floor. He pushes her onto the couch as
he pulls off his own clothes, frantically searching for the
dream that has passed him—them—by, and they make
love, oblivious to the outside world and its terrible war.

". . . affirmative experience, releasing my essence so I
could Become. After I dissolved that barrier . . ."

Twenty minutes earlier, Jace had mentally switched
off, no longer listening to Crysse Tanner's nonstop psychobabble, unable to glean any kernel of usable information. If he were actually writing a magazine article,
he'd be at a loss for material. Not so Risha, who had
only stopped shooting photographs for one ten-minute
period since they'd arrived; she'd apparently spent the
time "in the bathroom," but Jace hoped that she'd gotten
a chance to nose around in the rear of the spacious
apartment while he'd kept Crysse talking.

". . . a Scorpio, but he discharged his rage when he
started directing . . ."

Crysse Tanner looked like the girl next door that no
one, at least outside of southern California, actually
lived next to. Her straw-blond hair appeared tossed by
the wind and streaked by the sun, a testament to the art
of her hairdresser. Her face showed the faint hints of
freckles on a light tan that was out of place in the middle
of winter, and her blue eyes seemed almost to reflect
light at times. Her lips had that quality that only babies
and French women seemed to have, an innocent fullness

that held men's eyes captive. The nipples of her small, high breasts poked enticingly against her thin yellow T-shirt, and her tight jeans left no doubt that she wore no underwear. Jace wondered if the denim seam between her nether lips turned her on; it sure as hell had that effect on him.

". . . not to be understood as positive or negative, but for what it *is*, an affirmation of the inner child . . ." she continued.

Her Hollywood Hills apartment wasn't what Jace expected from a would-be actress. You don't get views for under $1500 a month, and this place was large enough to warrant an additional $500. He was about to ask Crysse what else she did for a living when he felt something heavy around his ankle.

Jace looked down, then froze. A thick snake was rubbing its upper chest against his shoelaces, all but a foot of its body still under the couch. Risha had just knelt next to the couch to get a good camera angle; she followed Jace's stare down, shrieked, and fell backwards against the heavy glass coffee table.

"Are you alright?" Crysse stopped babbling and leapt to her feet to help Risha up.

Jace tried to pull his leg up, but the snake had no intention of letting go. "Friend of yours?" he said to Crysse, trying to sound more casual than he felt.

The snake was gyrating oddly, almost as if trying to mate with Jace's Reebok. It appeared to be wearing a translucent collar.

"She won't hurt you. She's shedding—see? It's easier for her to crawl out of her old skin if she catches it on something. Just hold still, it won't take long. If I move her now, it'll upset her psychic balance."

Risha had regained her equilibrium and was already snapping photos of the snake undressing. Jace was not as calm, but he tried his best to hide it as more and more of the snake appeared through the old skin collecting on the side of his shoe. Its shiny head was now three feet closer to the kitchen; not only had the tail not yet emerged from under the couch, but its girth had not yet begun to taper.

"Uh, how long is . . . she?" he asked.

Crysse smiled, but Jace missed it because he was still staring at her pet. "I can't really be sure, because she won't straighten out to be measured, but I think she's about eight or nine feet. Greta's a boa constrictor," she added helpfully, "and they can get to be twice that long. They're not poisonous, you know."

"Greta?"

"Greta Garboa. Her previous person named her that, so she was just destined to become an actor's familiar."

Jace noticed with relief that the last eighteen inches of boa had appeared, so the shedding process was almost over. Her discarded skin looked like dried onionskin against his shoe, and bore the faint pattern of the snake's markings. The snake's new skin shone iridescently as Greta trundled off toward the kitchen . . . if a snake can be said to trundle. It was actually quite pretty, Jace thought, but a very weird pet, even for Hollywood.

"She likes to eat as soon as she sheds," Crysse said, going into the kitchen. "This'll only take a minute."

"What do you feed her?" Risha asked.

Crysse opened the freezer and took out a package, which she put into the microwave. "Rats," she called. "I'll be in as soon as I defrost one."

Within minutes, Greta had disappeared around the kitchen counter. Crysse opened the microwave, unwrapped the package, dumped the thawed rat, still covered with white fur, into a bowl on the floor; she washed her hands at the kitchen sink, and returned to the couch.

"She's a pacifist," she explained. "She won't kill. That makes it more convenient for me, because I don't have to keep live rats for her, but it would be easier if she'd eat veggies, fruits, or grains. The only meat here is Greta's. Now, where was I?"

Ten minutes later, Jace turned over the tape, and

Risha excused herself again to disappear into the back of the apartment.

". . . I'm sure Mrs. Anderson at the orphanage never thought I'd amount to anything, and if I'd stayed in Bakersfield, she'd be right; I'd probably still be a waitress at Bastanchury's Basque Family Restaurant, instead of where I am today."

"It's hard to make it in this town, too," Jace pointed out, trying to segue into his real question. "You have to put up with a lot, don't you? Casting couches and all that?"

Greta crawled out of the kitchen, a noticeable lump in her midsection, and curled up on the rug under the television.

"Oh, that. I had this dyke casting director come on to me once, but when she became aware I knew my center, she discharged."

Jace had no idea what that meant. "You got the role?"

Crysse shook her head. "She wouldn't have cast me even if I had let her violate my aura—they were looking for someone mousy; I had way too much power for them."

"Haven't men made passes during auditions? Producers, for example?"

"Nothing I couldn't cope with," Crysse said, waving off the question. "I'll bet you're a Sagittarian, right?"

"Well, she didn't have a cat," Jace commented to Risha as they drove down the hill.

"I thought the snake was kind of cute. You didn't enjoy it much though, did you?"

"What's to enjoy? It's not like it comes when you call it, or fetches the newspaper or anything. You can't even take it for a walk; it'd crawl right through the collar."

"I think the correct phrase is 'take it for a slither.' Did Crysse say anything about Robert Brandon while I was out of the room?" Risha asked.

"No, I couldn't even keep her focused on the subject.

She started blathering on about God-knows-what, and there was no opportunity to bring it up again. What an airhead! Did you snoop around while you were back there?"

"That's why you brought me, wasn't it? I didn't get much time in the bedroom; I was afraid she'd hear me if I opened drawers or the closet. She's got this . . . shrine, I guess it is. It had an Indian goddess, and candles and incense, that kind of stuff, but some of it looked like voodoo, dolls with pins, a candle in a glass marked SUC-CESS. There was a Chinese bowl on the shrine, filled with flower petals. She had business cards all around her dresser mirror—I saw Robert Brandon's, but there were cards for at least twenty other people in the industry, too."

"That means she met him," Jace said.

"You already knew that. He videotaped her, remember?"

"So he says. Anything else?"

He turned west on Sunset, which turned out to be a gross error in judgment; the Friday night traffic was heavy. He looked for a chance to turn left and get off the boulevard.

"I checked out her medicine cabinet when I was in the bathroom. Herbal toothpaste, ginseng, golden seal, vitamins. Two prescriptions: birth control pills and Valium."

"For when she can't affirm her center, I guess."

Risha laughed. "The Valium wasn't hers. The name on the label was William Tanner, but I didn't see any signs that anyone else lived there."

Jace turned south on La Cienega and quickly ran into traffic leaving the two theater complexes at Beverly. "She didn't mention a husband, but maybe they're divorced. If he's paying alimony, it would account for her lifestyle."

"She doesn't work? Other than acting, I mean?"

"I was just about to ask her when the snake put in an

appearance. Later, I forgot all about it. I can always do a follow-up if necessary." He honked at a Cadillac that swerved in front of him. "You know, I've never seen a Caddie signal. Do you think they make them without turn signals?"

"Probably. Well, it's only ten-fifteen. What do you want to do?"

"I dunno, Marty, what do you wanna do?" He finally reached Olympic and turned right. It was one of the fastest routes across town. "I wouldn't mind staying in and reading. I just started the new John Sandford before you woke up tonight."

"Would you mind if I went out? I thought I'd go down to the Third Street Promenade and shoot the crowd, maybe swing by Venice later for a feeder."

"Suit yourself. Just make sure you dispose of the body. If I'm asleep when you get in, wake me up. It's been two days since you last dosed me with venom."

"You used to want me to wake you up for sex," Risha chided with a smile.

"Come to think of it, it's been two days since we fucked, too. Come home early, I'll wait up."

Jace began to notice signs of change by the beginning of the third week. The cloying sweetness of Risha's venom, once so prominent, now seemed only a bare hint. And not only did it no longer cause unconsciousness, but the buzz was no more than he might experience from smoking half a joint. He missed the ecstatic rush from her venom, but sadly concluded that it was just as well that it eventually lessened; junkies were addicted to the drug rush, and would do anything to be able to experience it again and again. Jace wanted vampirism for the powers it gave him, not to give it power over him.

He lathered his face and peered into the mirror. Fortunately, he could still see himself; he'd have to switch to an electric razor after he crossed over—or get Elliott to shave him when he did Risha's makeup for her. At least he wouldn't be able to count his own gray hairs anymore.

While Jace could distinguish change in the high and the taste, the venom's effect on his disease was harder to discern. Although he hadn't had any more major episodes of spasms or memory loss, he still experienced the periodic tremors in his hands that he'd suffered for the last year and a half. Perhaps they didn't last as long, but he'd never timed their duration before—any difference wasn't more than a minute or so, and could just as well be wishful thinking.

He did seem to be getting by on less sleep. Although there had been many times, when he was still in the Job, when he would grab only three or four hours for days at a time, the practice had begun to tell on him by his midthirties, when his energy level suffered badly from the deprivation. With no need for an alarm clock after he retired, he usually slept about seven hours. But recently he'd been staying up with Risha almost 'til dawn, then sleeping until midmorning, four or five hours which now felt like a full night's sleep.

He finished shaving and got into the shower. He was getting a lot of reading done; he was planning to swing by the Midnight Special Bookstore to buy another bag of novels. Time enough to read all he wanted was the realization of a lifelong fantasy. As long as there were books, he'd always be entertained. There was another James Clavell due sometime soon, and maybe the new Robert Parker was out. Perhaps he might even search out some new authors—the dozen or so whose output he consumed usually wrote only one book a year, and he was going through two or three a month, even with the Brandon case.

He pulled on his jeans and his *New York Times* crossword puzzle T-shirt, sniffing the shirt before he put it on. Downstairs, he found Elliott outside the open kitchen door, staring at the woven grass mat under his feet.

"Must be all the rain," the older man said. "It's sprouting!" Indeed, there were four or five green shoots growing out of the mat. "You think something's just as dead as can be, and then one day, there it is, alive again."

Jace laughed, "Even the adornments here are vampiric. Is there any coffee?" Even though he didn't need the boost, he saw no need to stop having his caffeine in the morning.

"I was just about to put up a fresh pot—it'll be ready in a few minutes. I got some doughnuts while I was out," Elliott added, closing the door behind him as he handed a bag to Jace.

Jace looked in the bag—glazed jelly and chocolate-covered French doughnuts. Although they were among his favorites, he had no appetite for them. Another venom-induced change? He put the bag on the counter.

"Maybe with the coffee," he told Elliott. "Any calls?"

"You'll have to check the machine; I've been out all morning, getting Risha's prints to *City of Angels* and picking up darkroom supplies."

The machine flashed that two messages had been recorded. Jace sat at the desk, pen in hand, and hit playback.

"Jace Levy," the sultry voice began, "this is Joy Bonner." Immediately, Jace formed a mental image of the statuesque brunette that centered on the shape of her lips. "I'm calling to invite you to a play I'm in at the Morgan-Wixson Theater in West L.A. I would have mailed you an invitation, but I don't have your address. Anyway, it's called *Look Back in Anger* and it's Fridays and Saturdays for the next two weeks, but I play Alison only for the Saturday matinees. If you can come, give me a call, and I'll put your name on the guest list. I hope you can make it."

The other call was from Liz. "Jace, I've got some information for you. I'm going to see Ronnie Schaffer at the lab, but I should be back by ten-thirty."

Jace looked at the desk clock; it was twenty to eleven.

"Homicide. Robinson." She sounded rushed.

"Extortion. Levy," Jace responded.

"Hi, Jace—we were just about to leave on a call. Can we make it fast?"

"You tell me—you're the one with the information."

"Oh, right. OK, no U.S. passport has been issued to Tinah Powers. Maybe she's got a foreign passport, but I called TRW and ran the social security number you gave me, too. There's a credit history attached, but they wouldn't release it to me without a search warrant. What they did tell me was that the number doesn't belong to her."

"The name wasn't hers?"

"No, but it matched one of your other suspects," Liz said. "Hold on a second, I've got it somewhere. Okay, here it is. The social security number Tinah Powers used belongs to Crysse Tanner."

9

"Hi, Mr. Levy," Larry greeted Jace. "Mr. Roth told me you'd be by sometime today. He's—"

The phone on the desk rang.

"Excuse me." He answered "CineArts" and picked up a pen. "No, Ms. Hiser, he's out all day today. I can page him if—" He wrote rapidly. "Susan Dey attached . . . deficit financer calling 11 A.M. tomorrow. OK, I'll make sure he knows in time . . . Certainly. Good-bye."

Larry finished writing out the message, then turned back to Jace. "Sorry about the interruption. Mr. Roth apologizes for not being here; he's attending a memorial service for Arthur Ashe. He said you wanted to see the talent files?"

"I'd appreciate it," Jace said.

"I'll show you where they are. Will you need help?"

"I doubt it, but if I do, I'll let you know."

Larry led him into Marvin Roth's former office. "All the files are in this cabinet in alphabetical order. It's unlocked. Mr. Roth said you can go ahead and take anything you want; he's just going to recycle the paper anyway. Feel free to use the desk and phone. If you want to dial out, use the third line. Can I get you some coffee or a soft drink?"

"Black coffee would be great, Larry, thanks."

Jace located both Crysse Tanner's and Suze Daly's files immediately; he'd just laid them on the desk next to the résumés he'd brought with him when Larry returned with a steaming Time Warner coffee mug, which he placed next to Jace. "There're legal pads and pens in the top drawer," he added helpfully as he left.

The first sheet of Crysse's thick file was a form with her vital statistics and acting background, including the same social security number that had been on Tinah Powers's résumé. Two sheets of paper were stapled to the inside cover of the file, listing by date dozens of auditions to which she had been sent. Over half the entries bore dollar amounts, ranging from $1200 to $1700, in the "results" column. Robert Brandon was listed three times—twice at $1500, once at $1300; some of the notations bore parenthetical initials, including "T. P." Tinah Powers? Were Tinah and Crysse the same person?

Jace compared the statistics listed for Crysse with those on the résumé Brandon had given him for Tinah. Crysse was a five-foot-four blonde with blue eyes and measurements of 32-20-32; Tinah was a five-seven redhead with green eyes, 36-24-34. He compared their photos. Crysse had a pert little nose lightly dusted with freckles and wide-set large eyes; Tinah had a long patrician nose, no freckles, deep-set eyes. They were both beautiful, but they certainly weren't different appearances of the same person.

Jace sipped at his coffee. What was the connection between them? Was it as simple as two up-and-coming actresses sharing a social security number because one of them didn't have a green card? He turned the top sheet in Crysse's file, then passed half a dozen copies of her headshot-cum-résumé before coming to a sealed manila envelope at the back of the file. It was stamped PRIVATE.

Jace turned the envelope over and opened it. It contained more headshot/résumés, all different. The top one was Tinah Powers.

The next one was a stunning woman with large-lidded light eyes, full Negroid lips, and a bronze complexion. Jace turned the photo over to read her résumé. Her name was Hannah Williams . . . and her social security number was the same as Crysse's. Was Marvin Roth running some kind of illegal immigrant ring? Jace flipped through the Rolodex on the desk. No card for Hannah Williams. A check of the file cabinet also came up empty.

The next headshot in the package was a good-looking blond boy, late teens to early twenties, the kind of all-American kid teenage girls loved for their bedroom posters. His name was Harris Powers, and his social security number was the one Jace had come to memorize. Jace didn't find him in the Rolodex or files either.

The last photograph was a bearded brown-haired man named William Tanner. Jace recognized him immediately; it was the man who'd picked up the money from Brandon at Santa Monica Place.

"Crysse Tanner, William Tanner, Hannah Williams, Tinah Powers, Harris Powers," Risha read from Jace's worksheet. "They sound like they're somehow related—except for Hannah Williams—don't they?"

"Actually," Jace nodded, "they seem to be variations on the same group of names—besides two Tanners and two Powerses, there's William Tanner/Hannah Williams . . . and Tinah/ Hannah/Harris/Crysse, which might be stretching similarities. What they sound like are aliases; criminals commonly choose names similar to their own for new identities. I wouldn't be surprised if the mastermind behind this turned out to be named William H. Tanner Powers or something."

Risha laughed. "Did you try looking up that name?"

"Jeez, Rish, I've spent this entire week tracking down every name in the assortment, in every variation I could think of. The only one who seems to exist is Crysse Tanner. Maybe I should've looked up Greta Garboa, too."

"You couldn't find anything on any of the others?"

Jace shook his head. "I found a Bill Tanner in Glendale. He's sixty-eight years old, a retired anthropology professor from the Midwest. He doesn't know any other Tanners in California. None of these people have any record of owning property, paying taxes, using electricity, or owning a telephone. None of them have criminal records or driver's licenses either . . . and Liz has just about had it with running nonexistent people through NCIC and DMV for me."

"So what are you going to do?" Risha put down the worksheet and studied Jace. "Can you just come flat out and ask Crysse Tanner who these others are?"

"Not until I have an idea what the answer is likely to be. I'm going to have to do a more intensive investigation of Ms. Tanner—she's the key to this, possibly even Brandon's blackmailer. So far, Brandon's the only person who knows Tinah exists, whatever her name really is. I've got a lot of leads from Marvin Roth's file, other people who paid to 'audition' her. Plus, there's a dozen or more credits listed on Crysse's résumé—community theater and suchlike—and I can try to track down some of the people who have worked with her."

"Well, at least you don't have to interview any more starlets."

"Hey," he grinned, "that's the fun part. Marya Ashley's back in town, her agent called yesterday; I told her the article was on hold, but she made me swear I'd call if it got rescheduled. I'd still like to talk to Suze Daly, though—she's a convicted hooker from . . ." He paged through his notes quickly. ". . . Kansas. She might be willing to talk about the Marvin Roth connection, but she hasn't returned my call yet. I'm not dead yet, not by a long shot."

"Speaking of which, Jace—"

"Hmm?"

"It's been nearly four weeks since we started. You might want to give some thought to when you're going to cross over. Sunday's Valentine's Day," Risha hinted.

Shit. Thank God she reminded him. He could shop tomorrow while she slept. "I have to wait 'til I have fangs, don't I?"

"Have you tried?" When Jace looked confused, Risha elaborated, "You have to learn to use them. The first lesson is extending your fangs. You have to kind of stretch with your gums, like this." She opened her mouth and sneered back her upper lip.

Jace watched, fascinated, while her canines grew to almost an inch in length, extending from her pale gums much like a cat's claws. A drop of clear venom formed on the end of each fang. Although he'd felt her fangs enter him about a dozen times, he hadn't actually watched them come out. It was kind of scary . . . and pretty sexy. Risha's pale tongue licked away the venom as her fangs retracted.

"Now, you try it," she suggested.

Jace opened his mouth and growled like a lion, jutting his head forward as he roared.

Risha shook her head. "Not your jaw, use your gums. You'll feel a tingle when you stretch them. And the roar isn't required, my fine beast. Try it again."

Jace felt a little silly, like he was the butt of some enormous practical joke. He imagined his cop friends convulsing with laughter while they related the story of how Jace thought he was becoming a vampire. But he knew it was for real.

He stretched his gums as Risha had instructed. He felt something.

"That's it! You've got it—push a little more—there!"

Jace touched a finger to his teeth—*migod, she's right; I have fangs!* "I'm going up to look in the mirror," he cried as he bolted from the study.

But when he got into the bathroom, his fangs had retracted and his teeth looked like they always had.

"You waited too long," Risha said from the doorway. "They only extend long enough to inject venom. Try it now—and don't talk or they'll retract."

Jace faced the mirror and stretched his upper gums again. His fangs came out only partway, then retreated. He was disappointed. "They're not as long as yours," he pouted.

Risha laughed. "What is this—fang envy? They were plenty long downstairs. You'll get the hang of it." She sat on the sink, facing him. "Actually, the hard part is learning to keep them retracted. Until you know how to control it, when you're hungry and near a human, they'll extend. You have to remember to keep your mouth closed."

"Yeah, I can see how that could be a little embarrassing in a social context," Jace grinned.

Risha became serious. "It could mean a lot more than a little embarrassment. We're safe only as long as people don't believe in vampires; if you start showing your fangs, they'll find it a lot easier. It's not a big leap from belief to using wooden stakes to get rid of us."

"I guess that means we can't guest on *Oprah* or *Geraldo* either, huh? I was really looking forward to being on the *Couples Who Suck Blood Together* show. 'They're undead and they're in love. Tomorrow at three.' " He turned to the mirror again and, with slightly less effort, made his fangs appear. When they retracted, he turned back to Risha. "How come there's no venom on my fangs?"

"You won't actually secrete venom until you cross over," she explained. "And it'll be even longer before it's at full potency."

Jace hadn't been prepared for that tidbit of information. Was he going to continue into decline from the Huntington's even after he crossed over?

"How long?"

She shrugged. "Maybe a week before it's potent enough to drop a feeder on contact. Until you're up to strength, I'll eat first and then the feeder will already be unconscious, so you won't have any problems." She paused, thinking, then continued, "You won't be able to catalyze change in someone else for a good ten years, you know."

"Yeah, I remember, but when will it be strong enough to protect me?"

"Oh, that happens immediately . . . just like losing your reflection in mirrors, so you'd better get your fill while you can. Memorize that face—you won't be seeing it again, except in photographs."

Jace looked into the mirror again. His reflection looked back, a face he'd seen every day for forty-three years. He noticed a spot under his jaw he'd missed while shaving that morning. "I could have spinach between my teeth and not know it," he complained.

Risha smiled. "You're not going to be eating spinach, Jace. Elliott and I will keep an eye on your grooming, I promise."

The stores were filled with Saturday shoppers, their ranks swelled by men who'd waited until the last minute to shop for Valentine's Day. They were easy to pick out—they carried no bags of purchases and wandered alone through shops and past display cases, obviously without the slightest idea of what they were looking for. Victoria's Secret was packed with uncomfortable-looking men being helped by patient salesclerks, and Jace didn't venture in. He was making a major commitment this weekend; somehow, lingerie didn't seem to be the appropriate Valentine's gift.

Hallas's Fine Jewelry wasn't very crowded. A grand-fatherly-looking man was repairing a watch in a glass booth while a white-haired woman with a large nose wrapped up a purchase for a couple speaking Farsi to each other. A teenage girl was looking at men's identification bracelets through the glass case, craning her neck periodically to see the prices through the glass shelf. Jace wondered if teenagers still used ID bracelets to signify that they were going steady, then if teenagers even still went steady.

The clerk finished with the Iranians and turned to the girl. "Would you like to see some of these?" she asked.

"How much more is engraving?"

While the two discussed prices, Jace looked at gold earrings. There was a proliferation of hoops of varying sizes, buttons that looked like they went with business suits, cutesy little owls and hearts better suited to young girls. Nothing seemed unusual or creative enough to give to Risha.

"Can I show you some earrings, young man?" The old man was facing him over the case.

"I don't think earrings are going to do it," Jace said, despairing. "I need something special. This is an important weekend for my lady friend and me. Not just Valentine's Day," he finished lamely.

The man smiled. "Ah, an anniversary perhaps?" He studied Jace's face. "Or a proposal, hmm?"

"Something like that," Jace said, realizing that it was close to the truth. He wondered what the old man would say if he told him he needed a gift to mark his murder by the woman he loved.

"I have some lovely bracelets in the next case . . . or perhaps a ring?"

A ring. He was about to commit to eternity with Risha. Maybe a ring would be the right . . . He shook his head. "I don't know her ring size."

"No problem, sir. If it doesn't fit, the lady brings it back and we fix it to fit her. No extra charge," he added.

"Do you keep evening hours?"

"Yes, sir. Fridays until nine."

Jace was so nervous that night, he had trouble following the movie. Now that his last night as a mortal was here, he couldn't concentrate on anything else. Was he making a mistake? Would he be able to go through with it? Did he even have a choice at this point?

Apparently picking up on his anxiety, Risha squeezed his hand reassuringly.

On the screen, a bad guy doused a captive cop with gasoline and threatened to light it.

Jace wondered if he and Risha would still be together a hundred years from now. He worried what would happen when Elliott finally died of old age; where would they find someone like him?

The guy dying in a pool of blood shot the guy holding the matches.

"I knew he was the undercover cop," Risha whispered.

Jace nodded absently; he had no idea who was whom on the screen. What if he couldn't stand the taste of blood? What would he say if his fangs came out when he was talking to Liz? What if he and Risha broke up? What if it didn't take somehow, and instead of waking up tomorrow night as a vampire, he just died tonight when she drained him?

What if vampirism doesn't affect Huntington's chorea?

The lights came up and they stood. Jace had no idea how the movie had ended.

"You ready for dinner?" Risha asked as they got into the BMW.

"Huh?"

"I thought you'd like something special for your last meal. I made reservations at Le Chardonnay," she smiled.

The restaurant's Art Noveau decor was beautiful, the lighting romantic. Jace's salmon with avocado and lime sauce was excellent, but he barely tasted it. The waiter had been surprised when Risha ordered only a glass of port for herself, and looked downright concerned when he returned later to find that Jace had only poked at his food.

"If the salmon's not to your liking, sir, I'll be glad to bring you something else."

"No, no, it's fine. I'm just not very hungry. I'll have coffee." He looked at Risha. "Two," he amended.

"Certainly, sir. Would you like me to wrap this for you?" the waiter asked, indicating the uneaten fish.

"Sure." Elliott could have a salmon sandwich tomorrow for a change.

Risha came out of the bathroom in a black negligee. Jace sat on the bed, still fully dressed.

"Jace, you OK?"

"Yeah." He stood up and pulled off his shirt, dropping it on the floor where he usually hung his clothes. Risha never complained, nor did Elliott, who picked up after Jace each morning like a mother. "So we're really going to do this, huh?"

"Don't you want to?"

Jace caught the concern in her voice. He knew she'd be hurt if he appeared to waver. He unbuckled his belt. "Of course I do. It's just a little strange, knowing I'm going to die soon." He fumbled open his fly.

"Here, let me do that for you." She dropped to her knees and pulled down his slacks, planting a kiss on the bulge of his cock through the cotton of his red bikini briefs. "It won't hurt, you know."

In spite of his agitation, Jace's cock responded favorably. As he looked down at Risha, he could see through the neckline of her nightgown, her white breasts, her midriff, the hint of her dark auburn bush. She reached into his briefs and cupped his balls, carefully freeing him as she tugged off the last of his clothing. His penis stood out hard in front of him. She licked the head lightly, then stood to put her arms around him.

He pulled up her gown and held her tightly, his erect cock between her thighs becoming even harder as he felt her squeeze. His hot tongue drove deeply into her cool mouth and her firm nipples pressed against his chest.

They took their time, alternating between teasing and urgency in their passion, changing position several times. Jace almost came when he mounted her from behind, but he held back, knowing she couldn't bite from that position. He wanted to pump into her the same time her venom pumped into him.

He turned her over, facing him, and reentered her. She moaned, arching so he would thrust deeper.

"GodyesJace . . ."

"You want blood, Rish? You want to suck my blood?" He pumped hard and fast, close to climax.

"YesJace, yesIwantblood, Iwantyourblood . . ."

Harder, faster, pounding, nearly exploding . . .

"Now, Risha, now! Take it all!"

10

Jace awoke from a dreamless sleep suddenly, without noticeable transition. Although he knew the room was pitch-black, he could see most everything—not well enough to read, perhaps, but he could discern Risha's discarded black negligee from the dark bedspread it lay upon. He could even hear Elliott moving around downstairs. He turned his head. The red numerals on the clock next to him read 5:32 P.M. He put two fingers to his wrist, then shifted them slightly closer to his hand. Nothing.

"Checking your pulse?"

Even in the dark, he could see Risha's smile.

"Yeah," he admitted sheepishly. "Haven't got one."

"Well, actually you do, but you may have a long wait to feel it; it only happens once or twice an hour. How do you feel?"

Good question. Jace got up and took inventory. He realized that he felt great, like he could handle anything. He looked at Risha. On a whim, he bent over and slid his arms under her body and hoisted her up . . . over his head. She shrieked as he balanced her on one palm under the ceiling; he let her drop, catching her before she hit the bed. He grinned.

"Pretty good I'd say, particularly for a dead man." He stood her up next to the bed. "I'm famished, though."

She smiled, nodded. "You'll have to wait five or six hours, Jace. It's too early to get a feeder."

She opened the bathroom door and turned on the light. The smell of Ombre Rose wafted from the bath Elliott had run for her just before they woke. Jace heard Risha say, "Oh, how sweet." Then she called to him, "There's a surprise in here for you."

Jace joined her in the bathroom. On the counter was a covered wineglass, a note propped against it: *Congratulations, Detective. To your health. Elliott.*

The glass was filled with blood.

"Whose—"

"It must be Elliott's. Drink it before it clots, Jace."

Jace touched the glass dubiously. The blood was still warm; its distinctive copper smell made his fangs extend. He tentatively lifted the glass to his lips, tasted the tiniest sip. It was delicious, and before he was aware of it, he'd drained the glass. Trails of blood trickled down the inside of the glass as he put it down. He ran his finger along the bowl and licked off the fluid it collected.

"I want more," he said to Risha. "Let's go raid a blood bank."

She smiled and shook her head. "Doesn't work, I'm afraid; the anticoagulants they use interfere with digestion. I'm going to take my bath, then I'll give you your Valentine's gift. How about putting on some music?"

Valentine's Day. Jace got the gift box out of his sock drawer when he finished dressing. He hoped she'd like it. He took the stairs two at a time. God, he felt great!

He flipped through the CDs trying to find something appropriately romantic, and settled on *Red, Hot, and Blue*, a modern anthology of Cole Porter's songs. When Neneh Cherry started "I've Got U Under My Skin," he went in search of Elliott. He found the older man lying on his narrow bed, reading *The Bridges of Madison*

County. His left wrist was bandaged; a circle of blood on the inside was just turning brown.

"Hey, Elliott, can I come in?"

Elliott put the book aside and sat up. "Of course, Detective. How are you?"

"Just great. Never felt better. Jesus, that was some present you left me, man. I don't know what to say."

Elliott waved a hand. "Don't mention it. It was my pleasure. The flowers you ordered for Risha arrived this afternoon. They're in the kitchen."

By the time Annie Lennox had finished "Ev'ry Time We Say Goodbye," Risha had come downstairs. She found Jace in the study, arranging the long-stemmed apricot roses in a cobalt blue vase.

"For me?"

He turned around. She looked lovely. Everything looked lovely. He felt lovely, damned near euphoric.

"Of course they're for you. Happy Valentine's Day, Risha." He went over and kissed her. Her mouth felt warm for the first time. "I've got something else for you, too."

He led her over to the settee and took the box from under a cushion. He watched her pale eyes light up as she opened it and saw the black pearl ring.

"Oh, Jace!"

"It's engraved," he said proudly. "Look inside."

" 'Forever,' " she read. "Oh, it's so beautiful!" She threw her arms around him.

"I love you, Risha Cadigan," he whispered into her neck.

"I love you, Jace Levy, so very much." She pulled back. "I have something for you, too, but it's not this nice . . ."

"Shhh. You just gave me eternal life; anything else is gravy."

Risha went over to the desk drawer and withdrew a package about the size and weight of a brick. She handed it to Jace.

"Happy Valentine's Day."

He tore off the wrapping paper. There were two packages inside. Inside the small packet was a gold business-card case, engraved with his initials. It was empty. He opened the larger box. Inside were cream-colored business cards. He pulled one out, then laughed in delight.

The embossed cards bore a tiny bat in the corner and read:

JACE LEVY

FLY-BY-NIGHT INVESTIGATIONS

"Can we go now?"

Risha checked her watch. "OK. Change your clothes, and we'll leave."

Jace looked down, then back at her, confused. "What's wrong with this?"

"You should wear black when you feed. That way, if any blood gets on you, no one can see it."

Jace nodded and headed for the stairs, a bit embarrassed he hadn't thought of that, being an ex–homicide detective. He'd better start putting his training to work in reverse, now that he was going to murder people—feed, he mentally corrected. He sighed. This was going to take some getting used to. He pulled on his only black sweatshirt, imprinted with multicolored stylized umbrellas inspired by Cristo's environmental artwork. God, he was hungry!

"We're taking the Honda because the Beamer could be too conspicuous," he guessed as he rejoined Risha.

She grinned. "Now you're catching on. So, where do you want to go for your first feeding?"

"I don't care, just as long as—" He stopped. "Shit."

"What's the matter?"

"I was going to run down the current whereabouts of some particularly savory scum before now. I got so involved in the Brandon case, I completely forgot."

"Doesn't matter," Risha said, heading for the front door. "There're plenty of street people out there. You want to drive?"

"Wait. I want to get some stuff straight first." He hooked her arm and pulled her back. "I'm only willing to kill bad guys. There are enough of them out there so we don't have to . . . feed on the homeless."

"Suit yourself, Jace. Street people are just easier. Besides, cops don't usually bother if they go missing or are found dead—at least now that you're off the force. Hookers are real easy, too—they go with strangers all the time—but you should wait until you've had at least a couple of meals before you cope with AIDS. It can make you feel like shit, even with a fully operational system. I can go trolling for a mugger or rapist," she suggested. "They're not too hard for a woman alone to find in certain neighborhoods; you can hide behind a bush or something—"

"I'm not going to use you as a lure so I can feed!"

"It's what I do, Jace, what I've done for over twenty years—and what I'll be doing for hundreds more, whether or not you feed. In the jungle, it's the lioness who hunts, you know."

"Then what's the lion for?"

She grinned.

"Fucking."

"Get off here; this is Nordhoff," Jace told Risha.

"How can you tell?" The overhead sign for the freeway exit was so well covered by gang graffiti, its original message was invisible.

"I was stationed in North Hills for a while when I was a rookie. Turn right on Columbus—it's right after Sepulveda."

"Can't. There's a barrier here," she said a minute later.

"Take the next right. I forgot they put these up a few years ago to stop the drug dealing."

"So why'd we drive all the way out here?" Risha turned on Burnet. "Now where?"

"Pull over; let's figure out what we're going to do. They don't work," he said, answering her previous question. "That kid leaning against the barricade is dealing."

"OK," she shrugged. "Go get 'im."

Jace looked down the block, trying to find someone who looked a little more reprehensible than the skinny seventeen-year-old, but the only other apparent dealers were in groups. He got out of the car. "Keep the engine running."

When he was within three feet, the mixed-race punk mumbled, "Rock, blow, what choo know."

"Yeah," Jace replied, stopping. "How much rock you got?"

"How much cash you got, man?"

Jace pulled a bill out of his pocket and pretended to peer at it under the dim light. "Ten."

The punk laughed. "Dime rock ain't gonna clean me out." He took the ten and handed Jace a vial containing a tiny off-white irregular pebble.

"This good?"

"Sure, man, the best. You want more, you ask for Keno."

Jace slid the vial in his pocket and nodded. He walked a few steps away, then turned.

"No refunds," the punk said.

"I don't want a refund. You want to sell ten more?"

"You gave me your last ten bucks, man; where you gonna get a century?" Keno laughed.

Jace lowered his voice like he was afraid of being

overheard. "My woman's got it in the car. You help me get it, and I'll spend it with you. Otherwise . . ." He nodded in the direction of the dealers down the block.

"Fuck. Just go get it from her and bring it back. I be here." Dumb shit needed help to get money from his bitch!

"She won't hand it over until she sees you got enough rock to cover it," Jace explained. "I got ripped off last time we went to score," he admitted.

The punk shrugged. "Where she at?"

"Just around the corner."

As Jace and Keno neared the Honda, Risha got out, leaving the driver's door open and the car running. She got into the backseat.

"Get in with her," Jace instructed the punk. "I'll drive around the block until you've concluded your business."

"Can't go that way, man—barriers. Hang a right there." The kid got into the backseat and grinned at Risha. "Hey, sweet stuff—you got somethin' for me?"

By the time Jace reached the freeway, things in the backseat were quiet. His stomach was growling in anticipation and hunger. He got off at the next exit and found an overgrown dirt lot with two stripped and rusting car hulks. He pulled the Honda behind the farthest one. There was no traffic, the only noise the din of the nearby freeway.

The kid had his head against Risha's shoulder, his eyes closed. He was smiling.

"Come and get it," Risha said. "I only injected him. Have as much as you want; I fed last night."

"Yeah, I remember."

Jace got into the backseat on the other side of the punk. "Where exactly do I bite?"

"The side of his neck; you'll be able to smell his carotid."

Jace lowered his head dubiously, but the mother lode smelled so wonderful, his fangs flew out to their full extension; he clamped down so fast, he wasn't even aware of it until the hot blood gushed into his throat. It spurted in waves, seeming to be instantly absorbed, like water after a desert trek. The warmth rushed throughout Jace's body—almost a reverse orgasm, he thought. When he finally lifted his head, the kid's smile had gone, his face a blank.

"The blood stopped coming—did I drink it all?"

Risha touched the punk's arm. "It's dead. If you want the rest, you have to suck. Are you still hungry?"

Actually, Jace felt quite full. "No. Let's get out of here."

He pulled the corpse out of the car and carried it over to one of the hulks. The trunk lid was still on, though open. He dropped the feeder in the trunk.

"You want to do this part, too?" Risha said from his side. She was holding a bowie knife in her hand.

"Yeah, okay." He took the knife and placed it against the punk's throat so the point was centered between the fang scars. "Here?"

"Up just a tad—there. Push."

Jace pushed the blade into the waxy skin until the sides of the blade swallowed up the fang marks. When he pulled it out, blood gushed out of the wound and all over his hand and arm.

"I guess I didn't drain him. I should have gotten out of the way."

"That's why we wear black." Risha handed him a rag.

Jace wiped his hands and tossed the rag on top of the body. He closed the trunk lid. It didn't latch. He frowned.

"What's the matter?"

"He might be found before he decomposes."

"So what? A crack dealer got stabbed and left in an abandoned car. No one saw us." She turned back toward the Honda.

"Wait," he called to her softly, "I need another rag."

"Just lick it off. It's only blood."

"I've got to wipe my prints off the trunk," he explained.

Risha laughed. "No you don't. C'mon, Jace, let's get out of here."

He caught up with her as she opened the driver's side door. "Look, Rish, whenever that body's found, they're going to dust the trunk for prints—"

She looked at him with a patient smile. "You never found my prints when you were investigating my feeders, did you?"

"So? You wore gloves. I used my bare hands here."

"Look at your fingers."

Even in the dim light from the streetlights on the corner, Jace could see his fingertips easily. They were smooth.

He got into the car shaking his head, wondering what other surprises awaited him in this new life.

"So, what's there to do at 2 A.M. on a Sunday?" Jace dropped the towel on the floor and pulled on the sweater he'd been wearing before they left to feed.

"I usually take photographs or work in the darkroom. You're welcome to keep me company . . ."

Jace began to realize how much crossing over would affect his lifestyle. He wasn't going to be able to do much detective work in the middle of the night.

"No, you'll work better without me hanging over your shoulder. I'll read or something."

Was he going to have to find a hobby? He'd never really had a hobby, hadn't tried to build anything since high-school shop (when his teacher had dubbed his bird house *The Leaning Tower of Parakeet* just before it collapsed). David South had once invited him to do an article about being a homicide detective; maybe he could try his hand at writing. He'd been thinking about getting a computer with a modem anyway, so he could research various records for his cases—all one of them—from home. He could even buy some games for the computer; they eat up a lot of time. He wondered if there were any all-night computer stores.

Apparently picking up on Jace's loss for something to do, Risha said, "Some bowling alleys are open twenty-four hours. Do you like to bowl? I could bring my camera."

Bowling? Well, maybe once. "Will they have polka music?"

"I can't promise that," she grinned, "but country and western is a good possibility."

" 'You Sucked My Blood and Now I'm Blue'? Okay, get your camera. I don't know if I want to play, but I can have a couple beers while you shoot."

The bowling alley was surprisingly crowded for the hour—a dozen or more insomniacs, truck drivers, and off-shift workers manned the lanes in ones and twos, and another five or six were planted at the bar, obviously working on serious drinking problems. One lone floozy—an overblown platinum blonde in her early fifties, stuffed into jeans and a low-cut leotard two sizes too small—looked up expectantly as Jace walked up to the bar to order a beer, but sadly returned her gaze to her cocktail when Risha came up on his far side.

"Lean back about two inches," she whispered to him, surreptitiously positioning her camera on the bar facing the floozy.

He obliged, coughing ostentatiously to cover the sound of her clicking shutter. "Get it?"

"I think so. I'll swing back and get her from the door-way later; she doesn't look like she's going anywhere soon. Wanna bowl a game?"

Jace paid the bartender and picked up his bottle of beer, leaving the glass behind. "I don't know. Are you as good at bowling as you are at Scrabble?"

"Nowhere near. I haven't even played since I crossed

over, but my all-time high score was something like one-twenty-five. I'm an intellectual, not an athlete." Risha laughed.

"Me too, but I can beat one-twenty-five with my eyes closed."

"Wanna bet?"

"Ah, a challenge. Okay, Vampira—when I win, you have to give me a blowjob."

"Here?" she grinned. "Size seven," she told the shoe-rental guy.

"Ten," Jace added. "No, I'll wait 'til we get home."

"What about if you lose?" She picked up the shoes and Jace paid for a lane.

"Whatever you want."

"Okay," she said, "a foot massage—"

"No problem."

"—and an hour's worth of head."

"An entire hour? You're not hustling me, are you? You can go first," he said, waving magnanimously toward their lane. "It's the last time you'll get ahead."

"Was that a pun?"

When the game was over, Risha went back into the bar to shoot a few more pictures while Jace returned the shoes. He was mildly annoyed; it wasn't that he minded paying up—as a matter of fact, he was looking forward to it—but he was getting tired of being bested by Risha every time they competed. He would never have admitted it, but it occurred to him that a Real Man wouldn't get beat by a Mere Woman. On the other hand, he thought as they left, "real" and "mere" were odd terms to use in regard to vampires.

11

Brandon's tic was going full speed.

"Are *both* these bimbos blackmailing me, Levy?" He stabbed a finger against Crysse's and Tinah's headshots. "What is this, some kind of ring?"

It was six-thirty and the drone of rush-hour traffic on the street was beginning to mute. Jace was grateful for that—he hadn't adjusted yet to his accentuated hearing.

"It's possible," he admitted, "but I don't know yet. I've got some leads on other 'clients' who I want to follow up, see if anyone else has been approached. What do you remember about these particular women?"

A poke at Crysse's photo: "Ilsa Lund in *Casablanca*—" then at Tinah's: "—and she was Bonnie Parker, *Bonnie and Clyde*." Brandon stopped to squeeze his eyes shut twice; the tic halted for the moment. He sighed, nodding toward Tinah's, "She gave great head."

"Were either of them on the stolen tape?"

Brandon shrugged. "Beats me. Maybe."

Big help. "Can I see the tapes you have left? Maybe by the process of elimination, we can figure out—" Jace stopped midsentence because Brandon was shaking his head. "Why not? If you're worried about—"

"I destroyed them," Brandon said flatly. "I didn't

want to take any more chances. How much longer is this all going to take? It's been almost a month since the last payoff."

Jace took a deep breath, rather than futilely berate the producer for destroying potential leads. "It depends, Mr. Brandon. It could break tomorrow or two months from now; there's no way to tell. I warned you that you'd have to continue payments while I investigate this. These actresses are mixed up with the man who picked up the last drop, but I haven't figured out how yet. I want you to tell me everything you remember about them."

Brandon launched into a description of the scene he'd taped with Tinah from *Bonnie and Clyde* and reiterated how skilled she'd been at fellatio.

"Did she talk about anything off-camera?" Jace asked.

"Heck, I don't know. They're always talking about their careers; I wasn't listening."

Jace sighed. "What about Crysse Tanner? What do you remember about her?"

"I saw her twice; something went wrong with the tape the first time, so I reshot the scene a month or so later."

"Same scene?"

Brandon nodded. "*Casablanca*. She wasn't going anywhere as an actress, I can tell you that. Even apart from the taping problem, she couldn't handle the range of emotions Ilsa should show in the scene."

"So why didn't you hire someone else to do the scene the next time?"

Brandon's eye twitched a little. "She looked good and she threw herself into the work with enthusiasm. If it hadn't been for the *Casablanca* screwup, I probably would have hired her again anyway, for a different scene." He looked down at the photograph. "She had one of those high, round asses—you know the kind that begs to be spanked?—and tits that just about leapt into your mouth. I was thinking of using her to play Marilyn

Monroe in something—*Some Like It Hot* maybe," he said wistfully. "You know that scene where Tony Curtis is playing a Cary Grant playboy and he invites Sugar Kane to seduce him . . ."

Jace spent most of that night setting up his new computer while Risha worked in her darkroom. It was after four when she came into the study and put her arms around him.

"How's it going?"

"Damned if I know. I got WordPerfect installed, but I'm getting garbage out of the printer." He rubbed his face. "You don't know anything about this shit, do you?"

Risha laughed. "I can't even type. Elliott might. Why don't you leave him a note and see if he can figure it out in the morning?"

Jace turned off the computer. "Yeah, OK. How'd your work go—anything good?"

"I've got a great shot of Candra Mason and her plate of 'hors d'oeuvres,' but I'm not sure about where the cropping looks best. Got time for an opinion?"

"Sure." He stood. "Where is it?"

"Drying in the darkroom."

They spent ten minutes discussing the relative merits of including Candra's wall decor in the shot; although the painting had probably been purchased at a garage sale, its original home undoubtedly had been a cheap motel. Unfortunately, the kitschness of the Venice gondola scene hadn't been clear in the shot. They finally decided it was better to crop it out.

Risha glanced at the wall clock.

"Time for bed?" he asked.

"We've got an hour 'til dawn. I thought you might want to snuggle." She smiled.

"At your service, ma'am." He dropped an arm around her shoulder. "Let's go fool around."

Risha's mouth was hot around his cock, a new sensation—until he'd crossed over, her body temperature had always seemed cool—but maybe that was the problem; it felt great, but his erection never got hard enough to penetrate her.

"I'm sorry, Rish. I guess I'm just worn-out. I haven't gotten used to this yet. How about I go down on you?"

"If your tongue's still functioning after last night's orgy. If not, we can just go to sleep," she offered.

Jace stuck his tongue out and wagged it. "Seems to be working just fine"—*unlike my cock*, he thought, spreading her legs—"but you can give me a second opinion."

The smell of blood woke Jace; his fangs were out. With newly acquired instinct, he licked his lips but tasted only a drop of the wonderful flavor. He opened his eyes.

Elliott was standing next to the bed, his index finger showing a drop of blood where he'd stuck it with a pin. Risha still slept. Jace looked at the clock—it was only 4:15, not yet sunset.

"Is something wrong?" he demanded. "Why did you wake me?"

"I'm sorry, Detective, but I got through to one of the names on your list. He'll see you in Beverly Hills at five-thirty. If I waited 'til sundown to tell you, you'd miss it."

Jace got out of bed. "Yeah, okay." He looked wistfully at the spot clotting on Elliott's finger. "Why didn't you just shake me?"

"Has no effect, I'm afraid. Neither do lights or noise. It's hell trying to wake the dead, you know."

Jace smiled at the man's ingenuity and headed into the bathroom. "Who am I seeing?"

"Reese Hamilton, the CPA."

Jace flipped on the light, leaving the door open, and started the shower. When he turned toward the sink, he was shocked for a moment to find only the bathroom reflected in the mirror. "Jeez, that's disconcerting."

"I'll remove it this week. Would you like me to shave you before or after your shower?" Elliott asked.

Now that he was faced with it, Jace was sure that having the factotum shave him would be one step away from having him hold his cock while he pissed.

"I'll use the electric razor, thanks." Was he imagining it, or did Elliott look disappointed? "Just let me know before I go if I missed any spots, okay?"

"Certainly, Detective. I'll have coffee waiting for you downstairs when you're ready," he said as he left.

Jace thought that he'd rather have a nice cup of warm blood, but coffee would have to do. He realized they would feed again tonight. It had been two days since he'd had the crack dealer in North Hills, and Risha hadn't fed since the night she drained Jace. He was going to have to start researching some appropriate feeders so they didn't have to keep taking potluck, but there probably wouldn't be time tonight. He wanted the responsibility for getting their feeders, providing for his woman rather than being dependent on her.

That must have been why he didn't get it up last night.

Reese Hamilton's office was on an upper floor of a Beverly Hills office building on Doheny. The receptionist took Jace's business card, and said, "I'll tell Mr. Hamilton you're here," before moving silently down the hall on thick carpeting.

According to the register in Marvin Roth's file on Crysse Tanner, Reese Hamilton had "auditioned" Crysse once, for $1700. Another date, for $1500, had been coded "H.W." Since Hamilton was an accountant, Jace thought it unlikely that the auditions had been for movie roles.

"Mr. Hamilton will see you now, Mr. Levy. It's the door at the end of the hallway."

Hamilton was in his mid-forties, tall and handsome in

a WASPy, Ivy-league sort of way. Jace wondered why he would find it necessary to hire women to fuck him. Maybe he was kinky.

"Please close the door behind you." The deep tones bore a faint trace of Boston Brahmin. The accountant held Jace's business card by a corner. "I didn't realize when your secretary made this appointment that you were a private investigator," he said with a hint of annoyance.

"What did he tell you?"

Hamilton lowered his voice. "Just that you needed to see me with regard to some of Marvin Roth's business dealings."

"Were you Mr. Roth's accountant?"

"Not that it's any of your affair, but no, I wasn't."

"Then why did you agree to see me?"

Hamilton took a deep breath, then motioned Jace to a chair. "Why don't you tell me why you're here, Mr. Levy."

Jace sat. "I have a client who is being blackmailed. I understand you've had some contact with one of the suspects, a client of Roth's."

Hamilton's face had taken on an ashen pallor. He went over to a lacquered cabinet and opened it, revealing a full bar. He poured himself a stiff scotch and downed it without offering Jace a drink. He poured a refill and carried it back to his desk.

"What, specifically, did your client instruct you to do about the blackmail?"

Jace shrugged. "Stop it."

"Not get back the evidence?"

"If that stops it," Jace conceded. "Otherwise, I'll convince the blackmailer that it isn't in his or her best interest to continue. Do you know something about this, Mr. Hamilton?"

"I might. Are you a discreet man, Mr. Levy?"

"Mum's my middle name."

"If I tell you what I know, will you protect me as well as your client? I'll pay you. I just can't allow unfavorable publicity . . ."

"I have a client already—and I'm not a bodyguard or a contract killer, Mr. Hamilton."

"No, I didn't expect you were." He sighed, took a substantial swallow of his scotch. "Can you destroy evidence for me also?"

"You're being blackmailed." Jace didn't make it a question.

Hamilton nodded. "I've been paying $2000 a month for the last three months. I don't often use call girls, you understand. But most of my clientele is in the entertainment business, and one of them introduced me to Marvin Roth at a screening early last year. My date had made a bit of a scene in the lobby—about what is not important—and Roth suggested a solution to . . . 'strongminded women' that . . . had merits."

"A beautiful woman who'd be paid not to 'make a scene'?"

"That's right. I'm separated from my wife; she's living with my children on the East Coast. The divorce is going to be costly. If I'm indiscreet, things could get messier. Roth offered to take care of my . . . social engagements."

"Crysse Tanner."

"Among others."

"Do you know who is blackmailing you?"

The accountant drained his glass and rolled it between his palms. "No. A young man tells me what day to withdraw funds and picks up the money. Twice he was waiting in the parking garage when I left work, another time he came to my home late at night."

"What does he have on you, Mr. Hamilton?"

Hamilton looked at the bar, but didn't get up for another drink. "He said he has audiotapes of my phone calls with Roth, arranging for . . . appointments."

"Did he play any of these tapes for you?"

"No, but he told me that he got access to them after Roth died; that they were in his files."

Jace wondered if Larry, the reader at CineArts, was involved. "Did you ever talk to anyone at the agency, other than Marvin Roth?"

"I never talked to anyone at the agency at all; Roth gave me his home number, and I called him there."

"Can you describe the man you gave the money to?"

The description matched Harris Powers, the all-American kid in Crysse's file. Jace confirmed the identification with the headshots he'd brought along. There was still a possibility that Larry—or Jeffrey Roth?—was involved somehow, though Jace doubted it.

"How did your conversations get into the agency files—any idea?"

"None. As a matter of fact, from the start, I've doubted the story about the tapes."

"Then why are you paying extortion?"

Hamilton sighed. "In my business, rumor—even an unsubstantiated one—could sink me. He doesn't need tapes—he knows that I've hired call girls; all he has to do is have one of them talk to my wife or go to the tabloids about it and I'm dead, both professionally and personally. It seemed a small price to pay."

"Who did Roth fix you up with, besides Crysse Tanner?"

"Suze Daly and Hannah Williams. I hired each girl once. Since I wasn't building a relationship, I saw no reason not to switch." He looked at the bar again, and this time he stood. He carried his glass back to the bar, poured a shot, and turned back toward Jace. "Would you like a drink?"

"No thanks." *Not unless you'd care to offer your jugular.* "I need to know everything you can tell me about each of them, including as much conversation as you remember."

Hamilton had met Suze Daly first. He remembered

her as a woman who laughed a bit too much at his jokes, but she seemed quite comfortable with the situation and quickly put Hamilton at ease. After his second climax, she'd asked if he'd like her to leave now; he'd said yes, and she'd smiled and said she hoped he'd had a good time and would ask for her again.

"A bit like a stewardess asking if you had a good flight and hoping you'd fly United again," Hamilton told Jace. "It was considerably easier than getting rid of a real date. She didn't expect dinner, much less breakfast."

A few months later, he'd called Marvin Roth to set up a date with "an exquisite black woman," Hannah Williams, for an accountants' yearly banquet.

"I knew it'd shock everyone, bringing a black date, but I was feeling . . . frisky. I'd just landed a major studio account and I was . . . full of myself. It turned out to be a mistake, but not because she was black."

Hamilton went on to explain that Hannah had spent the entire evening babbling about astrology to the great discomfort of the others seated at their table. "I couldn't wait to get her out of there."

"So you didn't sleep with her?" Jace asked.

Hamilton smiled for the first time since Jace had walked into his office. "Of course I slept with her. Fifteen hundred dollars' worth. If you'll pardon the vulgarity, she sucked like a Hoover."

Crysse Tanner had been the last, a month or two before Roth died. "She was a bouncy blonde. We had champagne at a borrowed beach house and went for a midnight swim. I don't remember what we talked about, except that she said she was raised in an orphanage—someplace in central California, I think. The only reason that stuck with me was that one of my first clients was an orphanage."

The parking lot at the Forum was chained shut—and empty. They knew they'd missed the start of the hockey game, but it couldn't have ended yet—it was still before ten. The car behind them honked impatiently. Jace pulled over to the curb.

"Are you sure the tickets are for today?" he asked Risha. "Maybe the game was last night."

"David South sent them over by messenger this morning." She shrugged while rummaging through her purse for the envelope. "OK, let's see: 'Kings vs. Vancouver, Great Western Forum, Wednesday, February 17'—oh!" Risha shook her head.

"That's today," Jace confirmed.

"—at 1 P.M. Oops." She grinned. "It was an afternoon game. Sorry. I should have looked more closely."

"That's OK. I'm not much of a hockey fan anyway. Want to go to a movie?"

"Not in this neighborhood." She shuddered. "It's only good for feeding."

For a woman who'd never encountered the upper class before she died, Risha could be quite a snob, Jace thought. "So we'll feed. We were planning to do that later tonight anyway, right? Let's go find some gang-bangers," he said, pulling out.

Over the next hour, they saw several clusters of teenagers, mostly black, who looked vaguely threatening—at least to white yuppies—hanging out on the streets but none of the groups looked small enough for the two vampires to handle without the risk of witnesses.

"We could get out and walk," Risha suggested. "Maybe someone will try to mug us."

"One can always hope."

Jace turned down another side street and parked the Honda in front of a dark house with an extensive weed garden. He locked the car. "Which way?"

Risha shrugged. "There's a big street over there. Maybe some alleys."

As they headed toward the lights, Jace filled Risha in

on his meeting with Reese Hamilton. By the time he finished, they were at La Brea Boulevard.

"How did the blackmailers get audiotapes of Hamilton's calls to Marvin Roth?" Risha asked.

She nodded toward an alley running parallel to the boulevard and they turned to walk among the dumpsters and garbage behind the discount and closeout stores.

"It's doubtful they've got 'em. That's just what they claimed."

They passed a snoring bundle of smelly rags. Risha touched Jace's arm and pointed to the sleeper with her eyebrows raised in question. Jace shook his head and continued down the alley.

"So why doesn't he just tell them to prove they've got the tapes or go fuck themselves?" Risha wanted to know.

"He said it didn't matter if they could prove it or not, if they could get one or more of the hookers to make it public. He's got a messy divorce coming up and doesn't want to take the chance."

Over on La Brea, a car peeled rubber and a cacophony of horns responded. The sounds were so sharp that Jace clapped both hands over his ears. "Shit! Let's get away from the boulevard." They turned right at the corner, away from the traffic noise.

Risha smiled sympathetically. "Still sensitive, huh? You'll adjust soon. I remember a fire siren the day after I—"

"Shh," Jace interrupted, putting a hand on her arm to stop her. "Look," he whispered.

At the end of the block, not far from their Honda, a bulky figure wearing a backwards Raiders cap was dropping a metal shim down the driver's window of an aging Caddie.

"I'll get him. Wait here," Risha told Jace.

"No, you wait. It's my turn."

Jace moved along the shrubbery toward the car thief,

pretending not to hear Risha's whispered objection, although he could make out quite clearly, ". . . not strong enough."

The thief had pulled up the lock assembly by the time Jace reached him. He was sliding into the driver's seat when Jace yanked him back, pleasantly surprised that it was so easy. The man must have weighed over two hundred pounds, but Jace tossed him like he was child-sized.

"Wha—!" The thief twisted to look at his assailant and was astonished to find it was one dinky white dude.

Jace didn't waste any time. He pulled the guy's jacket collar back and dived for the blood he could smell pulsing in the dirty neck.

"Fuckin' fag honky!" the thief yelled as he broke Jace's hold and pushed.

Jace landed hard on the sidewalk. Surprised, he jumped to his feet and launched another attack. A knife appeared in the burly car thief's fist.

It didn't stop Jace. He leapt on the bigger man, pinning him to the hood of the Caddie. He dived for the man's neck again and this time got his fangs planted, even while he could feel the knife between them enter his belly. It hurt, but the blood shooting into his mouth made up for any pain. God, it was good!

After feeding for a few seconds, he felt the man go limp under him; the venom was finally kicking in. Jace shifted slightly to ease the pressure of the knife, when he heard Risha yell behind him.

He pulled out and twisted his head to look back over his shoulder. His feeder slipped off the car hood, taking the knife with him, and slid to the ground, smiling. Another black man, this one tall and wiry, was coming on fast from seven or eight feet back, swinging a tire iron above his head.

Before Jace could react, the man pulled up sharply, dropping the tire iron with a clang to the sidewalk. Jace could see a pair of delicate hands—Risha's—frame the man's head from behind and jerk it hard. The man dropped like the deadweight he was, his neck broken.

Risha came over to Jace, noticing the hole in his shirt and belly. "Are you alright?" she asked, worried.

He followed her eyes down. The knife wound was already closing. The shirt was a write-off, though.

"Of course I'm alright," he said testily. "I can't be killed, remember? Why did you have to butt in? I was doing fine on my own." He bent down and pulled his feeder back up to the car hood, holding him there with one hand. "You hungry? I'll wait 'til you're done," he offered.

"You have to keep an eye out when you're feeding," Risha chided. "That tire iron could have finished you."

"What are you talking about? I wouldn't have died—you know that!"

Risha shook her head. "No, you wouldn't have died. But if I hadn't stopped him—" She took a deep breath just to regain her composure. "If he'd bashed your skull in, you could have spent eternity as a vegetable. There's a *brain* in there, dummy!" She knocked his skull. "Or at least I thought there was," she muttered.

It finally got through to Jace how stupid he'd been. He'd been so full of his own power, he hadn't thought things through. But he didn't like Risha knowing it.

"I only drank a little," he said, gesturing to the feeder again.

Risha nodded wearily. "Finish feeding. I'll take what's left. But hurry—we've been here too long already."

12

Jace didn't talk all the way home.

When they got into the house, Risha put her arms around him. "What's bothering you?"

He shook her off. "Nothing. Forget it."

"It's not 'nothing.' C'mon, Jace, let me in."

Instead of his providing for Risha, she'd had to save him. He felt like shit. "Drop it. I told you it's nothing."

She obviously wasn't convinced, but apparently chose not to press him. "Whatever you say." She looked at her watch. "It's only one. You want to play Scrabble? Watch a video?" Her light tone sounded forced.

"You go ahead. I'm going to work at the computer."

He didn't wait for her response, just left her standing in the middle of the living room while he went into the study, slamming the door behind him.

He booted up the computer, but spent the next half hour staring, unseeing, at a blank screen. "Eternity as a vegetable" revolved in his mind like a mantra. Why did she always have to be right? Now that he'd crossed over, they were at least equals, weren't they? Why was she in charge?

He went over to the cabinet that served as their bar and poured himself a tumblerful of Glenlivet. *She doesn't know everything* . . . was he going to spend hundreds of years being less capable than her? *She has more experience, she has more money* . . . He threw back half the scotch, savoring the heat.

He was the *man* in this fucking relationship, wasn't he? If she'd wanted a mouse, she had Elliott—she sure as hell didn't need Jace just to follow her lead. What the fuck did she want from him, anyway? He'd killed for her! He'd fucking *died* for her, for crissakes!

He drank another inch of scotch, impatient for the effects. *What am I good for around here anyway? I can't hunt right, I don't bring in much money* . . .

But there was one thing he could do that she couldn't.

He downed the rest of the scotch and went upstairs.

"Stop it, Rish." Jace gently pulled his nearly limp cock from her mouth.

She lifted her head, her eyes still in that dreamy half-mast position they had when she got hot. "Doesn't it feel good?"

Yeah, it felt great. The only problem was, nothing was happening. He had only a slight erection, and Risha's considerable skill wasn't making him any harder.

"I had too much scotch," he said, almost defiantly.

He wanted it to be the truth, the reason he couldn't get it up. The only thing he could do that she couldn't. It must be the booze; he'd slammed back a good seven ounces before he'd come upstairs. (*Unless this relationship has emasculated me.*) It was just the booze. He wasn't used to hard liquor anymore; he usually just drank beer . . . and blood, he added mentally. (*So where's the blood in your cock, asshole?*)

Risha was rubbing against him like a horny cat, her tongue flicking at his neck. Usually that drove him wild. He kissed her, shoving his tongue deep into her throat. He reached over for her breast and began to pinch her . . . hard. She moaned and wrapped her thighs around his leg. He could feel her wetness against his hip. He felt a twinge in his cock—nothing more.

He pushed her back against the pillows, using his other hand to spread her legs. He shifted down until his chest was between her knees and touched her clit lightly with the tip of his tongue, teasing again and again.

Risha groaned and arched up, pursuing his tongue, trying to attract it to her like a magnet. He gave her a little more, a little harder, a little longer. He looked up, past her erect nipples, at her face. Her eyes were squeezed shut in ecstasy, her mouth had that complete pout he loved seeing, her dark auburn hair was messed over the pillow and her shoulders; one strand lay diagonally across her face, the end lying against her full bottom lip like a line of blood. God, she looked hot! Jace wanted to plunge into her—now was the time. He reached one hand down to his cock . . .

. . . which wasn't hard enough to penetrate Jell-O, much less the muscles currently pulsing against his tongue.

(*What if it's the Huntington's?*) He instantly lost what little erection he had. (*Is impotence a symptom?*) His mind dodged the word, the concept. It was the booze, just the booze.

"Jace," Risha purred, "honey, why did you stop?"

He couldn't do anything right! He rolled off her to the other side of the bed. "It's close to dawn. Let's just go to sleep. We can finish tomorrow—when I'm sober."

He saw her glance at the clock next to the bed. He followed her eyes. It was two-fifteen. He didn't look back at Risha. He turned over, his back to her.

She snuggled up to him, her lips soft against the nape of his neck, her arm over him, searching for his.

He didn't respond. A little while later, she got up and quietly got dressed, then tiptoed out of the room.

He was still awake when she returned three hours later and got into bed with him. He pretended to be asleep.

SCREEN TEST—SUZE DALY

"You left the phone off the hook, Blanche."

Stanley hangs it up. He's wearing pajamas and smoking a cigarette. He goes to the door. Blanche makes a frightened move, but he's just gone to throw out his cigarette, so she aborts, clutching her feathered wrap around her.

"Let me—Let me get by you," she says.

"You want to get by me, go ahead." Stanley stands between her and the door, amused by her timidity.

"Stand over there." She points to the other side of the room.

He shoves the chair aside with his foot, allowing her a few more inches. "You got plenty of room to get by me now."

". . . got to get out . . . I want out—"

Blanche scrambles the few feet to the door; Stanley stops her easily with one hand, but a single finger would be just as effective.

"You think I'm gonna have an affair with you?" he challenges.

She looks down—ashamed? demure?—and backs up a step. Stanley turns his back, and she makes another feeble try for the door. He slams it shut just as she reaches it and turns to face her, grinning.

"Stay back!" she warns him. "Don't you come toward me another step, or I'll—" She backs across the room.

"You'll what?" He follows her, taunting her with his smile.

"Some awful thing will happen—it will!"

She yanks the curtain across the doorway, as if it would stop him. But, of course, it doesn't. He rips the curtain open and steps toward her.

"I warn you . . . don't! I'm in danger!" she shrieks . . . but not loudly enough to bring help from outside.

She begins to faint, a Southern belle ploy, but grabs a liquor bottle by the neck and smashes it, holding the broken neck up threateningly.

Stanley stops his progression but leans toward her. "What'd you do that for?"

"So I could twist the broken end in your face!"

"Bet you would do that." He grins.

"I would. I will if you—"

"Oh?" He circles her to the side, his eyes never leaving hers. "You wanna have a little roughhouse, huh? C'mon, let's have a little roughhouse." He grabs her and they struggle. Her weapon smashes into the wall mirror and disintegrates. "Tiger, tiger, roughneck, whore—" he calls her, increasing his excitement—and hers?—while he rips off her tattered finery and takes her.

Common and crass as he is, Stanley Kowalski's strong young body is what Blanche DuBois has really wanted ever since she arrived on the Desire streetcar.

Suze Daly crossed her impossibly long legs and Jace's eyes followed until he lost them in the shadows under her black-leather miniskirt. She saw him watching.

"That's why they pay me the big bucks," she said with a smile.

They'd been at a sidewalk table at trendy Tribeca for under an hour, and already Jace had seen several men— walking by, driving by, other patrons—turn to look at her. That in itself was quite complimentary—that particular stretch of Sunset Boulevard had a high percentage of beautiful women at any given time—and Suze Daly could hold her own with any of them. With her looks, she had to have been one terrible actress not to have made it in Hollywood. Suze dangled one high-heeled fuck-me sandal off the end of her foot while Jace supressed an urge to run his tongue along her arch. She knew he wasn't a *City of Angels* writer; in fact, she'd only agreed to meet with him after he'd told her he was a private investigator and that anything she told him would be kept out of the press.

"How big?" he asked.

She shrugged. "Depends on the john—and who set it up. I usually got about a thou when I worked through Marvin, unless someone wanted something kinky. But this other person I work for once got me $2500 to do this sheik from Kuwait; he had a limo pick me up and bring me to a Bel Air mansion for a private party—you wouldn't have believed this place: It had two swimming pools, indoors and outdoors, a movie theater, and a zoo! I mean, there were these, what-do-you-call-'em, alpacas—and monkeys and this miniature pig and this huge snake—"

"One of Marvin Roth's clients has a pet snake," Jace offered.

"That little blond chick, Crysse? Yeah, I saw her snake once when she brought it to this party Marvin threw, but the one at the sheik's mansion was much bigger—must've been this big around!" She held her hands in a circle about the size of her thigh.

"So you know Crysse?" Jace asked.

"Not much. I've just seen her a couple of times with Marvin. We shared a john once."

"At the same time?" Jace formed a mental picture of pixie Crysse and amazon Suze naked in a Bel Air mansion with him. It was a great picture, and he reluctantly filed it away for later.

"No. I did him later. Marvin gave him a discount on me because the guy was complaining about his date with Crysse. It came out of Marvin's cut, though—he wants to keep the john's business, fine, but why should I take less money for something she did?"

"What was the problem with Crysse—do you know?"

"Not exactly. Marvin told me it was a load of shit and the john was probably just trying to get a refund. That happens sometimes; a yard doesn't seem too much when the trick's hot, but after they get off, they remember that when a fuck's over, it's over—you can't hang it on the wall, or wear it, or show it off to your buddies." She laughed and tossed her big hair. "All they have left are some great memories and holes in their wallets."

"So why did Marvin give him a discount?" Jace couldn't imagine paying a thousand bucks for a roll in the hay, but if he had it to burn, Suze would tempt him.

"I guess the guy gave him a lot of business. I got the impression that he referred a bunch of his friends. When I fucked him, he told me that Crysse wasn't who she was supposed to be, so maybe Marvin just sent him the wrong girl. Anyway, he told me he never even asked Marvin for his money back because she was great in bed, he just thought Marvin ought to know that she was weird."

"Did you ask him what he meant?"

"Hell no. It was like—what's that old phrase?—the kettle calling the pot black, because this john was a little weird himself. Maybe Crysse wouldn't play his game," Suze shrugged.

A middle-aged man and woman passed by six feet away. The man's eyes were on the exposed curve of Suze's leg and he stumbled on a crack on the sidewalk. His companion snapped a look of annoyance as they continued on.

"Game?" Jace asked.

"Golden showers, that kind of thing. You run into that once in a while. They pay for it, I'll do it"—she shrugged—"but I won't let anyone do it to me, no matter how much dough they've got. You got to have some limits." She leaned forward and put her chin in her palm. "You'd be surprised what some tricks want—I've heard it all. It seems like every man over forty has some kind of sexual problem. Either they can't get it up or they can't keep it up; they come too soon or they can't come at all. But I'm not complaining—their problems support me very well."

Over forty? Have I lost it because of age? Jace forced

his mind off his own problems—which wasn't easy, considering the topic they were discussing—and back to the investigation.

"Did you ever meet any of the other women Marvin ran?" he asked.

"Sure, six or eight."

Suze opened her mouth and slowly ran a pinky finger along the corner, touching the long red nail with the tip of her tongue. Jace thought it was just about the hottest thing he'd ever seen, then she bit down lightly on the nail and dropped her eyes to half-mast. Jesus, was she coming on to him? He was having trouble remembering what they were talking about. He watched the finger trail down from her mouth. She winked.

There was no mistaking the signal. He went for it. "Do you want to get out of here?"

"Oh, sorry, but I think I have other plans."

Like a drenching with ice water, Jace suddenly realized she wasn't coming on to him—she was looking over his shoulder at someone. He barely controlled the impulse to turn and look.

"One last thing—" he said, somehow managing to ignore the feeling that he'd made a fool of himself, "I'd like to talk to some of Marvin's clients—the johns. Can you help me?"

"Sure," Suze said absently. "Give me a call tomorrow, and I'll see what I can set up."

Jace felt someone standing right behind him. He turned. A distinguished-looking man with silver hair and an expensive suit was waiting for Suze.

She stood and offered Jace her hand, her eyes glued to the other man's. "Not until afternoon," she added. "I expect to be up late tonight."

Jace got home a little after three. The house was dark, except for the porch light. Elliott was undoubtedly asleep; Risha must be out shooting photos. He was a little disappointed that she wasn't home—even though he'd avoided her last night and before he'd left earlier in the evening, he was feeling randy and was sure that tonight he'd not only get it up, but that he could pound on her 'til dawn.

He had a list of the current whereabouts of nearly a dozen potential feeders, all scum who'd managed, one way or another, to avoid prosecution. He felt pretty good about it: He'd "taken charge," and they wouldn't have to resort to potluck tomorrow night. He was sure his venom would be strong enough by then to drop a feeder himself. Everything would be fine now.

He hadn't noticed Risha in the dark living room, but as he headed for the computer in the study, he heard her call to him.

"What are you doing sitting in the dark?" he asked, turning on the lamp next to the couch.

Risha shrugged. She was in her bathrobe. Her eyes were puffy; she'd been crying.

Jace felt a pang of guilt which he shoved aside. "What'd you do tonight?" he said casually, plopping down in the chair facing her.

"Nothing. Waited for you," she said in a small voice.

"What's up?"

He rummaged in his pocket for a joint and a match. He lit up, took a deep drag, and offered it to her. She shook her head.

"Where have you been?" she wanted to know, her tone just short of accusatory.

"Working."

"Last night, too?"

He blew out his hit. "Yeah. Why?" He took another toke.

"I thought you were avoiding me," she admitted. "You'd already left last night when I got up, and tonight you took off while I was in the darkroom without even telling me you were going."

"I wasn't avoiding you, Rish," he lied. "I've just been

busy with the Brandon case. Am I supposed to check in and out with you?"

"It's just common courtesy, Jace. I didn't know where you'd gone or when you'd be back—"

"I can't keep to a prearranged schedule when I'm working. If I get a lead, I have to follow it where it goes; it could take one hour . . . or six. What's the sense of telling you what time I'll be home when I don't know myself? I'm back now." He exhaled. "Sure you don't want some of this? It's Hawaiian bud, it'll knock your socks off." He took another hit, held the joint out to her. "C'mon, Rish, lighten up."

She took the grass from him and inhaled so deeply, a perceptible portion of the joint disappeared. They sat silently until she finally exhaled a few minutes later . . . and smiled.

"That *is* good weed," she said. "I'm sorry if I sounded like a shrew, Jace. I just—I was—" She stopped. "Are you seeing another woman?" she blurted.

Jace laughed. "Is that what you're worried about?"

She looked at the carpet, nodded.

"That's dumb, Rish. Jesus! It's been less than a week since I died for you—why would I want another woman?"

He got up and sat down next to her on the couch, took her hand. She was still looking down.

"Look at me," he said softly. When her eyes met his, he enunciated carefully, as if speaking to someone not fluent in English, "There is no other woman."

She smiled tentatively. Jace was flattered that she'd been jealous, worried; she *did* need him. He put his arms around her.

"I love you, Jace."

"I love you, too."

He kissed her to reassure her, but the kiss deepened and he felt familiar stirrings in his groin. Tonight, everything was going to be just fine. He slid his hand up the nape of her neck into her thick hair as he probed her hot mouth with his tongue.

She unbuttoned his shirt and he felt her fingers play over his chest, passing teasingly over his nipples without lingering. His cock swelled a little more. He pulled off her robe and took one of her nipples in his mouth.

"Let's go upstairs," she said huskily, standing up and pulling at him.

"No."

He yanked off her panties, then stood. He tossed one of the couch pillows on the carpet, then hooked the ottoman with his foot and dragged it closer.

"Sit there, facing me," he ordered.

She sat on the ottoman. Her nipples were hard.

"Scoot up to the edge . . . yeah, like that." He kicked off his pants and fell to his knees on the pillow. "Hook your feet around the corners; open your knees."

She did as he commanded, leaning back on her hands, her lips swelling into a pout. Jace drew his right thumb up Risha's exposed vagina to her clitoris; she was already wet. He rotated her clit under his thumb while he slid a finger into her, feeling her muscles clamp around him.

"Mmm . . ." she moaned.

"Pinch your nipple, Rish . . . pull it—yes!"

He added a second finger to the mix, pumping digits in and out of her as he watched her eyes close in ecstasy. He manipulated her to the edge of orgasm, then over the top. When her spasms abated, he slowly pulled out his fingers, sticky with her juices. He stuck them in his mouth, enjoying the smell and her taste, and sucked on them noisily. She finally opened her eyes and looked at him, smiling in satisfaction.

He stood.

"On your knees, wench," he grinned, pointing to the cushion on the floor.

He held his semierect cock in front of her, and she enveloped it with her mouth. He could feel her teeth scratching lightly along his length as he pushed into her.

"Play with your nipples," he told her, holding on to her hair as he watched her suck him. "That's good, baby . . . that's right . . ."

She dropped one hand from her breast to cup his testicles as she drew circles around his glans with her tongue.

"Yeah, oh yeah . . . just like that . . ." he groaned, trying not to think about the fact that It Wasn't Happening.

He pushed her back on the carpet and dropped on top of her, his cock between her legs where he could feel the heat radiating from her sex, her juices wetting him enough to slide right into her . . . but he couldn't get in!

He shifted, tried another angle. *Not hard. Goddamn cock's not hard!* He pulled Risha up, then turned her belly down onto the ottoman so her beautiful ivory ass was presented to him. He slid his cock between her thighs and pumped against her, his belly slapping against her buttocks.

It's not working! He replaced Risha with an image of Suze, the thousand-dollar piece of ass, but the words that came with the fantasy weren't as welcome: "*Every man over forty has some kind of sexual problem. They can't get it up . . .*"

Jace lost what little erection he had. He went over to the chair and sat down, leaving Risha splayed across the ottoman, and relit the joint.

"Jace?" she said, turning to look. She got up and went to him. "Honey, what is it?"

"I . . . can't," he said in a choked voice. "I've lost it . . ."

"It doesn't matter," she said to Jace's utter amazement. "You don't have to be hard for us to—"

"I can't fuck you if I'm not hard!"

Does she think this is temporary? Migod, this is the

third time in a row it's happened! He dropped the joint in the crystal ashtray and put his head in his hands.

"We can have fun without fucking, Jace. Gregor and I had a great sex life, and he never had an erection in the whole twenty years—"

"He *what*?" Jace's hands dropped and he stared at her, aghast.

"He couldn't—"

"Jesus Christ! It's the vampirism! That's what's made me impotent!" He stood and looked about frantically, then picked up the heavy ashtray and threw it against the wall, where it shattered into big shards. "How could you not tell me?" he yelled at Risha. "You didn't tell me because you knew I wouldn't cross over if I knew, didn't you? You fucking *tricked* me, you bloodsucking bitch! My life wasn't all you took!"

"No, Jace, I wouldn't—I didn't know! You have to believe me! Gregor was three hundred years old; I didn't know it was the vampirism—honest! It didn't affect me—" she pleaded.

" 'It didn't affect me,' " he mimicked. "Of course it didn't affect you—you don't need to be hard to be able to fuck! What's the fucking use of living forever without erections? What have you done to me?" he yelled.

"But it doesn't change anything," Risha tried again. "It doesn't matter. I still love you just as much—"

He balled up his fist, then slammed it into the wall to avoid smashing it into her face.

"Love? Love? What kind of love is it to emasculate me?"

To evade the hurt and shock in her face, he looked at his throbbing hand—it was obvious he'd broken two of his knuckles. The surging pain served to bring down his anger several notches.

"I'll get some ice," she said, rising.

"Forget it," he said in resignation. "It'll heal, unlike . . . other things." He dropped into the chair. "I thought it was the booze, the Huntington's . . ."

"The Huntingtons?" she asked, confused. "Who are the Huntingtons?"

"It's a genetic disease. Huntington's chorea." He stared at his hand. The bones were already starting to knit, the swelling beginning to disappear.

"It's fatal, isn't it?" Risha asked.

He nodded, miserable. *Eternity without erections? Without orgasms?*

"You never told me before, Jace." She stared at him. "We've been together more than a year, and you never told me you had a fatal disease?"

"It's not contagious."

"*That's* why you crossed over, wasn't it, Jace? It wasn't because you love me—it was because you were going to die if you didn't cross over! Oh, Jace!"

She ran from the room.

Jace didn't follow her. He hardly noticed she'd left.

13

Steve Osten cultivated the rock-star look; his sculpted black hair was worn quite long, his high-cheekboned gaunt face was appropriately pale, as if he never saw daylight, and his skintight leather pants cost $600. He sniffled frequently, a result of constant cocaine use. He claimed to be a record producer, a director of music videos, or a Hollywood stunt man, but he was none of those and never had been; Osten was a pimp.

Several times a week, he drove his customized van to the Greyhound Depot, parked nearby, and went in to wait for the busses ending journeys from the South or Midwest. He usually lounged insouciantly at the magazine rack as if he were expecting someone in particular but had arrived too early. Not a week went by without a potential score. The bus doors would open and the weary passengers would disembark, glad to be at the end of their long trip, and among them would be a girl, sometimes a pair of them traveling together, lugging backpacks or battered suitcases.

The runaways would be young—fourteen, fifteen, sixteen—and excited that they'd finally made it to Hollywood, sure this was the beginning of a new, wonderful life. Their wallets would hold as little as fifty bucks—or as much as three hundred, saved from a summer job at the Dairy Queen back home—and a photo of the family they couldn't wait to get away from. More often than not, their suitcases held a stuffed animal treasured from the childhood they'd not yet left.

Osten never had any trouble approaching them; they seldom had any idea where they were going to go after they arrived, and spent a lot of time looking at the brochures for local attractions. He'd be friendly but not pushy, willing to direct the runaways to the hippest places to hang out. In fact, he'd be more than willing to give them a lift—and if they needed a place to stay for a while, his house in Laurel Canyon had a spare bedroom. ("I work a lot; you can practically have the house and hot tub to yourself.")

He never had any trouble with them at all. Caught up in the fast lane they'd always imagined Hollywood to be, they happily accepted the new clothes, the drugs, the wild parties, the money Osten doled out when their meager savings were gone. ("As soon as I find the right video/role/song for you, you can pay me back.") They never realized how fast their debts would rise or that, soon, the only way they could keep going, keep snorting or shooting, was to party with some of Steve's "friends."

Sometimes—not very often—they called home tearfully and a frantic parent would wire travel expenses to come home. Kathy Faulkner's father wouldn't accept her collect call. She died making a snuff film that Osten had assured her would be her big break. Her only friend, Dawn Mallory (née Donna Sue Mulligan) had agreed to testify against Steve Osten, but before the case went to trial, she died of a heroin overdose in the bathroom of a grungy dance club. The charges were dropped for lack of evidence, and Osten went back to work, unhampered by overworked police with bigger fish to fry.

Jace was waiting in the back of the van when the pimp returned alone from the depot between busses on Saturday night. He watched Osten look around before he got in to pop off the panel of the console next to the driver's seat. Even without a dome light, Jace could see several packets of white powder inside. Osten removed one, along with a small mirror and a razor blade, then closed the panel. He picked up his goodies and climbed into the back of the van to chop up his coke.

The struggle lasted ten or fifteen seconds. The razor blade that Osten might have used to defend himself fell to the floor of the van, along with the mirror and the packet of cocaine, when Jace pinned him in a bear hug the pimp couldn't break. It only took a few moments before Jace's venom had subdued him.

Jace lifted his head from Osten's neck and wiped his mouth against the back of his hand. There was probably still plenty of blood left, but Jace was full. If Risha had been with him, there wouldn't be any waste. Jace used Osten's razor blade to disguise the healing fang marks, slicing the pimp's neck from one side to the other from behind so the gushing blood wouldn't drench his clothing. He opened the cocaine packet and poured it on top of the body; let the investigating cops assume it was a drug murder. He took the rest of the coke from inside the panel and dumped it down the sewer before he drove away.

It was after 3 A.M. when Jace got back. Risha still wasn't home. He didn't know where she'd gone or when she'd be back. He wasn't sure he cared. They hadn't slept together; Jace had camped out in the study, angry and unwilling to face her.

She'd been soaking in her bath when he'd gone in to shave earlier this evening; she'd looked up expectantly—hopefully?—when he came in, but didn't say anything. He'd merely nodded to her, brushed his teeth and shaved, then left the room without speaking. Although by then he was more hurt than pissed off at her, he still felt betrayed; how could she not warn him that impotence was part of the package he bought into when he crossed over? He'd gone into the study, planning to work, but had only stared at the State Search Menu without commanding Marriage Records as he'd intended. All he could think about was never again being able to fuck. When he'd come out, Risha had left. Elliott wasn't around either; perhaps he'd gone to a movie, but the Honda was still in the garage. Jace had waited for Risha to return to feed, but finally had gone out on his own.

He stripped off his clothes—his black sweatshirt was stiff; he must have gotten some of Osten's blood on it after all—and dropped them on the bathroom floor before he got into the shower. As an experiment—or perhaps to torture himself—he used his soapy hand and a succession of erotic images in an attempt to reach a full erection, if not orgasm. All he got for his efforts was a squeaky clean cock. With no one there to hear, he broke into sobs, which only seemed to confirm his lost manhood.

Pulling himself together, Jace forced himself to work. At least it would take his mind off his personal life. A session at the computer gave him the information that there was no marriage license or divorce decree filed for Crysse Tanner or William Tanner. While he was at it, he ran Tinah Powers, Hannah Williams, and Harris Powers. Nothing. Robert Brandon was going to get hit for another extortion payment, probably next week, and Jace hadn't gotten very far with his investigation. Apparently the bedroom wasn't the only place he was impotent. He turned off the computer and got up.

The light on the phone machine was flashing; he'd missed seeing it earlier. He hit playback, expecting a message from Risha, but it was from Suze Daly, returning his call; she left instructions to meet one of her johns at 8 A.M.

Shit. How was he going to get up for a morning appointment? If Elliott were home, Jace could leave him a note to wake him in time, but Elliott's room was empty, the bed neatly made. Where the fuck were they? Jace knew that if he went to sleep at dawn, there was no way he could wake up by himself before sundown. His only option was to stay awake until it was time to leave for Beverly Hills. He picked up *A Suitable Vengeance* and started to read.

The narrow strip park in Beverly Hills ran for at least a dozen blocks along the north side of Santa Monica Boulevard. Suze's message said Jace should meet her john in the cactus garden between Camden and Rodeo Drives. When he got there, the small park was deserted; he sat on a bench to wait. Even wearing sunglasses, Jace found the daylight glare painfully bright. A pudgy man in an unflattering dark purple jogging suit huffed by. A hummingbird hovered at an early flower on a barrel cactus, then chittered in disappointment before darting off in search of a more succulent bloom. Jace closed his eyes against the glare.

"You Levy?"

He opened his eyes. The pudgy jogger was standing in front of him, wiping his sweaty red face and bald head with a towel. His belly pushed at the dark purple velour, making him look a little like an eggplant.

Jace stood and offered his hand. "Right. And you're—?"

"Wiped out." The eggplant shook Jace's hand and dropped onto the bench. He motioned Jace to sit. "Fucking doctor said if I don't run every morning, I'll drop dead before I'm sixty, but I swear this shit's gonna kill me faster. You run, Levy?"

"Not unless someone's chasing me."

The eggplant laughed heartily, much more than the comment had called for, then stopped for a paroxysm of coughing which went on so long, Jace began to look around for a water fountain—or an ambulance. The coughing fit finally subsided and the eggplant hawked up a gob of phlegm onto the path.

"You don't happen to have a cigar, do ya?"

"Sorry, don't smoke."

"I'm not s'posed to, either . . . fucking doctor don't let me enjoy diddly-squat," the eggplant growled. "No cigars, no fat, no salt. Least he ain't told me to stop eating pussy, gotta say that for him. What's the good of living longer if you can't get your rocks off, I always say." He wiped his face again, then hung the damp towel around his neck. "Well. Suze said you wanted to talk to me about some of Roth's cunts. Whaddya want, a recommendation?"

"You've been with a lot of them?" Jace asked.

"Depends on what you call a lot. I fucked maybe five or six of his little starlets—they were all Grade A Prime Pussy, I'll tell you that. Some of them could suck you inside out so fast, you don't know if you're coming or going. Get it? Coming or going!" The eggplant chortled. "You're gonna have a hard time finding some of them broads, though—Roth's dead. Heard he kicked with a mouthful of snatch—way to go!" He scrunched up his face while he scratched his jowls. "There's other people running good cunt in this town, though. You a friend of Suze, I could make some calls for you."

"I appreciate the offer, Mr.—?" The eggplant was pointedly nonresponsive, so Jace continued, "But I'm investigating Roth's stable in an extortion case." He handed the eggplant one of his business cards and waited while he read it.

"Fly-By-Night Investigations? I like that—you got balls, Levy! So Roth's bimbos are blackmailing some poor slob? Ha! Stupid schmuck probably used his real name, gave the cunt a credit card or something? Serves him right. Ya fuck 'em, ya suck 'em, but you gotta be some kinda idiot to tell 'em who ya really are. Now me, fer instance, I give 'em my answering service, don't use my real name, and sure as fuck don't have 'em to my house—not that my wife would notice, too busy shopping. That woman's a world-class shopper, but can't fuck to save her life."

"Suze said you complained about one of Marvin's girls before he died," Jace said.

"Didn't have nothing to do with blackmail, Levy. I told you, those broads don't know who I am, just like I ain't told you. Suze tell you I was blackmailed?"

Jace shook his head. He opened the manila envelope he'd brought with him and pulled out the photos of Crysse, Tinah, and Hannah and handed them to the eggplant. "You meet any of these?"

"Yeah, these two." He handed Jace the headshots for Crysse and Tinah. He looked at Hannah's. "Don't do no dark snatch," he said as he passed the last photo back to Jace. "Pussy hair's too stiff."

"You had a problem with Crysse?" Jace indicated the blonde.

"Wasn't exactly a problem, Levy. She just wasn't who she was supposed to be. I told Roth I wanted that one." The eggplant tapped Tinah's photo. "Had her once before—big redhead, big tits she could wrap around your cock. Told Roth to send her to me at my room at the Hilton down the street—that's where I usually meet the cunts; they're discreet there, you ever need a place to fuck—but this one shows up instead." He pointed to Crysse's photo. "Short, didn't have no meat on her bones, looked like a fucking teenybopper—little tits couldn't wrap around nothin'. I was pissed off—you pay fifteen hunnert bucks to shove your boner between some good-sized hooters, but all you get is these little pimples . . ."

"Did Crysse say why she came instead of Tinah?"

"Gave me some line about scheduling—load o' shit if you ask me. Told her I wanted bazongas, wasn't going to pay no fifteen hunnert bucks to cum on her little pimples. She starts tellin' me Roth is going to drop her if I ask him for a refund, bats her big blue eyes at me and begs me to give her a try—says if I don't like her afterward, she'll tell Roth I sent her away without fucking her and I can get my money back anyway. So I let her stay—at the worst, it was free cunt, you know? She gave great head—I got a real blue steeler, didn't mind so much she wasn't the cunt I ordered. She creamed real good when I ate her out, too."

The eggplant's attitude made Jace feel ashamed of his gender, but he kept his distaste at bay.

"So you never asked Roth for a refund?"

"Fuck no. Got my money's worth. Even fucked her between her titties—they were bigger than they looked. Spewed about a gallon on her freckled tits, told her cum'll make 'em bigger." He laughed, grabbing his crotch. "Can't figure out how she made 'em grow like that. Must be about a million broads pay a fortune for that secret . . . not to mention the guys that fuck them!"

"Did you ever see Crysse or Tinah again?"

The eggplant shook his head. "Roth sent Suze the next couple times, then kicked the bucket. Took me a while to find a new source with clean cunt—don't want to get no AIDS, you know; gotta find someone tests the bimbos regular. You pay fifteen hunnert bucks, you don't wanna wear no raincoat, you unnerstan' what I'm saying?"

Jace nodded.

"You gotta be careful," the eggplant said. "Ain't no pussy worth dying for."

"I hear you," Jace said.

The postcard was in their mailbox when Jace checked Monday night. It was a picture of Los Angeles International Airport, the kind you'd buy just before a flight. The note in Risha's handwriting was terse: "We both need some time to think. Tell Elliott I'm OK.—R."

So Elliott hadn't gone with her. Where was she by herself? The card was postmarked Saturday night; she could be anywhere in the world by now. Maybe she'd told Elliott where she was going, but her assistant hadn't come home yesterday at all. Thinking he might have returned during the day, Jace checked Elliott's room, but it was still empty. He dropped Risha's postcard on the bed in case he came back while Jace was out. So what had happened to Elliott? Jace tried to remember when he last saw him—sometime last week was the best he could come up with.

The suitcases and a steamer trunk were in the garage. Jace thought it was possible a couple of suitcases might be missing, but he'd never paid much attention to their luggage; Elliott always took care of the packing and unpacking when they traveled. He went upstairs and opened Risha's closet and drawers, but couldn't tell what clothes were missing, if any; most of her wardrobe appeared to be still neatly folded or hung. Her camera was gone, but that didn't tell Jace anything.

He put on a CD and cranked up the volume; Risha hated Springsteen. With "Born in the U.S.A" blasting, Jace got a Harp lager out of the fridge and knocked back half of it before he lowered the bottle. OK, he was on his own. Nothing to be uptight about—he'd been alone before he met Risha and Elliott, and he sure as hell didn't need them now. He had friends he could see. He picked up the kitchen phone and dialed the Blooms' number from memory.

"Got any money you want to lose?" Jace asked when Phil answered.

"Are you sure you can afford to play poker, now that you're retired?" Phil laughed.

"I'm not retired, I'm freelancing," Jace corrected. "I make more money than you do at that shitty nine-to-five."

"Must weigh down your pockets something awful. I'm always willing to help a friend lighten his load. I'll call Marc and Gnat. How's Wednesday for you? Wait, hold on."

Jace could hear Robyn talking in the background.

"Shit, can't you go without me?" Phil said to her. "OK, OK—what about Thursday then?"

Again, Robyn's voice; Jace couldn't make out what she was saying, but her tone was annoyed.

"Look, I'll go to your folks' on Wednesday, but I want to play poker here on Thursday—Jesus, don't cry, Robyn! Jace, let me call you back."

Jace sighed. "You've got the number?"

"Yeah. Ten minutes."

It was more like half an hour and when Phil called back, his voice was resigned. "You think women are hell on wheels when they've got PMS? Let me tell you, it's nothing compared to when they're pregnant! Robyn doesn't want us to play poker here—can we use your place?"

"Yeah, why not." Jace gave him the address and directions. "Thursday?"

"Yeah, I'll call the guys. Can we start a little early—like seven? Robyn wants me home by midnight," Phil muttered.

"You're pussy-whipped, Bloom. See if you can get an advance on your allowance for the game."

"Fuck you, Levy. See you at seven."

Jace hung up and tossed the empty bottle from his second Harp into the glass recycling bin. That took care of one night this week. He figured he'd feed Tuesday and Friday nights. That left tonight and Wednesday . . .

He wondered what Risha'd meant by "some time to think." How long does thinking take? And what the hell is she thinking about? How to apologize? *Whether she really wants to stay with me when I can't*—Jace shied away from completing his thought. *Maybe she's looking for another man, one who can fuck her the way I used to; she wouldn't make the mistake of forcing him to cross over, leaving his erection behind. She won't have any problem getting laid—she's a hot-looking woman . . .*
An image came to him of Risha in her crimson teddy

and lace choker, her dark auburn hair pinned up with a few wispy tendrils against her neck, her pale eyes at half-mast, her lips in a pout. Jace felt stirrings at his groin. He slid his beer-cold hand under his waistband to his cock. He had a partial erection! He altered his mental image so one of Risha's straps slipped off her shoulder, revealing a full breast with erect nipple begging to be bitten . . .

. . . *by a hunky blond beach boy*. Jace's cock softened. He rejected the image of someone else with Risha, but couldn't regain the titillation. He pulled out his hand and refastened the snap on his jeans, almost elated to have gotten as far as he had.

Maybe it wasn't the vampirism after all—maybe it was Risha! She'd been systematically stripping him of everything he was, ever since they'd met—his job, his income, his freedom—and she certainly didn't need him to protect and defend her . . . no wonder he'd felt useless and emasculated! "It doesn't matter," she'd said Friday night. Did she think he was stupid, too? "It doesn't matter" that he's not hard? Maybe he didn't even love her, he thought excitedly—he'd just been deceiving himself so he could justify crossing over, becoming a vampire so he wouldn't die of Huntington's. He'd certainly never been in love before he met her—he might not even be capable of loving anyone. It was terribly convenient to think he was in love with the woman he'd died for, but was that really what was going on? Now that he was immune from Huntington's, he didn't need her anymore. Risha had served her purpose. Good riddance.

There were other women to fuck. Joy Bonner had been hot for him—she'd turned down an extra fifty bucks with "buy me dinner sometime" and a smile that had told him he could have her for dessert. Jace remembered the actress's full lips and dark eyes, the way her ass moved when she walked. If anyone could make a dead man hard, it was Joy. With a woman like her, Jace wouldn't have any problems. In fact, with his vampiric strength, he might actually wear *her* out, so she'd have no energy left to continue begging him to fuck her again!

He'd been with only Risha since crossing over, a woman he probably didn't love, one who regarded him as inferior. No wonder he hadn't been able to get it up! He didn't have a sexual problem, he had a relationship problem. Risha had taken off—he had no obligation to be faithful to her.

He got Joy's number and dialed.

Jace brought the glass to his mouth, then noticed it was empty again. He tipped the bottle over it, but only a mouthful trickled out. He downed the last gulp and dropped the scotch bottle on the couch. There was a dusty bottle of Galleano and some of that sweet white port Risha liked left, but nothing else. He thought about smoking some grass, but it didn't promise oblivion. Where could he buy liquor this time of night—and what time was it anyway? He attempted to look at his watch, but couldn't focus. He went into the kitchen to look at the big clock over the stove. Almost five. It'd be dawn soon, too late to go out.

The date with Joy had started out just fine. She'd opened her door wearing a clingy black dress with a high neck and cutouts to show her warm golden shoulders. The sounds of soft jazz came from hidden speakers.

"I'm really glad you called," she said with a big smile. "When you didn't come to any of my performances, I thought you weren't interested."

She turned to lead him into her living room, revealing that the dress plunged below her waist in back. It was obvious she wore no underwear. Jace wondered how she kept up her black stockings.

"What are you drinking?" she asked.

You, he thought. "Whatever you're having. This is a

nice place." He didn't mean it—the living room was furnished with nondescript, generic pieces and poster art; there were no books in sight—but a comment was expected.

Joy uncorked a bottle of Chardonnay and poured them each a glass. "Want the nickel tour?" she asked, handing him his.

"Sure."

The bedroom was better. Her cherrywood four-poster bed was made up with bronze satin sheets and matching comforter and a pile of red and gold satin pillows; pseudo-Tiffany lamps flanked the bed on either side, their soft amber glow complementing her cherrywood armoire and dressing table. A painting of a topless odalisque lounging in harem pants faced him over the bed, plump in the way thought to be most feminine seventy years ago; the painting had a patina of age.

Joy had followed his eyes to the painting. She smiled. "That's my grandmother, Maria. Grandpa Valentinetti was an artist and she was his model. He gave that to me before he died; it was his favorite painting of her. I guess it reminded him of why he fell in love with her." She sat on the bed. "He told me I look like her. What do you think?"

Joy reclined under the painting in the same position as the odalisque. Jace pretended to compare them while his eyes traveled over the line of Joy's thigh to her hip, still trying to figure out how she kept her stockings up— there were no garter-belt lines.

"You have the same coloring—and her lips are like yours—but the rest is a little hard to tell with your clothes on. She looks a lot heavier than you."

"But not nearly as fat as I remember her. Grandma was really obese by the time I was born." Joy smiled in that enigmatic way she had and sat up again. "So, where are we going for dinner? I hope what I'm wearing is all right." She stood.

Jace hadn't thought about actually taking Joy out to

dinner, but that had been the ostensible reason for calling her earlier. "How about going up the coast to Moonshadows for lobster?"

If Joy had noticed that Jace only moved his food around his plate without eating, she'd said nothing about it. She talked about the difficulty of a New Yorker adjusting to California mellowness, the roles she'd had, the ones she'd auditioned for but lost. She asked him about his time with the LAPD and had laughed easily at his more amusing stories, countering with a few of her family's cop stories from New York.

By the time they got back to her place, it was understood that he was invited in. They were necking on the couch when he slid his hand up her leg and discovered her thigh-high stockings had elastic tops—and that they, and the dress, were all she had on.

"You want to go in the bedroom? I've got scented oils and condoms in there," she said huskily.

"You've convinced me."

She opened the bedside drawer pointedly, then sat on the edge of the bed and leaned back on her hands, smiling. He pushed her dress up to her waist and admired the sight of her flat belly and dark bush above the dark stockings and high heels. He kicked off his shoes and unbuttoned his shirt while he peered into the drawer. In addition to the oils and condoms, the drawer contained scarves and a massive vibrator. He tossed a couple of condoms on the bed and pulled out a silk scarf.

"What are these for?"

He drew the scarf lightly up the inside of her thigh and along her vaginal lips. She quivered deliciously and Jace dropped to his knees in front of her, sliding his hand up under her dress to her warm breast as he put his tongue where the scarf had just been.

"The bedposts . . . Mmmm, that's nice."

And there she'd been, naked except for her stockings and high heels, her wrists tied to the bedposts with silk scarves, her dark hair spread across the satin pillows, her pussy gleaming with her juices and his saliva, and . . .

. . . he couldn't. His cock had swollen some, but hadn't really gotten hard. He'd used his tongue, his fingers, the vibrator, and she'd had at least two orgasms. Her deep voice moaned a nonstop stream of dirty words and encouragement, but eventually just kept pleading, "Fuck me, please fuck me!"

Jace wanted her so badly, wanted nothing more than to ram into her, to hear her beg for mercy.

"Not yet," he'd said, "you don't want it enough yet. Come again, Joy—that's it, let yourself go—"

In the end, he'd just gotten dressed and left without saying anything. He hadn't even untied her wrists, didn't care how she'd get loose. As the door closed behind him, he heard her swearing at him in Italian. All he'd wanted to do was get out of there, away from his humiliation.

It had been a mistake. Everything he'd done recently had been a massive mistake, and there was no way to undo any of it. He was no longer alive, no longer a man. His life had turned to shit.

14

Although Jace believed things couldn't be worse, that was before he went into the study Tuesday night.

He woke famished and went to the desk to get his list of potential feeders. The light on the answering machine was flashing furiously. He hit playback and the machine announced, *"Please wait."* It took forever to rewind. When had he last checked it? Sunday?

BEEP. "It's Elliott. I've changed my plans—I'm leaving Tucson and renting a car to tour the Grand Canyon. I don't know which flight I'll take back, but I'll be home no later than Friday morning. I'll get the shuttle from the airport." The time/day stamp announced *Six-forty-three, Sunday*.

Elliott was on vacation; that explained one mystery. Apparently he didn't know about Risha's absence.

BEEP. "Jace, this is Robert Brandon. It's Monday morning. Please call as soon as you get this message." *Ten-fifteen, Monday*.

BEEP. "Levy, it's Brandon. Where the hell are you? I've been trying your cell phone all day. Call me—the pickup is at two tomorrow!" *Four-fifty-seven, Monday*.

Oh shit, this wasn't good. It was past seven Tuesday night. Too late. Jace put his head in his hands.

BEEP. Risha's voice: "Jace, are you there? Please pick up the phone." She paused. "I'll . . . I . . . never mind." *Eleven-four, Monday.*

She'll what? Call later? Be home soon? Never see him again?

BEEP. "You fucking sonofabitch, it took me two hours to get untied after you left! I suppose you think that was cute? If you get near me again, I'll rip your fucking eyes out! And don't even think of ever showing up in New York!" *Eight-nine, Tuesday.*

No problem figuring out who that was; another satisfied customer heard from. So now the entire NYPD would be keeping an eye out for him? Nice to be wanted.

BEEP. Dial tone. *Ten-fourteen, Tuesday.* A hang-up. Daytime—couldn't have been Risha. Probably Brandon.

BEEP. Brandon's voice: "What am I paying you for? I'm supposed to make the payment in two hours; you'd better be here! I'm going to take an extra thousand dollars with me and try to bribe the messenger . . . Where the hell are you, Levy?" *Eleven fifty-seven, Tuesday.*

Bribe the messenger—not a bad idea, Jace thought. He wondered if it had worked.

BEEP. Brandon again: "Levy, you're fired! I should have known better than to trust your kind." *Three-twelve, Tuesday.*

Jace wondered what his "kind" was: Jews? Vampires? Out-of-work private investigators? Men who couldn't get it up?

Beep-beep-beep-beep. The messages were finished—and so was Jace.

Stan Kelly, 40, was the prime suspect in a series of follow-home robberies which targeted the elderly in up-scale areas. Stalking his victims long enough to ascertain their routines, Kelly usually hid in the bushes near their front doors or carports, his face hidden behind a mask, confronting them with a gun when they returned home at night. Forcing them inside, he'd steal their cash and jewelry, threatening to come back and kill them if they called the police.

One of Kelly's victims, a feisty man of eighty-two, had feigned a heart attack at the front door. Kelly had bent over the old man to check his pulse; the man grabbed the mask while pleading for a doctor and got a good look at the thief's face. Kelly had left without calling an ambulance, apparently hoping the old man would die before anyone found him, but the victim had picked Stan Kelly out of the mug books later. However, when the police had brought him in for a lineup, the old man had been unable to make a firm ID.

Kelly's Culver City tract home was dark when Jace drove past at 10 P.M. He parked the Honda on the next street over and walked back to case the house. For someone who specialized in theft, Kelly was less than cautious about security at his own home: A loose screen over an open bedroom window at the back of the house gave Jace access in seconds.

Even without light, Jace's vision allowed him to see easily about the small house. Although he could find no concrete evidence linking Kelly with the crimes—like a gun or jewels—he found a pile of newspaper clippings in a drawer which detailed the police frustration with finding the follow-home robber, and that was enough. Jace left the drawer ajar and sat in Kelly's battered vinyl recliner to wait.

He wished he'd brought a book with him—he could read without turning on a light, but he certainly couldn't turn on the TV without giving away that someone was in the house. He tried to remember how he'd kept himself alert during stakeouts, then realized that talking with Liz had made the time pass as fast as it ever did—not an option here.

He wondered where Risha was, what she was doing—and with whom—then wondered why he cared.

She'd lied to him, by omission at least. *What else has she lied about? Where she's really been when she's supposedly out shooting pictures?* He shoved out a budding fantasy that she'd had another lover all along.

What was he going to do for money if Risha didn't come back? He didn't feel comfortable using their joint account because most of the money was hers. Maybe Kelly had some cash someplace Jace hadn't looked yet, but he didn't know when the thief would return home and didn't want to be caught off guard in another part of the house. Brandon still owed him a couple of thousand dollars, but Jace thought it unlikely he'd be willing to settle his bill now. His pension check wouldn't go very far without supplement. He could use a new case, but Brandon certainly wouldn't give him a reference.

It was nearly midnight. He was ravenous. What if Kelly were gone for the night, or out of town? If he waited all night, and Kelly didn't return, it'd be too late to get another feeder. Hadn't Risha or Elliott said something about falling into a coma if he didn't feed every three nights? It had been three days since he'd fed off the Osten pimp.

He'd just pulled the feeder list out of his pocket to study it when a car turning into the driveway threw bands of light through the blinds. *Show time.*

Jace flattened himself against the wall and listened. The lights and car engine turned off, the car door slammed. Jace heard the rustle of a paper bag and footsteps coming up the stoop. A key in the lock. The door opened and Kelly came in, kicking the door closed with his foot as he entered, one arm holding a full grocery sack. He'd taken a step toward the kitchen when Jace clamped an arm around his neck from behind, yanking him off his feet. The bag dropped to the floor—Jace heard glass break—as Kelly flailed, trying to loosen Jace's deadly grip on his windpipe.

The smell of beer rose from the bag, but that wasn't the odor Jace noticed. His fangs extended at the tantalizing aroma of surging blood, and he snapped at the man's neck, missing it by centimeters. Kelly twisted, swearing, and actually got loose, but before he could regain his balance, Jace had him pinned again. This time he got his fangs planted, and as soon as he injected Kelly with venom, the feeder went limp and Jace was able to drink his fill.

When he finished, Kelly was still breathing, but his heartbeat was slowing noticeably. Jace got a serrated knife out of the kitchen and used it to stab Kelly several times, then to disguise the fang marks; the rest of Kelly's blood pooled beneath him.

Jace got a good look at his feeder for the first time and was shocked. It wasn't Stan Kelly. It was a young man, little more than twenty. Jesus. He'd killed the wrong guy. But the clippings—this had to be Kelly's place! Jace searched the body for a wallet, finally finding it in the bag with the beer. He flipped it open to the driver's license. Preston Kelly, twenty-one—Stan's son.

Jace wanted to feel guilty, wanted to berate himself for not making sure, but he was still high from feeding and didn't really care. *One feeder's as good as another—they're just containers, right?* It had taken him less than two weeks to adopt Risha's cavalier attitude toward prey. Were the last vestiges of his humanity gone so soon?

He began to trash the place to make it look like Preston had walked in on a burglar, but anger took over and Jace was no longer satisfied with pulling out drawers and yanking off mattresses. Howling, he upended furniture, then kicked in the television tube, satisfied by the implosion. In the bedrooms and bathroom, he smashed hateful mirrors which no longer reflected his face, as if he didn't actually exist, and was somewhat gratified that they now would reflect no one.

Eventually, he calmed and remembered that Stan Kelly could still return home—it wouldn't do to be found here with his son's body. He realized he might have been making enough noise for neighbors to call the police, too. Time to leave.

Jace was picking his way through the debris to climb out the same window he'd used to enter when he saw a thick envelope taped against the back of the shattered bedroom mirror. He picked it up and a diamond ring fell out. He looked inside. There was a string of black pearls, worth a small fortune if they were real. The envelope was filled with cash.

Jace dropped the necklace on the rug near the ring—the cops could return them to their owners—and started to climb out the window, the envelope full of money tucked into his pants, but stopped. A burglar wouldn't have left the jewelry behind; to do so would red-flag this as an unusual case, worth careful investigation. He kicked the ring under the bed, but picked up the necklace and pocketed it—*Risha loves black pearls*—and left.

He might have killed the wrong feeder, but the evening wasn't a complete waste: He was full and twelve thousand dollars—and a pearl necklace—richer. He should have felt better than he did. Was this what his life was going to be like now? What was the fucking point?

He stopped at a liquor store on his way home.

Elliott paid the shuttle driver and took his bags around to the back of the house, letting himself in by the kitchen door. It wasn't yet two o'clock; Risha and Jace would be asleep for hours yet. He opened the box with the silver-and-turquoise squash-blossom necklace he'd bought Risha and straightened it out on the cotton, thinking again how nice it would look with her pale eyes and dark auburn hair. He closed the box carefully and placed it on the kitchen counter, next to the red-clay reproduction of an Anasazi cliff dwelling he'd brought Jace.

He turned to pick up his bags and clucked at the state

of the kitchen: Three empty ice-cube trays sat in pools of water around the sink, an empty beer bottle and a couple of bottle caps lay on an open newspaper forgotten from two days before, dark shoe prints smudged a sticky patch in front of the refrigerator. The trash can was filled with empty bottles and newspapers which no one had bothered to separate for recycling. Elliott sighed. He'd been gone only five days, but everything had gone to hell.

He carried his luggage into his room. There was a postcard on his bed, addressed to Jace at the house, not the maildrop. "We both need time to think. Tell Elliott I'm OK.—R." Risha's handwriting. It was postmarked the day after he'd left on vacation. What had happened? Where was she?

He grabbed the postcard and ran into the study to call the London house. Even if she weren't there, she might have left a message for him on the machine. He waited for the circuits to complete the call, frantic that he didn't know where she was. What had happened here after he left? Had Jace done something to her?

The machine answered after the second ring—there were messages, otherwise it would have gone four rings—and Elliott punched in the three-number code which prompted playback.

"It's me, Elliott." It was Risha's voice. He let out his breath, which he hadn't realized he was holding. "It's Sunday, I think. I didn't want you to worry in case I'm not back by the time you get home. Jace and I had a fight—" Her tone was flat, as if talking took too much energy. By God, if Jace had hurt her—! "We both . . . anyway, I just need to get away by myself for a while. If I'm not home by next Sunday, I'll leave another message for you here. I'm not real happy, but I'm OK, so don't worry . . . Elliott, please take care of Jace for me."

Elliott listened to the message again, erased it, then hung up, no longer frantic, but no less concerned. There were a couple of calls on the answering machine in front of him. Maybe Risha had left a more recent message here? He listened to them—one was for Jace from Reese Hamilton, the other from *City of Angels* with a question about Risha's new batch of photos. When he finished writing them down, Elliott took his first good look at the state of the room.

A jacket lay haphazardly over the arm of the couch, one sleeve trailing to the floor. An empty scotch bottle nestled in the couch cushions, another sat on the bar; ten empty Harp lager bottles sat in bowling formation a few feet from the couch—all standing except for the ten-pin bottle, which lay on its side, downed by the antique ivory puzzle ball which lay near it. Elliott picked up the puzzle ball and placed it carefully back on its pedestal on the desk.

He took Risha's postcard back to his room. He obviously had a lot of housecleaning to do before sundown, but he wanted to unpack first. Risha hadn't said where she was staying, but Jace might know . . . if he were sober enough to remember.

By four, Elliott had both the study and the kitchen back to normal. He finished mopping the kitchen floor and took his cleaning equipment into the living room. Jace apparently had not spent much time there; Elliott would have to dust and vacuum, but it could wait until tomorrow. He turned to go upstairs and walked face-first into a pair of Reeboks.

The shoes swung lazy circles for a moment before coming to a stop, dangling five feet off the floor. Elliott's gaze followed up from the shoes, along denimed legs, past a darkened area at the crotch, over a T-shirted torso to a dark face with bulging eyes and protruding tongue. The slipknotted electrical cord had bitten so deeply into Jace's neck that it was invisible except where it rose past his left ear to tie on the stair post.

Elliott was stunned, unable to move. His first clear thought was for Risha—thank God she hadn't found the body! She had nearly been destroyed by the Baron's suicide—to have another mate kill himself to leave her would be more than she could bear.

Skidding a little on the wet floor, Elliott got a knife from the kitchen. He spread out couch cushions under Jace's hanging body, then climbed the stairs to cut him down.

Shortly after sundown, Jace opened his eyes. He was lying on something soft at the bottom of the stairs. Elliott was coming down, carrying a hamper full of dirty clothes.

"Elliot . . ." His voice was a barely audible croak, but Elliott turned to him, his face stern.

"Stay there. I'll come back," he told Jace as he took the hamper toward the rear of the house.

Jace's neck hurt. He put his hand there, found a deep furrow that circled his neck; his throat felt like it had been sandpapered from the inside. His head ached, even his eyes felt sore. He sat up, a big mistake—his head reeled; he groaned in pain and lay down again.

He remembered enough to know that he'd bungled a drunken suicide. Why not? He'd failed at everything else—what made him think killing himself would be any different? If he'd been within shouting distance of sobriety last night, he probably would have realized that committing suicide wasn't a simple matter for a vampire. He knew it was possible—Gregor had done it, although Jace didn't know how—but apparently hanging wasn't the answer. Maybe he should have tried to stab himself in the heart with a wooden stake.

"I have some tea for your throat." Elliott had returned with a steaming mug.

"Yeah, OK." Jace's voice was as painful to his ears as to his throat. He tried to rise again.

Elliott put the mug down on a stair and helped him get up and into a living-room chair, then went back for the tea. When he returned, Jace opened his mouth to speak, but Elliott cut him off.

"Shut up, Detective. You can listen to me for a while." He shoved the mug at Jace. "Drink it—the honey will help your voice."

Jace took a sip of the tea. It was too sweet, but soothed his throat as he swallowed. Elliott put the cushions back on the couch and sat down facing Jace, glaring. It was impossible to miss the older man's anger; it radiated through his voice, his posture, the stern expression on his face. Jace didn't know what Elliott was pissed off about; Jace hadn't done anything to him. *He knows how Gregor committed suicide; I can still opt out if I can get him to tell me how.*

"You planned for Risha to find you, didn't you?" Elliott began accusingly. "You know what Baron Bathory's death did to her! What kind of man are you?"

Not much of one; that's already been established. Jace looked away from Elliott, staring without seeing at the table next to the couch. Had he thought as far as Risha finding him? He didn't remember, didn't care. Oddly, he thought of the string of black pearls; where had he left them?

"I don't know what you and Risha fought about, but whatever it was, she never could have deserved this treatment—"

I could slash my wrists . . . can a vampire bleed to death? Unlikely. Jace drank more tea.

Elliott continued to rail at Jace, telling him that he had made a commitment to Risha, that he *owed* her "—for supporting you, for giving you immortality, and, most of all, for the very precious gift of her love! And you threw it all in her face! She deserves better than you, but as long as you're who she wants, you're going to stick around! If she hadn't told me to take care of you, I'd kill you myself—"

"You talked to her? She asked about me?" Jace's voice was improving; the tea and the curative powers of vampirism were taking effect. "When? Where is she?"

Elliott shook his head defiantly. "If she wanted you to

know where she was, she'd have told you—and for her sake, I hope she never does! You don't deserve her; none of you deserve her." Jace had no idea whom else Elliott was referring to. "Now listen to me and listen good: When I talk to Risha, I'm not going to say a word about this. And, if and when Risha wants you back, you're not going to tell her either. You're *never* going to tell her—and you're never going to try something this stupid and cruel again! As long as she wants you, you're going to do your very best to make sure she's happy. You hear me?"

Make her happy? I can't even make her come! If she wanted him, he had no idea why—he couldn't be more useless.

"Did you hear me?" Elliott repeated, belligerently.

Jace had never seen the little man so impassioned. No one could love Risha as much as Elliott did. No one had ever loved Jace like that . . .

. . . except Risha.

He nodded, ashamed.

It wasn't until he changed his clothes that he discovered the stain on his jeans. He'd seen men killed by hanging before—they usually fouled themselves as their sphincters relaxed—but Jace no longer urinated or defecated, so what—? He felt the spot—it was sticky. He'd ejaculated, he realized excitedly. If hanging could do it, maybe there were other ways!

15

Risha was naked on top of him, her head thrown back as she rode his massive erection to yet another climax; he could feel her vaginal muscles spasming as he pushed up against her, driving himself deep within her contorting body, but he wasn't ready to come yet—not yet, but soon; he could feel the pressure building and he knew that he would spew about a gallon on her freckled tits.

Freckles? Risha doesn't have freckles.

Jace woke, grasping his somewhat tumescent penis. A dream, just a dream. He stroked his cock while he conjured up the mental image he'd awakened from. He pictured Risha's sexy open mouth, her fangs dripping venom, then imagined her sharp pale tongue circling his glans. He clamped his hand around the base of his cock, trying to keep the blood there, remembering what it felt like to be hard, but it was in vain. He dropped his uncooperative member and sighed. Okay, this was going to take more than wishful thinking; he was going to have to do some experimenting if he were to find a solution.

He got up and took a shower, realizing as he washed his face that he had several days' worth of stubble. He had toweled off and picked up the electric shaver when Elliott knocked on the door.

"Come in." His voice was back to normal. His throat no longer hurt, and he couldn't feel the furrow in his neck anymore. How come vampirism could cure everything but the one problem it caused?

"Would you like me to shave you, Detective?" Elliott spoke as if the previous night's events had never happened; Jace was glad not to have to continue their discussion.

"Yeah, a close shave sounds like a good idea, thanks."

He put down the shaver and got shaving cream out of the medicine cabinet. He slathered it over his face and sat on the closed toilet lid. Elliott shaved him quickly and efficiently. When he finished, Jace got up to wash off the lather.

"You have a phone message from yesterday; I apologize for not giving it to you last night," Elliott said. "Reese Hamilton called. He wants you to call him; he left a home number."

Reese Hamilton. The CPA from the Brandon case. The case Jace was no longer on. "Yeah, OK. Any other calls?"

They both knew he was asking about Risha.

Elliott shook his head. "Just the one. His number's on the desk in the study."

The phone rang downstairs. Jace started for the door, but Elliott said firmly, "I'll get it."

A minute later he was back. "It's someone named Phil who wants to know if he should bring beer or food."

"Is this Thursday?" Elliott nodded, so Jace said, "Tell him I've got enough beer, but he can bring some munchies."

Poker night with the boys. Jace was grateful. Poker was something he was good at.

* * *

Jace placed a pad of paper at Gnat's chair at the card table in the living room; since Gnat had been known to draw on any available surface, the tabletop wasn't safe otherwise. Gnat Donner, four-foot-ten-inches and black, had been a promising cartoonist—his strip, *The Donner Party*, had won a couple of awards—but he had a family to support so he'd reluctantly taken over his parents' carpet-cleaning business. His published cartoons were now limited to advertising flyers, but that didn't prevent him from drawing whenever his hands weren't otherwise involved.

The doorbell rang. Phil Bloom and his brother-in-law, Marc Rosenberg, came in carrying paper bags. Marc was as dark as his sister was fair, with brows that met over his prominent nose; he wrote computer guides that were outdated as soon as they were published.

"You want this in the kitchen?" Phil asked Jace.

"Whatsit?"

"I dunno, Robyn packed it. Food."

"Yeah, I guess so. That one too?" Jace asked Marc.

"Beer and cards," Marc explained, tossing the decks on the card table.

They followed Phil into the kitchen, and Jace got beers out of the fridge and passed them out while Marc chilled the ones he'd brought.

Phil unpacked the bag. "OK, we got assorted raw veggies, guacamole, and some kinda white dip—" He stuck his finger in the bowl and tasted. "Clam." He reached into the bag and pulled out a covered paper plate and removed the foil. "Miniature quiches."

"Quiche for a poker game?" Marc complained.

"Hey, she's your sister." He removed a casserole from the bottom of the bag. "Chili." He read the piece of paper taped to the top, "Nuke for three minutes on high." He crumpled the bag and arced it into the wastebasket. "You gotta watch out for this stuff—Robyn's got an asbestos mouth," he warned.

"No chips for the dip?" Marc asked.

"Guess not," Phil frowned. "You got any, Jace?"

Jace was about to admit there was no other food in the house (*except for you guys*) when Gnat walked in and tossed Phil a giant bag of tortilla chips.

"At your service. Your butler let me in," he told Jace, shaking hands.

"He's not my butler. . . . You want a beer?"

"Does the president inhale?"

Jace got another beer out of the fridge and they went back to the living room. Elliott finished putting coasters at each place and left the room without speaking.

Gnat got a throw pillow from the couch and put it on his chair before sitting down. "So who is that guy?" he asked Jace, indicating the departed Elliott with a nod.

Phil shuffled the cards and pushed the deck to Gnat, who tapped it with a knuckle.

"Risha's assistant," Jace shrugged. "He lives here."

"We could use a fifth," Phil suggested.

Jace shook his head; he couldn't imagine Elliott playing poker.

"OK, the game is five-card stud, nothing fancy, quarter ante, dollar limit." Phil dealt a round face-down.

Jace checked his hole card: queen of clubs.

"Hey, Bloom, is it my imagination or have you got more hair?" Gnat said.

Phil ran his hand suavely over his pate. "At sixty bucks a bottle for Minoxidil, I better have." He dealt a five, a king, the seven of spades to Jace, and a queen. "King bets."

"King's good for fifty cents," Marc said. "Phil plans to have a ponytail someday."

"He didn't have enough hair for one the last time they were in style." Jace laughed. "I'll see that," he said, matching the bet.

Phil flipped Jace the finger. "I'm in. Can't you tell I have more hair?" he pleaded.

It was Gnat's turn, but he was already drawing furiously on the pad.

"Gnat!"

He looked at the cards. "Oh, why not?" He tossed in money and went back to his drawing.

"So where's your lady tonight?" Phil asked Jace, dealing third cards.

"She's out of town for a while." *Or forever?*

"Seven to the five, red ace to the king, a six for the seven—possible flush, and two red ladies to me. Like the way I shuffle? I'll bet a dollar."

"Baching it, huh?" Gnat looked up from his cartoon at Jace. "See the dollar."

"See it and bump twenty-five cents," Marc said.

Jace looked at his cards, trying not to think about Risha. He had a six and seven of spades showing. He tossed in $1.25. He wondered if she'd come back, suddenly realizing that he missed her.

Phil added a quarter, then dealt. "Ten going nowhere, another ace to the king—look out, ten to the spades, possible straight flush—and a worthless deuce to the dealer. Aces, it's your bet."

Marc: "Aces bets—oh, fifty cents."

"Trying to keep us in the game, huh? I'll bite," Jace said, remembering he'd have to get another feeder tonight or tomorrow.

"Too sweet for my blood." Phil folded. "One more bet, anyone?"

Gnat stared at the back of Jace's hole card like he had X-ray vision. "You're bluffing," he announced. "Bet a dollar."

"Raise that dollar a dollar," Jace retorted with a grin.

The phone in the study rang twice before Elliott got it. *Maybe it's Risha*, Jace thought.

"You're not bluffing," Gnat decided. He paused another moment, then folded.

Jace turned his cards down and pushed them to Phil, then raked in the pot.

Gnat snarled at him. He tore off his drawing and started another one. Marc picked up the finished cartoon and laughed, passed it over to Jace. It was a drawing of Phil as a lion. The caption read: "I owe my mane to Rogaine."

"Lemme see it," Phil demanded.

Elliott came in and walked over to Jace.

Jace passed the cartoon to Phil as he turned to Elliott. "For me?"

"It's Reese Hamilton again," Elliott told him. "He sounds like it's important."

"Can I have this?" Phil asked Gnat.

Gnat was shuffling. "Sure," he said without looking up.

Jace stood. "I'm out of this hand; I've got to take a call."

When Jace picked up the phone, Hamilton immediately launched into a chronology of his last few days, beginning with a call to have money ready for another payment.

Jace interrupted. "Sorry, Mr. Hamilton, I'm no longer on that case."

"You haven't solved it," Hamilton said. It wasn't a question.

"No. My client decided not to continue with the investigation."

Elliott passed the study door carrying a tray filled with food. Jace could smell chili. The sound of raucous laughter came from the living room.

"No problem. You can send your bills to me," Hamilton said. "You want a retainer? I've got some new information for you; can you come here tonight?"

A new client . . . and money. Things were looking up. "Uh, I've got some company here right now . . ."

"Tomorrow morning then, my office."

Morning. Not the best time for a vampire. It was only 8 P.M. now, maybe he could . . . "How late will you be up tonight?"

"Ten, eleven."

"OK, Mr. Hamilton, I'll come over. Where do you live?"

When Jace got back to the living room, Elliott was sitting in his chair, shuffling the deck of cards.

"Five-card stud, nines are wild, trey in the hole is wild, trey-up buys the pot or drops out, four-up gets another card, fifty-cent ante, two-dollar limit," Elliott said, dealing.

Jace's mouth dropped open.

"You're too late for this hand, Levy," Gnat said unnecessarily.

"It's just as well. I've got some business I have to deal with." He picked up his money from in front of Elliott. "Play with your own money," he told him. "I'll be back in an hour."

Hamilton's Brentwood condo was furnished with quiet elegance, the museum-quality artwork lit by recessed spots. The accountant was wearing a handknit teal-and-black sweater with Armani slacks. Jace almost felt guilty sitting on his ecru silk couch in his thirty-dollar jeans. Unfamiliar classical music drifted in from another room.

"Is that a Modigliani?" Jace asked, looking at a painting on the opposite wall.

Hamilton looked surprised that Jace recognized it. "Yes. My father gave it to me when I graduated from Harvard."

Jace mentally bumped up his hourly rate by twenty percent. "So you got tapped again?"

Hamilton nodded. "Tonight, when I left the office, he was waiting next to my Mercedes."

"Same guy as the other times?" Harris Powers, the all-American kid.

"The same one. I know something else about him now."

"That the new information you mentioned on the phone? What did you find out, Mr. Hamilton?"

"Where he lives."

Jace was impressed. "How—"

Hamilton interrupted. "I followed him. I thought it would be helpful to know with whom I was dealing."

Jace grinned. "Good idea. He didn't see you, huh?"

"I had the keys to my secretary's car and used that instead of the Mercedes. Just a moment, I'll get the address."

Hamilton went into the other room and returned immediately with a sheet of small notebook paper, which he handed to Jace. "It's in the Hollywood Hills, nice building with view apartments."

"You're helping to pay the rent there," Jace pointed out. He looked at the paper. The street name, Vista Terrace, was familiar. "You said it was an apartment building? Did you get the unit number?"

"No. He drove into a gated garage. If I'd stopped to look in, he might have seen me. I got the license plate of the car, though. It's on the other side."

Jace turned the sheet over. It read Tan VW, CA 1FSC 598. Where had he run across a tan VW recently?

"Good work, Mr. Hamilton. I'll run this and see what I come up with."

Hamilton nodded, then passed Jace an envelope. "Here's a fifteen-hundred-dollar retainer. Will that be sufficient?"

Jace put the envelope in his jacket pocket. "That's fine. I get sixty dollars an hour, plus expenses."

"I'll pay you in cash; I don't want a receipt, or any other record of our transactions. If you supply a bank account number with your bill, I'll have the cash deposited directly within two business days. You're authorized to continue until you've made sure the extortionist is no longer a threat to me. I don't care how you do it—in fact, I'd rather not know," he added pointedly. Hamilton rose. Their meeting was apparently over.

Jace stood and shook his hand. "I'll be in touch."

"If you need to see me, don't come to my office. You have the number here?"

Jace assured him he did and left. He patted the envelope in his jacket. He hoped Elliott had left the other players with some money.

Gnat crumpled up the paper from his last roll of quarters. "That's my limit, gentlemen; I'm out of here."

Phil looked at his watch. "It's late anyway. Robyn's probably waiting up. You ready?" he said to Marc.

Marc glanced at Elliott's neat stacks of quarters and pile of bills. "Yeah, he's got enough of my money." He turned to Jace. "You ought to pay this guy so he doesn't have to hustle poker for a living."

"With that face, poker's bound to be lucrative," Jace said ruefully. "He's got thirty bucks of my money, too."

When the guys left, Elliott started to clean up the living room.

"Just leave it," Jace said, "it'll be there in the morning." Aware that he knew next to nothing about the little man, he asked, "Where'd you learn to play poker like that?"

Was that a hint of a smile on Elliott's face?

"Prison," he replied. Scooping up his cash, he headed for his room, leaving Jace standing openmouthed.

It took only minutes on the computer for Jace to find out that the Volkswagen Harris Powers was driving was not registered to him. It was registered to William Tanner at the address on Vista Terrace. *There's something incestuous about this group*, Jace thought; *they're too close-knit yet couldn't be more different*. He wondered what had happened when Brandon had tried to bribe the mule; maybe he'd talk, now that he was no longer paying Jace.

He turned off the computer and spread out his case files over the desk. In spite of her spacey demeanor, Crysse Tanner was obviously the key to the whole extortion plot: Her file from CineArts held references to all the others, she had taken Tinah Powers' appointment with the eggplant, Hannah Williams and Harris Powers used her social security number, William Tanner's name was on a prescription in her medicine cabinet and Harris Powers was driving William Tanner's car . . .

Suddenly Jace remembered why Vista Terrace was a familiar address: That's where Crysse Tanner lived! It was time to investigate Ms. Tanner more thoroughly, perhaps get into her apartment for another look around, preferably when she wasn't home.

He spent the next several hours transcribing the tape of his interview with her and going over his notes. He knew that no clue was too small to study, but wading through the snake owner's endless psychobabble was cruel and unusual punishment. He sent the file to the printer and got up.

He left a note for Elliott to wake him an hour before sundown so he could catch Brandon before he left for the day, and went upstairs. It was almost an hour 'til dawn; if Risha were here, they could have . . . *fucked? With what?*

Elliott had changed the sheets; the soft percale pillowcases now smelled faintly of fabric softener, not the dusky rose scent he associated with Risha. As he got into the empty bed, Jace thought maybe he'd be less likely to dream about her now. He picked up the Elizabeth George novel and read until he lapsed into dreamless sleep.

Jace listened to the news while he waited, parked in the slot next to Brandon's Cadillac Seville. Elliott had told him about the massive explosion at the World Trade Center when he woke him; the Feds still didn't know what had caused it. Like everyone else, Jace feared that it had been a bomb, that terrorism had finally hit U.S. shores. They were still accounting for the dead and missing. Unbelievable.

Brandon arrived carrying a briefcase, fumbling in his pockets for car keys.

Jace turned off the radio and got out. "Mr. Brandon? May I have a few minutes of your time?"

Brandon looked annoyed. "I don't have anything to say to you, Levy. I wouldn't hire you again if you were the last private eye in the city." He unlocked the Seville. "You've really got a nerve, showing up here."

It was starting to rain again; just a sprinkle so far, but the angry clouds threatened deluge.

Jace put out a placating hand. "I know you're pissed off, Mr. Brandon; you have every right to be. I wasn't there when you needed me . . ."

"You didn't even have the courtesy to call me back!"

"I know. It was unavoidable, but I'm not going to make excuses; I fell down on the job and you were justified in firing me. I've torn up your bill," he added.

"I wouldn't have paid it anyway, after what you did," Brandon snapped. "So why are you here, Levy?"

"Look, can we get out of the rain? Go back to your office—or at least sit in the car?"

Brandon looked at Jace for a long moment; without speaking, he opened the Seville and got in, unlocking the passenger door for Jace. Jace slid in and closed the door. The rain spots on the windshield had amassed enough to run, washing dirty streaks across the glass.

"Terrible about that explosion in New York, huh?" Jace said conversationally.

"You come here to discuss current events?"

Jace shook his head. "One of the other extortion victims has hired me—"

"His mistake," Brandon interrupted curtly.

Jace accepted the slur with a modicum of grace. "Nevertheless, I need more information from you. If you can help, I might still be able to get the blackmailer off your back, too, and you won't have to pay me," he said reasonably.

Brandon thought about that for a while, finally nodded. "What do you want to know?"

"What happened with the last drop? You left me a message that you were going to try to bribe the mule—" he stopped at the confused look on the producer's face, then clarified "—the person picking up the money. What happened?"

Brandon's eye began to twitch. "It was a young girl, maybe twelve years old. What kind of animal uses a child for criminal activity? She barely had breasts, she was so young. It was at the McDonald's down the block." He gestured south. "I was told to sit in the back, and she came in and sat down across the table from me. I passed her the envelope under the table, just like she told me. Then I asked her, 'Want to make five hundred dollars for yourself?' or something like that." The twitch sped up. "She asked me what she'd have to do for the money." Brandon looked down at his hands, then at the rain on the windshield. "Actually, what she said was: 'That's a lot of bread for a blowjob.' " He finally looked Jace straight in the eye. "I swear to God, Levy, those were her exact words. Twelve years old . . ." He shook his head. "I told her I wanted her to help you find the blackmailer . . . or get the tape back for me. I said there could be more money for her if she helped in a significant way. At first, she seemed to be considering it. I was even thinking about getting her into a Christian foster home or something."

He squeezed his eyes shut twice, and the twitching stopped. The rain, however, did not; it was coming down heavy, drumming on the top of the car.

"You said 'at first'—what happened then?" Jace asked.

Brandon looked out the window at a homeless person in a cheap plastic rain poncho pushing an overloaded cart full of belongings.

"She laughed," he said finally. "It was a nasty laugh, mocking, scornful. She told me to . . . go fuck myself." Brandon said the word like he'd never spoken it out loud before. "She said if I tried to stop her or follow her, she'd scream. Then she left."

"Did you follow her?"

"Good Lord, no! If she screamed that I was bothering

her . . ." He left the rest of scenario unsaid; Jace could see where it was going. Brandon's eye began to twitch again. "There was something else about her, something wrong," he added hesitantly.

"What?"

"You wouldn't believe me."

"I have no reason to doubt you, Mr. Brandon; what did you observe?"

"Her voice. Her voice was wrong. It was too deep, not the voice of a girl at all. Satan was in that little girl—she had a man's voice, Levy, I swear!" The tic started to contort Brandon's whole face, it was so strong. "It wasn't until later that I realized it was the voice of the man who called me about the blackmail." Brandon's twitching face had paled. "The Devil has taken my soul for my sins, God help me!"

If the extortionist's aim were to drive Brandon over the edge, he was doing a good job of it.

Jace wondered why the producer saw a different mule each pick up, while Hamilton always saw Harris Powers. Just what the hell was going on with this case?

16

Jace could see Crysse's apartment from where he'd parked around the side of the building. Through the curtains, he could see lights on in both the living room and the bedroom. He waited, hoping she'd leave for the evening so he could get in—he'd arrived before seven and it was a Friday—but, shortly after eleven, the living-room light went out, followed half an hour later by the bedroom light. The rain was still pouring down—only idiots (and private investigators) would go out in it. He could have waited another couple of hours to make sure she was sound asleep, then let himself in to look around, but it would be an unnecessary risk; better to wait until he was sure she was away for a while.

Besides, he still had to feed tonight.

Wesley Nizen had served time for arson and was the main suspect in the 1990 fires, but it was a hard charge to prove, and he was currently a free man. As Jace obliterated the fang marks in Nizen's neck, he reflected on the advantage of timing this particular feeder now. All this rain meant a lot of new growth in the drought-starved hills, and it would all turn to tinder come summer. An active arsonist wouldn't be able to resist. One less firebug; Jace had done good.

He stopped at a dive in Hollywood for a drink before the 2 A.M. cutoff, but the heavy metal music played at top volume drove him back out into the rain. He got on the freeway and headed home.

He heard Risha's voice in the study as soon as he came into the house.

"Well, the French Quarter *is* famous for its fine food," she was saying lightly.

"People stay up late there, too, don't they?" Elliott.

Jace paused, out of the line of sight from the study. His stomach churned as he tried, in vain, to make sense of his conflicting emotions of elation and dread.

"New Orleans is a vampire's playground, that's for sure. I can see why Anne Rice sets her novels there," Risha said. "It was Mardi Gras last week and the streets were filled with drunken revelers at all hours—" She stopped as Jace appeared in the doorway.

Elliott got up. "I guess I'll go to bed now," he said. He looked at Jace, but spoke to Risha: "Wake me if you need me."

She nodded. Elliott sidled past Jace to get through the door, the warning expression on his face quite clear.

"Hi," Risha said. Her hair was loose and she wore no makeup. She looked even younger than usual—and more innocent, somehow.

"Hi, yourself." He leaned against the doorjamb.

"You going to stay there?"

Jace shrugged more casually than he felt, then came fully into the room. He pulled out the desk chair and sat down a good eight feet from Risha on the couch.

"New Orleans, huh?" he said.

"Yes. God, what a great city! Have you ever been there?" Before Jace could answer, she continued. "How have you been?"

He wagged his hand. "*Comme çi, comme ça.* You?"

"Comme çi, comme ça." She smiled. "I missed you, Jace."

"Not enough to come home." He tried to keep the sullen tone out of his voice, but it was evident anyway. "You weren't alone, were you?" As soon as he said it, he regretted it; it not only sounded petulant, it sounded accusatory. He was doing a good job of getting this off on the wrong foot. He went over to the bar and opened the scotch. "You want a drink?"

"No. And I'd rather you didn't either. Elliott told me you've been hitting it pretty hard—"

He slammed the bottle back down. "None of his fucking business what I do—or yours, for that matter!"

But he didn't pour a drink. He turned and leaned back against the cabinet, trying to keep his anger in check. She hadn't answered his question about being with someone; he admonished himself not to repeat it. He stared at her guileless pale eyes. "Who were you with?"

"What makes you think I was with someone?" she asked reasonably.

He shrugged.

"I was by myself, Jace. I wanted time to think, not another man. Did you . . . see anyone while I was gone?"

A statuesque brunette I couldn't get hard for. "Some guys came over for poker last night. Feeders. Clients."

"Clients plural? You got a second case?" she asked with interest.

"Same case, different client."

"Tell me about it?"

He sighed, sat down in the chair again, told her about losing Brandon and gaining Hamilton. She asked a lot of bright questions, and by the time he'd gotten her up-to-date, the tension in the room had abated noticeably. For the moment, it almost seemed like nothing bad had ever been said between them.

"You haven't had any trouble feeding alone, have you? I mean, your venom's up to strength, isn't it?" she wanted to know.

He smiled. "No problems. Dropped a pimp, a robber—" *Well, a robber's son, anyway.* "—and just had an arsonist tonight." He patted his stomach. "Venom seems to be working just fine."

"Good," she nodded. "Did you think about me at all?" she asked shyly.

"Of course I did."

Risha waited, but he didn't illuminate further.

"And?"

"I missed you," he conceded. Her smile looked relieved. "Look, I'm sorry for what I said the other night. I shouldn't have taken out my frustration on you. We've both had secrets . . ."

"I wasn't keeping secrets from you, Jace. It never occurred to me that Gregor's impotence was linked to vampirism. Vampirism is why I stopped getting periods, so now that I've thought about it, I guess it's sort of the same thing."

Jace felt a flash of anger. "Not by a long shot; not being fertile isn't even close to not being able to perform in bed! You can still fuck," he pointed out, unconsciously looking at the scotch bottle.

"So can you, Jace! Gregor and I—"

"Shut up about Gregor! I don't want to hear about your sex life with him, how good he was, or any of that bullshit! What makes you such an expert on male sexuality? If he was so fucking comfortable with never getting a hard-on, why did he kill himself, huh? Tell me that!"

Risha looked as if he'd hit her: She physically recoiled from his anger, her stung expression eliciting a wave of guilt in Jace that he refused to entertain. He was leaning forward, still belligerent, waiting to pounce on whatever she said, and she knew it. She opened her mouth to speak, but closed it again without a sound. He didn't wait for another attempt.

"You put Gregor on a fucking pedestal! The suave, rich, powerful baron who loved you, right up until the moment he opted out; *he* wasn't bothered by impotence—oh no, not Gregor, The Perfect Lover! It wasn't a problem for *you*, as long as he could make you come, but you never once thought about how it affected *him*, did you? What it was like for him to never hear a woman say, 'Fuck me harder!,' to know he'd never have an orgasm again! Well, I know what it was like for him, because it's now that way for me!" He strode over to the bar and poured two fingers of scotch, downed them. "In fact, it's worse for me, because I still remember what it feels like to drive a steel-hard cock into a hungry woman—I haven't had three hundred years to forget what being a man is all about!—and I *know* why he committed suicide, Risha: It's the same reason I tried to kill myself two days ago! Your fucking vampirism isn't a blessing, it's a curse—and I could kill you for destroying my manhood so casually, as if it didn't really matter!"

He picked up the bottle again, looking hard at her, daring her to say something, but her devastated expression hit him harder than any words could.

He threw the nearly full bottle hard against the wall over the couch, the satisfying explosion spewing glass and scotch on her head. He was vaguely aware that he was strangely excited, even had a partial erection. Risha didn't flinch, didn't even wipe her face or remove the fragments of glass from her hair.

Elliott came rushing in, still dressed, holding a .38. He looked at Risha first, then at Jace, threateningly.

"Get out of this house." Elliott's tone was dangerously quiet.

"No," Risha said in a whisper. "Go to bed, Elliott."

"But—"

"I'm not in danger. Go on, Elliott; I'll call you if I need you."

Reluctantly, Elliott left. The sound of his bedroom door snicking closed never came.

"You're right, Jace," Risha said softly. A drop of scotch rolled down her face like a tear; she ignored it. "I don't know how it was for Gregor, how it is for you. Your erections aren't important to me, but I realize they were to you." Jace winced at her use of the past tense. "If I could do anything to give you back your . . . virility, I would—but vampirism isn't reversible, and that's a fact I can't change, that no one can change. If you choose not to be with me anymore, I'll have to live with it, just like I've had to live with Gregor's choice. But killing yourself? Jace, you haven't given this time; it's only been two weeks since you crossed over. Don't throw away your life without trying to regain your self-esteem, without giving me a chance to prove to you that I love you just as much without erections as I did when you had them every night."

Overwhelmed by guilt and Risha's compassion, Jace turned away so she wouldn't see he was on the verge of tears. She came up behind him, gently touching his shoulder.

"Let me in, Jace; I do love you, so very much."

He turned to her, wrapping his arms around her, holding on tightly. He buried his head in her hair, feeling glass fragments and the dampness of the liquor, not caring.

"God, I'm sorry, Risha. I don't know how you can still love me, but I'm incredibly grateful that you do. I'll try, I promise. I do love you, Rish. We'll work it out. Somehow, we'll work it out."

They woke Saturday night in the same position they'd gone to sleep in—lying spoons, Risha behind—but the previous bedtime had begun a little awkwardly.

Jace had already been in bed, reading, when Risha

finished her shower and came in. She slipped in next to him wearing only an oversize T-shirt—neither seductive nor forbidding. He closed his book and placed it on the bedside table. He'd been planning to make love to her (the best he was able), not only because he'd felt it was the Right Thing to Do, but because he badly wanted to (even though it wouldn't be the best of which he was once capable). He put his arm around her and she snuggled in, her head on his chest.

"I'm glad you're back," he told her honestly.

"Me too. I missed this." She kissed his chest, then added, "The snuggling, I mean. We don't have to have sex if you don't feel like it. I understand that it might take a while to . . . adjust."

Jace suddenly felt like he'd been challenged—dared!—to do something he was already planning, his ability even to give head called into question with Risha's "understanding." Now he was damned either way: If he did, she would think it only because she'd said something; if he didn't, she'd think him incapable, both of sex and of handling a crisis. Either way, she'd emasculated him again, and he began to think that he really didn't want to fuck her after all.

As the soupçon of anger began to cook, Jace felt his cock stir, just as it had a few hours earlier when he'd hurled the scotch bottle against the wall. He slid his hand under the hem of Risha's shirt and up to her right breast, squeezing her nipple hard as he planted his lips on hers. She gasped, and he pulled off her shirt, sucking and biting at her erect nipple as his fingers teased her clitoris. He felt her hand at his cock, the long fingers grasping as if to pull more blood into his uncooperative member, but he concentrated his attention on her body, determined to reduce her to an orgasmic puddle, regardless of the state of his erection.

When her eyes had half closed and her mouth had swollen into full pout, Jace leaned over the bed and pulled his thin leather belt out of the loops of his jeans.

He removed her hands from his body and tied her wrists together, fastening the belt to the bedpost. She lay on her back, her hands over her head, her legs spread as she squirmed below him. He ran his tongue along the side of her neck and down her chest, teasing her nipples before continuing on to her vagina. Reading her familiar moans and writhings, he expertly brought her to climax several times, giving her only a moment to recover from one orgasm before he orchestrated her next.

Eventually, with a grin, she'd gasped, "Uncle!"

"You sure?" he said, replacing his tongue in her vagina with a finger. "It's at least twenty minutes 'til dawn; I could make you come"—he stopped as she shuddered in mini-orgasm—"at least once more." He grinned.

"I know you could, Jace, but I'm still on Louisiana time—it's two hours past dawn and I'm worn-out."

Jace kissed her and untied her hands. She rotated her shoulders to get out the kinks, then smiled dreamily at him, like a feeder on venom. "Mmm, that was hot, Jace. I'm going to sleep like the dead today."

"You are the dead," he reminded her.

The sex *had* been hot. He realigned his pillow and put his head down. The last thing he'd been aware of was the warmth and softness of Risha's body conforming to his.

"Evening," he said when Risha opened her eyes.

"Mmm." She smiled and stretched. "Sunset already? I was just starting the nicest dream—"

"What about?" he said, caressing her nipple.

She dodged him with a grin. "Oh no you don't! If you start that, we'll never get out of here." She kissed him and got out of bed. "I need to shoot tonight, Jace; I've got a deadline coming up at *City of Angels*, and I can't use the photos I took in New Orleans. It's Saturday night—we can hit some of the clubs or something, party down with the younger set."

She opened the bathroom door and the scent of Ombre Rose wafted from her bath. Jace followed her in to brush his teeth.

"Can't, Rish—I've got to work tonight, too." He ran a hand over his stubbled cheek and reached for the electric shaver. "You can come with me if you want, but stakeout's pretty boring, and there won't be much to shoot."

"Why don't I just check in with you later? You still have the cell phone?"

"Yeah, but you take it and I'll call you," he said. "I don't want it to ring while I'm breaking into her apartment—if she goes out tonight."

Getting into Crysse Tanner's security building was no problem. Shortly before eight, Jace saw the actress's lights go out, followed by a tan VW's exit from the security garage. Jace ducked down as the car passed his, but he got a glimpse of Crysse, dressed in black and wearing rhinestone earrings, her hair styled for evening, as she drove away; she obviously wouldn't be back for hours. It was only another ten minutes before Jace saw a man walk up to the main gate and ring a button. Jace grabbed the bulky gift-wrapped empty box from the backseat and ran up just as the man opened the buzzing security gate. Seeing Jace's arms full, he held the gate open for him.

"Thanks."

"No problem."

Picking Crysse's lock was almost as easy. Jace closed her apartment door as soon as he entered, then stopped. The television was on without sound, the only illumination. Was one of Crysse's co-conspirators in the other room? Jace froze, the decoy package still in his arms, and listened with augmented ability. Eventually, he could hear talking from inside a nearby apartment, but was assured that he had Crysse's unit to himself for now.

He stepped quietly toward the kitchen to put the box

on the counter where he wouldn't forget it, but went sprawling, crushing the box under his chest as he fell. He knew he hadn't been hit; did he trip over something? He sat up and looked.

Greta Garboa lay in front of the television set, the front third of her enormous body raised so her head was on a level with the flickering light. Jace laughed. The snake was actually watching TV, hypnotized by the light and movement of the Roadrunner once more outwitting Wiley E. Coyote.

"I'd love to see how this turns out, but I've got work to do," Jace told the boa as he got up. "Let me know what happens."

Before searching the apartment, Jace took photographs of each room from at least three different angles. He took his time on the search, being careful to replace everything exactly where it had been.

He found the Brandon extortion video almost immediately; it was in the cabinet under the TV and VCR, along with several other tapes labeled with play names and dates—obviously, records of Crysse Tanner's more public performances—and a few prerecorded self-help and spiritual-guidance titles. The videotape caught Jace's eye first because it wasn't the same format as the others—it was Beta—and then because it bore no label on the spine. When Jace pulled it out, the box had a Right Path Films sticker on it. He couldn't be sure it was The Tape, because Crysse's machine was VHS, but he took it anyway, leaving the empty box in its slot. Brandon was no longer his client, but Jace felt guilty for letting him down; besides, Brandon might pay him the balance due on his bill if Jace returned the video to him. He didn't have as much luck for his current client: he found no audiocassettes at all.

In the next hour, Jace found only two references to the others' names. He recorded the number, doctor name, and Bakersfield pharmacy on the Valium prescription for William Tanner. Then he found a yellowed clipping at the bottom of Crysse's underwear drawer about a 1972 fire, which had killed a family named Powers—Martin and Elise and their twelve-year-old son, Harris; there was no mention of Tinah. The clipping bore no city or newspaper name. Jace took several close-up photos of the clipping and copied the facts into his notebook before he replaced it in the drawer. The name was right, but the Harris Powers Jace knew of would scarely have been born in 1972, and certainly wouldn't have been of school age. Yet another puzzle piece that didn't quite fit.

As far as Crysse Tanner's background, Jace found remarkably little evidence of her past. Most people kept souvenirs—pictures with the family, the tassel from high-school graduation, photos of old beaus, but Jace found none of that. Most of the things Crysse used to personalize her home were the dregs of the various psychobabble movements she'd subscribed to, at one time or another. She'd apparently been through everything that had swept through California in the past decade, no small feat. And no small expense—some things, like Scientology, must have cost her a fortune. Is that what she used the extortion money for?

By the time Jace was satisfied he'd seen everything he could without staying too long, he'd decided he'd have to go to Bakersfield. It wasn't a place he would choose to visit under normal circumstances, but he had to find out what Crysse Tanner was hiding if he were going to convince her to go away.

17

Bakersfield, 110 miles north of Los Angeles, had been named after one of its early settlers and not because of its consistent hundred-plus-degree summer temperatures, as some would have it. A small city at the foot of the San Joaquin Valley, settled by Mexicans, French, Basques, Italians, and Portuguese, Bakersfield was strongly religious and family-oriented, not a city known for its nightlife.

When Jace walked into the motel office on Wible Road, the desk clerk was already snoring, although it was not yet 9 P.M. A small TV on the counter was tuned to CNN and broadcast news of the standoff some religious cult in Texas had begun by killing four ATF agents that morning. Jace cleared his throat loudly, eventually waking the man and getting checked in. Before he left his overnight bag in his room, he told the clerk that he slept during the day, so was not to be disturbed.

The community theater where Crysse Tanner had done several plays was a few miles from Jace's motel. He found it easily, but the theater was dark. A small marquee informed him that the next production would be *The Fantastiks* the following weekend, and gave a telephone number for information. Jace called it and got a recording about ticket availability, at the end of which was another number for further information.

"I'm a detective, up from Los Angeles," he told the man who answered his next call, "and I'm trying to get some information about someone who acted in your productions several years ago."

"I've been managing the theater for fifteen years," the man said. "What do you want to know?"

"It's rather involved. I'm in Bakersfield; would it be possible for me to come over and talk to you?"

"Now?" The man's voice was so incredulous, Jace double-checked his watch—it wasn't yet nine-thirty.

"If you wouldn't mind, sir, it shouldn't take very long."

The man thought for a second, then said, "My name's Ed Bisang. I'm on Dracena, across from Beale Park; do you know the area?"

"I'll find it."

Bisang's house was an older stucco tract home. As Jace walked up the driveway, he could see a large aboveground pool in the back. A kid's bike left on its side on the front lawn attested to either a trusting soul or a low crime rate; in L.A., it would have been stolen. The front door opened as Jace climbed the stoop's three stairs and a short, barrel-chested man came out, closing the door behind him.

"You're the detective? I'm sorry, I forgot to get your name."

"Jace Levy. Thanks for seeing me on such short notice, Mr. Bisang."

"Ed. I'm sorry I can't ask you in—my kid's got the flu and . . . well, never mind; my office is around back."

He led Jace up the driveway to the two-car garage, one-half of which had been walled off with faux wood paneling. They entered the office through a side door—Jace noticed it wasn't locked—and Bisang turned on the lights. The small room held a battered desk, where stacks of paper competed for space with soft drink cups from McDonald's; a couple of metal file cabinets, a chair, and a sagging couch. Trash overflowed the dented wastebasket under the desk. Posters from the community theater's productions were stuck on the paneling with thumbtacks. Bisang moved a mass of paper to one end of the couch, clearing a space for his visitor.

"I should probably say something like 'it isn't usually this messy,' but I'd be lying—it's usually worse than this." Bisang laughed. "They finally got me some storage space at the high school, so I moved a lot over there."

"You do theater at the high school, too?" Jace asked.

Bisang nodded. "When I can. I teach English, but I have a drama group whenever there's enough interest. I like to expose the kids to theater, but budgeting's so tight, there's not really enough money to put on a play each semester, unfortunately. For most of these kids, it'd be their first—and probably only—contact with the arts. The parents think it's foolishness—their kids don't need Shakespeare or Neil Simon to get jobs in the oil fields or sheep ranches—so I'm fighting a losing battle." He shrugged. "But you didn't come to hear my problems. What can I do for you?"

"I'd like to ask you about Crysse Tanner. I understand she was in some of your community-theater productions in the eighties." Jace pulled out Crysse's headshot from the envelope he'd brought. "This is what she looks like now, if it'll jog your memory." He passed the photo over.

Bisang looked at it, then shook his head.

"You don't know her, Ed?" Jace asked.

"Oh, I know Christine Tanner," Bisang said, "I'm just amazed to see what she looks like now. She wasn't this pretty when she was here, but it wouldn't be the first time one of my students blossomed late."

"Student?"

"Yes, at Vista High School. She wanted to act, so I encouraged her to try out for some of the community-theater productions after she dropped out. I wish I could have convinced her to continue her education, but she left Vista right after her sixteenth birthday. I suspect her home life wasn't the best, although she never talked about it. As I remember, she got a job at one of the Basque restaurants and earned enough to rent a room. About four years later, she just stopped coming for auditions; I'd heard she'd gone to Hollywood. To tell you the truth, I expected she'd come back as soon as she ran out of money, but it's been . . . oh, five years, I guess, so maybe she did better than I thought."

"Why didn't you expect her to last?" Jace asked.

Bisang scratched his head and grinned. "She wasn't the worst actress I've ever seen, but she was close."

"You cast her in several productions, though," Jace said, confused. "It says here"—he pointed to her résumé—"that she was in half a dozen plays . . ."

"Mostly bit parts and walk-ons, I'm afraid. This is community theater, and I try not to discourage anyone with enthusiasm, and Christine had a lot of that, but she couldn't make a line come alive if her life depended on it."

"What kind of person was she, aside from her lack of acting ability?"

"Well," Bisang said, leaning forward, "you remember when you were in high school, the girls who had 'reputations' for being easy?"

Jace nodded; he'd gratefully lost his virginity to one of them.

"That was Christine. I don't expect she was really having sex with all the guys who claimed it—you know what teenage boys are like—but she did change boyfriends a lot. She got caught smoking on campus a few times, cut classes a lot, small stuff like that. That's why I was pleased when she took an interest in theater; I thought it might turn her around. She didn't have a lot going for her; she had bad teeth, low self-esteem, a bad attitude. I was afraid she'd end up in some shack with a passel of kids by the time she turned twenty." He looked at the headshot again. "I sure didn't expect her to turn out like this."

"What about after she left school? You said she was around the theater for another four years," Jace prompted.

"Yeah, about that long. But I only saw her during rehearsals and productions, and I just wasn't privy to the same kind of gossip there. I know of a couple of people you might ask about Christine, but I'm not sure where you'd find them."

"Any leads would be a big help, Ed."

"OK. About a year before she left town, she was seeing one guy pretty regularly. He ran whitewater rafting tours down the Kern, may still be doing it, for all I know. His name was something to do with cars . . . Olds! Patrick Olds. He was a local boy, I think, so if he's not still doing tours, you might be able to locate him through his family."

Jace wrote down the information in his notebook. "Good. You said you knew of someone else, too?"

Bisang nodded. "Brenda . . . Belinda . . . something. Sorry"—he grinned—"she was kind of forgettable. Her father owned the restaurant Christine worked at . . ." He closed his eyes while he tried to conjure up the name of the restaurant.

Checking his transcription of the interview he'd had with Crysse Tanner, Jace offered, "Bastanchury's Basque Family Restaurant?"

"That's it!" Bisang exclaimed. "It's over on Union, north of Truxtun. The Bastanchury girl came to all of Tanner's performances and most of her rehearsals, but I never once saw her come to any play Christine wasn't in. She was a mousy little thing, and I think she looked up to Tanner's tough-girl image."

Jace cradled the phone against his shoulder while he twisted the cap off a Dos Equis; the clerk at the liquor store had never heard of Harp lager.

"I went by Bastanchury's, but they were already closed, and they're not open on Mondays," he told Risha. "I've got a lot of other leads to check out here, so I probably won't be back home until Wednesday at the earliest."

"Do you want me to drive up and keep you company?"

"No, you've got your own work and there's nothing to do at night here. They roll up the sidewalks by nine; you'd hate it."

Risha laughed. "It'd certainly be a culture shock after New Orleans. So what are you going to do all night?"

"I've got a novel with me, and the motel has cable TV. I'll have to work tomorrow morning, even though Elliott isn't here to wake me, so I'll take it easy tonight and try to get in a few hours of daylight sleuthing before I crash."

"Is there anything we can do down here to help? I could ask Elliott to follow Crysse, if you want," Risha offered.

"I don't think Elliott's in the mood to do me any favors," Jace said. "What you could do is get hold of a Betamax so I can check out that video I got from her place."

"Beta? Oh, that'll be a challenge." Risha sighed. "Maybe Elliott can find one in an antique store. So, can I call you there at night or what?"

"Sure, there's not much chance I'll be out in the wee hours, unless I'm feeding. Hell, for all I know, even the drug dealers here are in by nine."

An hour after ringing off, Jace began to regret not accepting Risha's offer to drive up. The Sunday late-night local TV offered a variety of devotional programming and test patterns, while all the cable stations were running *I Love Lucy* episodes or "Vanishing Son" film festivals. It wasn't even midnight yet, far too early for him to just settle in with a book.

He got in the car and cruised the streets of Bakersfield, looking for something that still showed any signs of life—a bar, a movie theater, a bowling alley, a potential feeder on the street alone, anything!—but the only places open were Mercy Hospital and the police station . . . and neither looked particularly busy. This city seemed to have as many churches as Los Angeles had Thai restaurants, but Jace was no more interested in praying than in eating. He was about to give up and head back to the Comfort Inn when he heard salsa music from around a corner.

El Borracho was a seedy little bar between a laundromat and a thrift store. Its sign was amateurishly lettered on a plastic light box which had been designed to alternate illumination between two bulbs of different colors, but one had burned out so the sign merely flashed from red to off. The door was open, and Jace could see a man stroking off a shot as he leaned over a pool table. Ah, playing pool in a Mexican dive called The Drunk—now, that's class! Jace parked behind a green pickup truck with a "Yo ♥ Tepic" bumper sticker.

The Hispanic man playing pool looked up as Jace walked in. Although the surprise on his face was clear, he nodded and said, "*Hola.*"

"*Hola,*" Jace replied.

He glanced around the small bar. The walls and windows had once been painted black and, save a variety of beer signs, were unadorned. A jukebox near the front door was the source of the salsa music Jace had heard from outside. The battered plywood-and-formica bar was long enough for half a dozen stools, one of which was occupied by a skinny Mexican whore in an improbably blond wig. Three tables were scattered on the other side of the room from the pool table, but their mismatched chairs were empty. A flimsy door in the rear banged open, and another Mexican man emerged, zipping his fly, and headed for the pool table; even from halfway across the room, Jace could smell a miasma of stale urine trailing after him. The place was everything its name had promised. Jace took a stool at the end of the bar farthest from the john.

The man who had greeted Jace put down his cue and walked around to the inside of the bar. *"Cervesa?"*

"Dos Equis, por favor."

The blonde got off her stool and moved over next to Jace and smiled at him. Given her profession, that was a mistake: one of her front teeth was gold, the others tended toward green. Jace motioned to the bartender that he'd buy her a beer, too.

The bartender put a plate of lime wedges and a salt shaker on the bar, and a bottle in front of Jace, but he poured the whore's beer into a glass before serving it.

After all, Jace reflected, she was a lady.

When the bartender had returned to his pool game, the whore smiled at Jace again and said, *"Gracias."*

"De nada." Jace drank off the top two inches of his beer.

"Joo not from here," she told Jace in heavily accented English.

He was relieved to be able to switch back to his native tongue. Although it was almost impossible to be raised in L.A. and not pick up some Spanish, Jace's vocabulary was small and his knowledge of grammar nonexistent.

"No," he agreed, "I'm just passing through." He poured salt into his beer, and when it foamed, he squeezed in the lime, then swigged the Dos Equis.

"Joo wan' some company?" the whore said, putting her hand on Jace's knee. Her fingernails were quite long and painted florescent pink. "Joo have a room?"

"No," Jace lied.

"But joo have a car, jes?" She moved her hand between Jace's legs. "Concepcion good fuck, good suck. For you, fifty dollars." She squeezed his crotch.

Oh, good; an ugly, skinny hooker (named Conception, no less!) would be sure to get Jace hard, yessiree.

"Twenty bucks," he countered.

Concepcion made a face to indicate the price was far too low, but then nodded. "An' a bottle of tequila, jes?"

Jace agreed and Concepcion called out to the bartender in rapid-fire Spanish. Minutes later, they left the bar, Concepcion clutching a brown paper bag containing a bottle of five-dollar booze for which Jace had paid twenty-five.

When they'd gotten into Jace's car, the whore demanded her money, then directed him to drive to where some dark warehouses deepened the gloom. As he pulled to a stop, Concepcion climbed headfirst into the backseat, her bony ass obviously bare under her vinyl miniskirt. If Jace had been capable of an erection, the odor wafting from under Concepcion's skirt might have killed it. He sighed, then got into the back with her.

She unzipped his fly and pulled his cock out of his pants. He had intended to feed, not fuck, but there it was . . . and he'd already paid for it. Her mouth was hot on him and, looking down at the blond wig bobbing over his lap, Jace forgot about her teeth. Concepcion hadn't lied about "good suck," but she wasn't good enough to get a vampire hard. Her attempts to get her client off became more frantic, more insistent. Jace finally pushed her off of him.

Concepcion began babbling rapidly in Spanish, her tone alternating between defensive and desperately apologetic; Jace managed to translate her repeated concern that he'd expect his money back if he didn't come. He told her in English that she could keep the money, motioned her to sit on his lap.

The whore's face lit up at what she obviously thought was a second chance, and she hiked up her skirt before straddling Jace's lap, facing him. Again, he smelled her unpleasant odor, but even stronger was the scent of blood coming from her neck. As soon as his fangs extended, he sank them into her carotid.

When he was done, Jace looked at the whore lying

across his lap. Her eyes were shut and her closed-mouth smile so beatific that she looked almost pretty. He lifted her out of the car and carried her unconscious body over to a Dumpster at the side of a warehouse, where he placed her gently on the ground.

What if he didn't kill her off? What if he just left her there? She might live, even with the blood loss. She hadn't done anything to deserve death, Jace thought; the whore was, ironically, innocent. He rocked back on his heels, looking at her sleeping smile, her cheap red-vinyl skirt and black lace blouse, and he was sorry. But he also recognized that if she lived, she would be able to identify him or would be brain-damaged; either way, he decided, it would not be right to leave the job unfinished.

He gently pushed her hair away from her face and neck. The two fang holes had healed already, but Jace could see where they'd been. He opened his pocket blade and slit Concepcion's neck from front to back, making sure to cut through both fang marks, remembering to stand clear as the rest of her blood spurted from the wound.

When she was gone, he dropped her body into the Dumpster, then covered it with cardboard boxes and debris from another Dumpster. He dragged the bin a few feet to cover the blood on the pavement; with luck, the body would be hauled away before it was discovered.

If she had been able to make him hard, he probably would have let her live.

The bright light outside the library was painful.

Fumbling frantically for his sunglasses, Jace dropped his stack of photocopies and reprints and had to scramble for them as they blew down the street. Nevertheless, an article on inflatable penile implants was flattened by a passing car and now bore tire tracks. Once his eyes were protected, Jace became aware that his skin was tingling unpleasantly—the sensation of aging two weeks in moments?—so he ran to his car, his arms full of now-disorganized paper.

Jace was not yet fully acclimated to being vampiric, and ruefully realized he'd expected it to be less of an adjustment than it was turning out to be; somehow, he thought his life would be only minimally changed from the way it had been prior to his death.

He suddenly flashed on feeding off the Mexican whore the previous night . . . and felt ashamed. Concepcion hadn't been the type of criminal Jace had planned to use—she'd made a living with her body, a victimless crime; the only difference from what Suze Daly did was the amount of money they got paid. In less than a week, Jace had killed two people no more evil than the homeless he'd blamed Risha for feeding on. Although he'd pardoned himself for Preston Kelly's death—he'd honestly thought he was feeding on the thief, not his son—Concepcion had been a different matter: Jace had been fully aware of what he was doing, and to whom, when he'd murdered her.

The twelve-block drive back to the motel seemed to be interminable, but Jace finally reached his room and pulled the blackout drapes closed. He began to feel somewhat normal again, but even as the discomfort in his eyes and skin stopped, he was overwhelmed by a need to sleep. Managing to stay awake just long enough to put the DO NOT DISTURB sign on his double-locked door, Jace didn't stop to undress before dropping heavily onto the bed.

18

He listened to the radio on his way to the Basque restaurant Tuesday night. An Arab suspect in the World Trade Center bombing had been arrested when he tried to get back his deposit on the rental van in which he'd left the explosives. Jace knew criminal stupidity was often the reason when a case got cleared quickly, but the Fibbies had lucked out with this Salameh terrorist—he was obviously too dumb to live. Meanwhile, the nuts in Waco had just released six more children, but Koresh, apparently shot in the stomach during Sunday's raid, had not yet surrendered, and the ATF was drawing analogies to Jonestown. Unfortunately, Jace reflected, not all criminals were idiots.

A few blocks past the Civic Center, Jace saw Bastanchury's Basque Family Restaurant on his right. Basques had come to Bakersfield a century earlier to herd sheep, but stayed to farm and run restaurants. Bastanchury's boasted that they'd been "Serving Bakersfield Since 1921," and was apparently still popular: The large parking lot was almost half-full and it was still early.

Inside, the restaurant had kept much of the original decor: The maize walls had been painted so many times,

their junctures were concave; the booths in the front
room and long tables in the back room were solid oak,
preserved with decades of lamb grease; the paintings of
the Pyrenees were yellowed with age . . . and lamb
grease. Ceiling fans pushed around warm smells from
platters and tureens; Jace wasn't hungry, but he regretted not having tasted Basque lamb, cassoulet, and pistou
before he'd given up the ability to digest them.

"You asked to see me?"

The dishwater blonde standing in front of Jace was
barely five feet tall, with a flat chest and a steatopygic
ass. Although her poorly cut hair and self-conscious
stance made her appear plain at first glance, her warm
brown eyes were wide-spaced, her small nose tilted up
pertly, and her bare lips were full. He guessed her to be
around thirty, older than he'd expected.

"Belinda Bastanchury?" He stood. "I'm Jace Levy.
I'd like to talk with you about Crysse Tanner, if I may."

She raised brown eyebrows in surprise, then waved
Jace back into his chair, though she remained standing.

She glanced at the gray-haired man at the reception
desk, then lowered her voice to a whisper. "Is Christine
in trouble?"

Strange first reaction, Jace thought. "Probably not,"
he dodged, "but perhaps you can help make sure. You
know her, then?"

When the woman nodded, Jace said, "It shouldn't
take too long . . ." and looked pointedly at the chair facing his.

"I . . . I can't." Again, she checked the older man, but
he was speaking to a waitress holding a tureen on a tray,
so she turned back to Jace. "We can't mention her in
front of my father," she added in a whisper.

"Can I meet you somewhere else?"

Belinda bit her lip, looked like she was about to cry,
but then nodded. "Dewar's. I can't leave for at least a
half an hour—is that okay?"

Jace felt that if he moved, Belinda Bastanchury

would jackrabbit into the next county. "That's fine; how about we meet there in an hour?" He smiled as reassuringly as he could.

Belinda nodded and skittered into the kitchen. Jace went to the phone booth to look up the address for Dewar's.

Jace had expected Dewar's to be a bar, but was delighted to discover it was an old-fashioned ice-cream parlor and candy kitchen. It had no tables, just a couple of dozen stools along an L-shaped counter. Even though it was no more than fifty degrees outside, several people were indulging in sundaes or malteds; one towheaded three-year-old was spinning around atop his stool, chocolate sauce covering the front of his shirt, while his mother attempted futilely to keep him facing his dish while she balanced a squirming two-year-old on her lap.

Jace recognized Belinda's full ass at the far end of the counter, her back to the door. He took the stool next to her.

"That looks good," he said, indicating her tin roof sundae.

"Oh! I should have ordered one for you, too," she fretted. "They can make you one; I'll get the soda jerk . . ." She tried to attract the attention of the teenager working the counter.

"No, that's all right," Jace said with a smile. "I'm . . . allergic to ice cream."

Belinda looked stricken. "Oh! I'm sorry—I should have picked someplace else."

"This is fine, Belinda. I'll have a Coke," he told the soda jerk.

"Just plain Coke?" the kid asked incredulously.

When his drink appeared and the soda jerk had left, Jace rotated his stool to face Belinda, but she continued to face the counter, her eyes pinned on her sundae.

"So, why couldn't you mention Crysse Tanner in front of your father?" he asked conversationally.

Without raising her eyes, Belinda mumbled something.

"Pardon me?"

Belinda turned/dipped her head, peering shyly at Jace from under her brow.

"He didn't like Christine," she explained quietly. "I'm sure that's really why he fired her—no matter what he said, she wouldn't steal money from him! Christine, she's going to be a famous actress in Hollywood soon," she informed Jace seriously.

"She's really good, huh?" he prompted.

Belinda swiveled to face Jace, her eyes lit up. "Oh, yes! She's got an agent and everything!"

"You've known Crysse a long time?"

"Almost ten years. We both went to Vista High, but Christine left before our junior year and I never knew her then anyway. We didn't become friends until she started working at the restaurant."

"How long did she work there?"

Belinda's eyes returned to her melting sundae. "Oh, a few years. Three? I don't remember for sure."

"So your father didn't mind you being friends with her then?"

Jace felt a tug. The three-year-old was clutching his pant leg with a chocolate-sticky hand while he tried to reach for Jace's soft drink.

"Mikey! Leave the man alone," the towhead's mother called. "Your ice cream's melting here."

"Firsty," the kid wailed.

"I'll give you something to drink," his mother promised, coming over with the two-year-old in hand to un-clench her son from Jace's pants. "I'm sorry," she told him.

As she dragged the little boy back to the other end of the counter, he started to cry. The young mother looked like she wanted to leave the planet and her kids behind. Jace blotted futilely at the chocolate on his pants before turning his attention back to Belinda Bastanchury, who was looking at Mikey with unabashed adoration.

"Isn't he just the cutest?" she gushed.

Jace grunted noncommittally. "I was asking about your father's attitude toward Crysse Tanner when she worked at the restaurant," he reminded her.

Belinda's fawning smile disappeared. "He didn't want me talking to her at all; he said she was a bad influence."

"But that didn't stop you, did it?" he asked conspiratorially.

Belinda shook her head. "No, but I'm no good at sneaking around like Christine does." She scraped out the last bit of ice cream, then pushed her dish away. "She's really good at it—because of the Home and the foster families and everything; her and the other kids were always sneaking out," she added with a trace of envy.

"The Home?" Jace prompted. "Is that the orphanage?"

"Chester Lane Children's Home," Belinda said. "That's mostly where Christine was raised. I met Mrs. Anderson—she's the lady who ran the Home?—when she came backstage after Christine's very first play at our community theater. Christine only had one line, but Mrs. Anderson brought her flowers; wasn't that nice?"

"It certainly was. Is Mrs. Anderson still at the Home? I'd like to meet her, too."

"I think the Home closed down, but I see Mrs. Anderson at Riverdale Retirement Home when I visit my gramma; she wouldn't remember me from Christine's play, but I remember her, because she was so nice to bring flowers, you know? I wrote to Christine last year that I saw Mrs. Anderson at the retirement home."

Poor Mrs. Anderson had apparently progressed from the Children's Home to the old folks' home without having her own home in between.

"So you're still in touch with Christine?"

Belinda looked down. "Well, I sometimes write letters to her, but she's usually too busy with her career to write back. I understand; becoming a famous star is a lot of hard work. Christine told me all about it after she got to Hollywood. I sent her five hundred dollars to help out until she made it," she said proudly.

Jace added Belinda Bastanchury to his mental list of people who'd been conned by Crysse Tanner, though she was blissfully ignorant that she'd been taken.

"Do you know Tinah Powers, Harris Powers, Hannah Williams, or William Tanner?" he asked her.

"I'm not sure about the first names, but Tanner is the name of the family that adopted Christine—and I think one of her foster families was named Powers, but I'm not sure. Maybe Mrs. Anderson would remember." She looked at her watch. "Oh! My father's going to wonder what happened to me—I have to go." She grabbed the check and fumbled in her purse as she stood.

Jace pulled the check gently from her hand. "My treat. Thank you very much for talking to me, Belinda. If I have more questions, would it be all right if I call you?"

"I guess so, but not during dinner. My father's always at the restaurant at dinner." She headed toward the door, then turned. "I'll tell Christine you said hello, Mr. Levy," she called.

"I miss you, too, but it's going to take me a few more nights to finish up here," Jace told Risha on the phone. It was nearly 4 A.M., and he'd been reading about testosterone patches when she called. "I've tracked down the woman who ran the orphanage where Crysse Tanner was raised, and she's agreed to see me tomorrow evening. I think she can lead me to the foster families, and maybe the old boyfriend, too."

"Well, it sounds like you're keeping busy at least."

"Believe me, Rish, I'll leave here as soon as I can;

I'm not having any fun. How're the pics for *City Of Angels* coming?"

Risha sighed. "I still need one more. I've got a fallback shot, but there's a lot of room for improvement. I'll have to see what the shots I got tonight at LAX look like, but I'm not real optimistic about them. Oh! Speaking of the airport: Elliott located a Betamax in Inglewood through a *Pennysaver* ad; he's going to get it sometime this afternoon."

Jace was eager to see the video; he would soon know what secrets Robert Brandon had shelled out nearly twenty grand to protect. Outside, he could hear a siren wail and wondered why the driver felt it necessary; surely, there couldn't be an appreciable amount of traffic at that hour.

"OK, good. Tell you what: If I haven't got this wrapped up here in another night or two, I'll come home for the weekend. We can go out, catch some music or take a drive up the coast—and it'll give me a chance to get some fresh clothes and look at the tape. How's that sound?"

"Sounds good," Risha said. "Friday night at the latest, then? Do you want to go see the *Chicago Conspiracy Trial* revival at the Odyssey? It's been getting great reviews, and I can leave a note for Elliott to pick up tickets when he's out today."

Ah, culture . . . or, at least, laughter (Jace wasn't sure the antics of Abbie Hoffman and Jerry Rubin would actually be considered culture).

"Make it for Saturday night, just in case I'm running late getting back to town."

"That's what I figured. Besides," Risha added mischievously, "I've got something else planned for the night you return."

Riverdale Retirement Home was a large white edifice on New Stine Road in southwest Bakersfield. It had a deep open veranda spanning the front and another, enclosed with screening, on the west side. Heavily shel-lacked wooden chaise lounges, like those once found on cruise ships, were neatly arranged in rows facing out-ward; card tables with chairs sat ready at each corner, although Jace was currently the only person on either patio. Just inside were a dozen oldsters, some having their hearts warmed by the obligatory precocious child on a saccharine sitcom, others playing chess or cards.

"Here we are, then!" Mrs. Anderson said cheerily as she reappeared through the side door. She was holding a tray with a china tea service. Jace jumped up to take the tray from her, but she said, "Thank you, dear, but I can manage quite well."

The former headmistress of the Chester Lane Chil-dren's Home looked close to eighty. Her once-porcelain skin had become nearly translucent; Jace could easily see the blood vessels underneath. Her wispy hair had been bobbed and tinted a pale lavender that matched her glasses' plastic frames.

He held a chair for her, and she sat gracefully, cross-ing her ankles demurely and closing her peach cardigan at the neck against the cool night air.

"Cook was out of Earl Grey," she told him, holding the pot over a cup. "I'm afraid this is just Lipton's. Lemon or milk, Mr. Levy?"

"Lemon, please. No sugar."

Mrs. Anderson placed a slice of pound cake on Jace's saucer before passing it to him. He was suddenly re-minded of a tea party his cousin Leah had once put on for several of her favorite dolls; he'd been five and had agreed to attend only because she'd said she was serv-ing cake. Leah hadn't mentioned the cake was make-be-lieve.

"I hope you're not too cool out here, Mr. Levy? But the sitting room isn't really conducive to privacy; there's always a biddy or two around to eavesdrop"—she leaned forward conspiratorially and lowered her voice—"and I assure you, they're all dying to know

what such a handsome young stranger wants with Callie
Anderson." Her pale blue eyes lit with mirth as she sat
back. "Let's keep them guessing, shall we?"

Jace found himself captivated. "Perhaps you should
say I'm a relative; I wouldn't want to sully your reputa-
tion, Mrs. Anderson," he said with a smile.

"Oh, pooh, sully away. I'm not a schoolmarm anymore"—she poured more tea in Jace's cup—"and I'm
tired of acting like one."

"I can certainly understand that," he laughed. "You
deserve to do what you want when you retire. How long
has it been since Chester Lane closed?"

"A fire destroyed the Home on October 31, 1989, and
the girls all had to be relocated. There was no longer any
need for me, so I was transferred here."

Mrs. Anderson's bitterness showed; Jace used it to es-
tablish rapport. "Isn't it terrible the way they force the
people who have all the experience to retire? When my
father was forced into retirement, it killed him."

"Oh, yes! I know what you mean! I see it here all the
time; no one knows what to do with themselves, so they
dry up and blow away. I have useful years left to me,
but . . ." She shrugged.

Jace clucked sympathetically, nodding, then observed, "October 31 is Halloween. Was the fire arson?"

"You're sharp, Mr. Levy; yes, it was. One of our girls,
I'm afraid. Fortunately, no one was injured, but we
weren't so lucky with the records—everything was lost:
adoption papers, medical transcripts, immunization
records . . ." Mrs. Anderson sighed. "There are nearly
thirty children out there with virtually no paperwork,
and another fifty with only the sparsest of records.
That's why I probably can't be of much help in locating
your niece, Mr. Levy."

Jace picked up his cue and tried to look crushed. "I've
been looking for her for so long, I'm afraid I got my
hopes up when I found where you'd gone. It just breaks
my heart, Mrs. Anderson. Breaks my heart."

He paused to milk the moment, then hesitantly produced the bottle of cognac he'd bought.

"Well, I brought this along for a celebration, but I guess I could still use a drink. If you wouldn't mind, I mean. Would you care for a splash in your tea, Mrs. Anderson?"

Callie Anderson shot a glance into the living room, then tossed the rest of her tea into a potted plant. She held her empty teacup out to Jace. "No sense spoiling good cognac with mediocre tea, Mr. Levy. Thank you."

It was close to an hour before Jace got the conversation turned back around to his "niece." While Mrs. Anderson put away a remarkable amount of cognac for her age and size, she talked about the orphanage.

"Arson was just the capper to a bad situation. The children at Chester Lane had a lot of anger—that was one of the reasons they were there: they were 'problems,' kids who'd failed at foster-home care. Although they were often placed again, it usually didn't work out any better, so most of the girls stayed at Chester Lane until they were old enough to be on their own. When I first took over in 1958, I thought I could supply all the love they'd been deprived of . . ."

Mrs. Anderson shook her head slowly and Jace got an inkling of how much thirty years of "problems" had taken out of her—and perhaps how she'd gotten her tolerance for alcohol.

"It couldn't be done, of course," she continued, "and certainly not by one middle-aged widow bucking an indifferent bureaucracy, no matter how determined I was. It was all I could do just to keep my girls out of serious trouble. Do you know that Kern County has the highest pregnancy rate for ten-to-fourteen-year-olds in California? I remember Sarah Troxler, the headmistress at Herbert Home in Santaroga, once bragged to me that over forty percent of her girls went on to college; I was lucky if forty percent of my girls finished high school!"

"Now, I'm sure some of your girls went on to better

things . . ." Jace ventured, hoping to segue toward Crysse Tanner's Hollywood career.

Mrs. Anderson dropped her cup and saucer to the table in a clatter and her cognac sloshed out. "In a pig's eye!" she exclaimed vehemently.

Jace had no idea what had set her off, but he knew that if he could maintain their rapport through a "crisis," she'd open to him and tell him what he needed to know. The alcohol might have been affecting her; her pale skin was slightly flushed. He splashed another drink into her teacup, leaned toward her expectantly, and said soothingly, "You can tell me, Mrs. Anderson."

So she did. "I spent the better part of my life defending my charges every time the bureaucracy wanted to close the Home. I told them, 'There are no bad children. With love and care, these girls can become valuable members of society; these girls will contribute!' I believed it, too, Mr. Levy, I truly did. Year in and year out, I spent much of my small salary on extras for my girls: field trips, pretty dresses to boost self-esteem, even—" she lowered her voice a notch—"even abortions when there was no acceptable alternative. When they had severe emotional problems—most of my girls had emotional problems, Mr. Levy—when they had problems, I arranged for counseling to help them through. I gave them all the security I could beg, borrow, or steal for them. It should have been enough, but it wasn't. I wasn't enough. My girls became arsonists, liars, thieves, and whores because Callie Anderson failed them!"

She stopped, suddenly aware that her frustration permeated the stillness of the veranda. She pulled a tissue out of a pocket and wiped angry tears from her eyes.

"I know this isn't what you expected when you came to find your niece, but I've stopped doing what's expected. In the years I have left, I intend to speak my mind." She tucked the tissue into her sleeve, drew a deep breath, then said quietly, "The Chester Lane Children's Home was inadequate because I was inadequate. I couldn't save any of them."

Jace was completely at a loss. He wanted to comfort the old headmistress, point out successes she must have overlooked, but he knew of none—in fact, he'd come specifically to find out more about one of her failures—so he did the only thing he could think of: He got up and went over to Callie Anderson and put his arms around her.

She sobbed into his shirt for a few minutes. A nurse opened the door to the veranda, concern evident on her face. Jace felt embarrassed, as if he were being blamed for causing the old woman to cry, but Callie Anderson impatiently waved the nurse back into the house and composed herself.

"I'm sorry, Mr. Levy, I truly am. Thank you for being so patient with this old biddy. Now, let's see what I can remember about your niece. Do you know what name she might have been given or when she might have arrived at Chester Lane?"

"Well, as I explained to you on the phone, my brother and I were estranged; I didn't even hear that he'd gone missing in Vietnam for a number of years. I have a photograph of his fiancée; perhaps you might notice a family resemblance to one of your girls. She'd be . . . oh, about twenty-five now, I should think, if that helps you narrow down the time frame any."

Jace pulled out a photocopy of Crysse Tanner's headshot, aware that it looked too contemporary to be her own mother, but it was the best way he had to leading Mrs. Anderson to an ID. He passed it over to her.

She got up and stood under the porch light to study the photo through the bottom part of her bifocals.

"There's something about her eyes . . ." she said, almost to herself. "And her mouth. But not the teeth . . . Christina! That's who this looks like, although much prettier—it looks like Christina Tanner!"

"Tanner?" Jace said dubiously, hiding his delight that

Mrs. Anderson had pinned the tail on the donkey. "Although I don't know what name my brother's fiancée gave their daughter, I'm sure the last name would have been Walker or Levy, not Tanner."

"Oh, Christina didn't start with that name—Tanner is the name of the family who adopted her. Before Christina came to us, she'd been placed with a couple named Powers, but they and their son died in a fire, so then—Gracious, this would be so easy if I still had my records!"

Records which had perished in a fire. A foster family who had perished in a fire. Was Crysse Tanner an arsonist and murderer, as well as an extortionist? Jace filed away the question for later; it could be exactly the information he would need to persuade her to drop the blackmail of Reese Hamilton, if not cause her incarceration—there was no statute of limitations on murder.

"Please tell me everything you remember, Mrs. Anderson!" he begged. "Do you know where I can find the Tanners?"

"Oh, dear. This isn't a pleasant story, Mr. Levy," she warned him.

"My niece is dead, isn't she?" he said with resignation, to show he was prepared for the worst.

"Oh, no—I'm sure Christina's still alive. Well, probably still alive," she emended.

Jace looked relieved. "I can handle the truth, Mrs. Anderson. Please."

"I think I might just have another little splash of cognac, if I may, Mr. Levy. Thank you." She stopped to swallow. "The Tanner household was . . . suddenly disrupted. I don't remember all the details, I'm afraid, but the gist of it is that Mr. Tanner killed his wife, shot her right on the front lawn, in front of the mailman and a neighbor. He swore up and down that he was innocent, but with the witnesses and all . . . I'm so sorry—I just don't know what happened to Christina after that. She was over sixteen and didn't have to return to the Home. Mr. Tanner's still in Atascadero State Prison, I believe; perhaps he would tell you."

The nurse came out on the veranda again. This time she saw the near-empty cognac bottle on the table between them and frowned. "I'm afraid your visitor will have to leave, Mrs. Anderson. It's almost lights-out."

Jace stood, and the nurse went back inside, leaving the door wide-open while she waited for the former headmistress to join her. Mrs. Anderson gave Jace her hand, and he bent over to kiss it.

She giggled like a schoolgirl. "Oh, Mr. Levy, you're too much for me! If you're ever in Bakersfield again, please come see me."

"It would be my pleasure. And next time, I'll take you out someplace nice, away from all these prying eyes." He smiled charmingly and walked down the steps, turning back as he hit the last one. "Oh, Mrs. Anderson? One last thing: Who was responsible for the fire at Chester Lane?"

The old woman hesitated, then said softly, "I'm afraid it was Christina Tanner, Mr. Levy, although no one was ever able to prove it."

19

"Liz, it's Jace," he told his former partner's answering machine. "I'm in Bakersfield on my extortion case and I need a favor. I want to get into Atascadero to interview a prisoner outside of regular visiting hours—can you please reach out and arrange it? Any day after 6 P.M.—tomorrow, if you can swing it. The prisoner's name is T-A-N-N-E-R, first name William." He added his phone number at the Comfort Inn and hung up.

He started to call Risha, but aborted before he finished dialing, deciding to wait until he heard back from Liz, just in case the prison visit changed their weekend plans. He wondered what Risha had planned for the night he returned; the tone of her voice had hinted at the sensual. He formed a mental image of her, naked and wet from the shower, on her knees, sucking him off, just like she had the night she'd consumed the feeder in the backseat while he drove. He remembered the feel of her cold wet hair in his hands and the sight of her pale lips enveloping him to the root, and his cock stirred. He unzipped his trousers and pulled it out, stroking for the sensation, no longer expecting to actually get hard, while the loop played in his head. It felt good, but when he later realized he was thinking about feeding, not fucking, he stuffed himself back into his pants. It had been three days since he'd drained Concepcion—he should be out finding a feeder, not playing with himself.

When Jace left his room, he stepped out into Bakersfield's infamous tule fog, a deep, impenetrable blanket, occasionally responsible for forty-five-car pileups at the Grapevine on I-5. Although Jace knew he'd parked less than twenty-five feet from the door, he couldn't see his car. He thought of returning to his room to spend the rest of the night reading more of the research papers on impotence he'd obtained, but hunger drove him out. He told himself that when he had the car lights on, he'd be able to see, but he knew better; even his amplified senses were stymied. He could neither see nor hear much of anything—how would he find a feeder?

He located the car and flipped on the headlights, illuminating the thick white curtain only a foot ahead. As he pulled slowly out of the parking lot, sticking his head out his window to see the road better, he was grateful that he would survive any collision he might cause, but any others involved might not be so lucky. (Would he be reduced to feeding on roadkill?) He switched off a radio interview with one of the people injured in the New York bombing so that he could hear any cars which might be sharing the road with him, and wondered what the fuck he was doing out in this fog when he could be inside, masturbating . . .

Desire. He still had desire! Maybe he couldn't get it up, but sex hadn't ceased to interest him. His recent research had taught him that a drop in testosterone levels resulted in a concurrent drop in sexual interest that Jace had not experienced, so his testosterone level was probably not affected by the vampirism and, therefore, was not the cause of his impotence. (Of course, he thought ruefully, that also meant it wouldn't be curable by using a testosterone patch, one of the more promising impotence treatments he'd been reading about.)

Damn this fog! He couldn't see the streetlights until

he was right under them, and could easily pass right by a feeder and not even know it. And the fog was deepening, if that were possible, so now Jace couldn't even make out the white line on the road, except by looking down as he drove alongside it. It was madness being out in this pea soup, but he couldn't wait another night to feed. He pulled over to the curb and got out of the car to walk, but hesitated, unsure of how he'd find the car again—or his motel, for that matter. He certainly couldn't read street signs through this.

He was still leaning against his car when he heard a voice and the mumble of a car engine. A man appeared out of the fog, walking the dividing line in the middle of the street, guiding the driver of a subcompact that tailed him down the street like a puppy.

"OK, honey, here's the corner; turn right," the walker told the driver.

The odd duo made the turn and quickly disappeared into the ground fog, never having noticed Jace. If those people were still out on the street, there could be others—maybe even someone alone to feed upon. Jace switched on the parking lights, then began to walk, counting his paces from the car. He didn't want to still be out at daybreak, waiting for the fog to burn off so he could find his way back.

One hundred and eighty-seven paces later, he heard a man's voice just to his right and stopped.

"Fuckin' tule fog. Couldn't make out a nigger 'til you was right on top of it."

"I'll see whut I kin do," another male voice laughed gruffly. "Can't really be blamed if'n I run over mud people 'causa fog."

Jace heard the distinctive slam of a pickup truck's door, but didn't realize that he was less than six feet behind the truck until the driver turned on his headlamps. The lights illuminated the first man standing outside a gated yard, an aging skinhead with a huge beer gut in an NRA T-shirt, who said, "See ya Sat'day, Beam." The pickup truck drove off faster than was prudent, considering the visibility.

Feeling a bit like the Invisible Man, Jace preceded the skinhead through the gate and ducked through the open door of the house without being seen. Suddenly, it occurred to him that it would have been better to ambush the feeder outside—there could be others in the house—but it was too late to duck out.

The skinhead came through the door, saw Jace standing there, and managed to get out "What the fu—" before Jace jumped him and planted his fangs. He yanked the skinhead into the room to his right and gulped as much blood as he could as fast as he could, all the while alert to any sounds from elsewhere in the house. If Risha knew how recklessly he'd attacked this feeder, she'd have read him the riot act.

When he was finished with the skinhead, Jace looked around the room they were in for the first time. A glass cabinet displayed a variety of old guns and knives which bore Nazi swastikas and SS insignia; the stained plaid couch and matted shag carpeting were littered with copies of *The Jubilee*, a white supremacist newspaper, and other Aryan Nations' literature. Jace smiled. Now, this was the kind of feeder he preferred! Although he had a knife with him, Jace used a particularly nasty-looking blade from the skinhead's own collection to obscure the fang marks and finish draining the body.

He turned off the lights and slipped back out the door seven minutes after he'd entered, seeing no one as he counted the steps back to his car.

"That bitch is just trouble, man. She's hot, but she rips people off without even thinking about it, like it just comes natural, you know?"

Patrick Olds, Crysse Tanner's old boyfriend, made a final adjustment to the Harley engine, then sat on a milk crate and accepted a beer from Jace with a nod. He was under thirty, but his dirty blond hair was already receding and his skin already leathery from working outside; he obviously spent a fair amount of time keeping his well-defined muscles toned—even with just the light from the garage, Jace could discern a washboard stomach under Olds' T-shirt.

"I heard something about stealing from a Basque restaurant . . ." Jace began.

"Yeah, that place on Union? Guy who owned the place lost his whole take one night—he, like, had it in his desk or something, ready to take to the bank, but when he went to get it, it was gone. He couldn't prove it was Tina took it, but everyone else who worked there was in his family, so he fired her anyway. I knew it was her—hell, she showed me the dough, musta been close to a grand—said she was finally gonna get out of here, go to Hollywood and be famous." Olds laughed and swigged back the rest of his beer. He crushed the can in his fist and lobbed it into a trash barrel against the side of the garage, then added, "Only thing Tina ever be famous for is blowjobs."

Jace passed the six-pack across to Olds, who pulled open another beer. "So she split right after she got fired?" he asked, taking a drink.

"No, man, I wasn't that lucky. Musta been another— what? two–three months?—'fore she left. I come home late one Sunday night after running a weekend whitewater group, and my stereo and my stash was gone, along with about two hundred cash I kept in my trailer. Never saw Tina again, but I figure I got off cheap, 'least compared to the dude what runs the restaurant. Hell, at least she fucked me before she screwed me."

"How long did you go with her?" Jace asked.

" 'Bout a year, I guess, but we wasn't exactly going steady. I never been a one-woman man, and didn't make enough money to keep Tina exclusive, anyway. She was always wanting stuff, but whitewater rafting don't pay shit—it's good work, but there ain't a lot of extra . . . and Tina liked a lot of extra. An' she knew how to get it, too: I once seen her turn an older, married guy inside out—in fifteen minutes, he followed her out the door just like she had a leash on his cock; sure as shit, by the time he came, his wallet was empty. She was back at the restaurant before her lunch hour was over." Olds shook his head in grudging admiration. "You ever seen a chick, you know right away you gotta nail her? Tina could do that to any man she wanted to. It wasn't that she was so pretty, but she turned it on you, you had to have it, that's just the way she was."

Jace stood; he had to leave if he was going to make Atascadero by seven-thirty. Olds held up the rest of the six-pack to him.

"Keep it. Listen, Olds, any of these names sound familiar to you? Tinah Powers, Harris Powers, Hannah Williams, or William Tanner?"

"Sure. Hannah and William Tanner adopted Tina from this orphanage she lived at, and before that she lived with some people named Powers—what was the first name again?"

"Tinah and Harris."

"Tina coulda used Powers, I guess, but she was already Tanner when I met her. I don't remember her saying anything about a Harris Powers, though."

On the drive to Atascadero State Prison, Jace mulled over all the names he'd heard for his suspect: Crysse, Christine, Christina, Tina, Powers, Tanner. They seemed to add up to a chameleon who was skilled at arson, theft, and blowjobs.

"You must have pull, Mr. Levy—even my lawyer never got to visit at night."

William Tanner was in his mid-fifties, a big man with thin, light brown hair, a deeply lined face and alert, sad eyes which matched his prison blues. The former driving instructor was serving twenty-five-to-life for murdering his wife.

"Apparently, my editor knows the warden here." Jace

shrugged, then handed a prison-inspected package across the table. "I didn't bring much, because I know you can't take anything back to your cell," he apologized, "but there's two different brands of cigarettes—"

"Don't smoke. Thanks for the candy and Pepsi, though—that was real thoughtful." He popped open a can and toasted Jace before drinking. "So, what do you want with me?"

"The only arrest on your rap sheet is the one which brought you here. I'd like to understand how a previously law-abiding man ends up in prison for murder, thought it might make an interesting article. Do you mind talking about it?"

"Mind? No—it beats lockdown. But there's something you have to know right from the git-go: I didn't kill Hannah. I don't know who did, but it wasn't me. We were married for nineteen years . . . you married, Mr. Levy?"

"No, but I live with someone."

"Not the same thing. You live with someone and things get to be too much of a hassle, you just leave; but if you're married, you stick it out, get through it. Problems always come up—arguments over children, over sex, over money—but after nineteen years, you been together long enough, you know you'll get past it eventually. I'm not saying Hannah never pissed me off, but I never laid an angry hand on that woman, and I sure as hell didn't shoot her in broad daylight in front of two witnesses. I never did understand how they could swear I did it . . ."

Tanner picked up a Milky Way bar and turned it in his hands absently. Jace's instincts told him that he was telling the truth: He hadn't murdered his wife.

"Tell me what happened."

Tanner sighed, then tore open the Milky Way and bit off a hunk. He didn't speak until he'd swallowed, then he put down the rest of the bar and looked straight at Jace.

"I only told the whole story to one other person, Mr. Levy: my lawyer. You can see it didn't do me much good"—he smiled ruefully—"but maybe it's time to trust someone else. The person who murdered my wife is still out there, free as a bird, while I'm spending the rest of my life locked in here with criminals. If nothing else, maybe you can figure out why Wini Street and Martin Kirk lied and said I'd done it."

Jace switched on his tape recorder and nodded. "Ready when you are."

Tanner looked down at his hands, took a deep breath, then faced Jace again. "Hannah was killed on Saturday, March 9 at eleven-fifteen in the morning. I wasn't there, because the night before, Hannah and I had had a fi—an argument, and I stormed out. I did a fair amount of drinking, spent the night with . . . a lady friend. In the morning, I went straight to work, but by the time Hannah was murdered, I was way the hell out at Lake Isabella, looking for some woman who'd called for driving lessons. Never found her, never even found the address she'd given me—later, my lawyer told me it doesn't even exist; it was a wild-goose chase, probably some high-school kids getting their kicks . . . could've even been Christy, I guess."

"Christy?" Jace asked, though he knew exactly whom Tanner meant.

"Our daughter. She was sixteen then. When Hannah and me got married, we planned to have children, but we—I—couldn't. Low sperm count. It wasn't that important to me—I guess it's just not the same thing for a man—but Hannah, she could never let it go. If we so much as saw a movie with kids in it, Hannah'd be crying half the night over not having one. She drove me crazy for years, until I finally said we could look into adopting one. To tell you the truth, I wasn't too happy about taking in a baby—I was forty by then and had gotten used to our routine, which was pretty quiet. The next day, Hannah found out we'd have to wait too long for a baby, but that we could have an older child as soon as all the background checks and interviews and whatnot were all taken care of. Well, it sounds a lot easier than it was, but almost a year later, we met Christy, who was twelve, at the Chester Lane Children's Home. I don't know what happened to Christy's biological parents, but she was the only survivor of a fire that killed her foster family. Hannah took to her right away, even though Christy was a lot older than we'd wanted. She thought it would be fun to raise a teenager." He snorted with bemusement.

He drained his Pepsi, then took another bite of the Milky Way before continuing.

"When we adopted Christy, Hannah set out to be the kind of mother she always wanted to be: She joined the PTA, baked cookies, all that stuff. Her whole world revolved around that girl. Half the time I'd come home from work and they'd both be gone, out gallivanting around the mall, buying clothes like they were best friends or something. Neither of 'em had much time for me, so when I met a woman who did, I—makes no difference; Hannah never knew . . . or if she did, she didn't much care. She had her daughter, and that was what really mattered to her. But by the time the girl reached the end of junior high school, things changed. Christy had her own friends, her own stuff to do. Hannah was . . . she felt . . . neglected."

Tanner stopped and rubbed his eyes with the heels of both hands. Jace checked the tape; there was about twenty minutes' worth left. He waited for Tanner to continue, not wishing to impede the flow of his narrative by speaking. Tanner finished the candy bar, popped open another soda, then resumed.

"The next year or so was hell around the house. Christy stayed out doing whatever teenagers do, while her mother went crazy trying to keep her a child, like I expect mothers of teenagers do. That last night, the two of them had a pretty big blowup. Christy hadn't done her chores, then came home a bit too late, and Hannah liked to have had a fit, demanding the girl tell her where she'd been half the night . . ." Tanner looked embarrassed. "I stayed out of it, mostly, on account of I didn't know who was right, anyway. After Christy went to bed, Hannah took off after me, yellin' at me that Christy was a monster because I wasn't a better father, and that she should have married Jud Goodman, because at least he could father children. . . . That's when I stormed out. I just couldn't listen anymore; I'd plumb run out of patience."

He looked into his soda can, then drank some. "The very next afternoon, the police arrested me for murder. They said that Wini Street, our next-door neighbor—and the mailman, a guy named Martin Kirk—told them that I just walked out of our house, cool as you please, and shot Hannah in the head while she was watering the flowers. They don't like to give bail in murder cases, Mr. Levy. They wouldn't even let me go to Hannah's funeral. I never saw Christy again either—my lawyer said she'd gotten some kind of emancipated minor paper from the court, so she could be on her own. I sent her some letters, but"—he shrugged—"she sent them back unopened. She just wrote 'refused' on them."

"Hannah called Christy a 'monster'?"

Tanner nodded. "By that point, both women were calling each other names quite a bit. Christy called Hannah a dried-up old hag, which wasn't the best way to get on her mother's good side, I'll tell you. It had been building for a while. A few months earlier, Hannah had some bee in her bonnet and told me Christy had a split personality—God knows where she got that, but she dragged the girl off to some psychologist to get tested for it. Cost me $175 to find out Christy was just a normal teenager; hell, I coulda told her that for nothin'."

A split personality had occurred to Jace, too, although he couldn't make a psychiatric aberration fit the case profiles. "Christy didn't go to your trial?" he asked.

Tanner shook his head. "I guess I didn't really expect it. Christy wasn't too fond of authority, policemen and courts and the like, and I guess she didn't think too much of me, either. A year or two later, I heard she got picked up for shoplifting at a dress store, so I guess she had to face the system a little then; got probation, my lawyer said. She moved out of Bakersfield five or six years ago, never got a forwarding address. Hell, she could be dead, too, for all I know."

The guard stuck his head in the door. "Time."

Tanner finished his soda, then said, "I've been straight with you, Mr. Levy—told you everything, just how it happened. Will you do me a favor?"

"Sure, Mr. Tanner. What do you want?"

"Hannah's buried at Greenlawn Cemetery. I'd really appreciate it if you'd put some flowers on her grave for me. Tulips, if you can find them; Hannah was always partial to tulips."

Jan Van Bever, night editor of the *Bakersfield Californian*, took off his plaid cap, smoothed the remains of his gray hair forward over his bald pate, then replaced the cap.

"Powers? Yeah, I remember. It was the only arson I covered as a reporter. Father, mother, young son. Sometime in the early seventies, wasn't it?"

Jace nodded. "Nineteen seventy-two. The clipping I saw said nothing about arson, though."

"The fire was definitely arson—someone poured lighter fluid all over the furniture and tossed a match—but the cops never located a suspect, or a clear motive. Arsonists prefer better accelerants, like gasoline, so the detectives didn't think it was a professional hit. As I remember, the family was squeaky-clean—churchgoers, no enemies, like that. The only survivor was a little girl, and she didn't see anyone."

No little girl was mentioned in the article Jace had

seen at Crysse's apartment. "Who was she? The article I read reported only the three people in the family: Martin and Elise Powers, and their son, Harris."

Van Bever scrunched up his face in concentration, then shook his head. "Let me call up the piece from the morgue."

While they waited for the file to come up, Van Bever asked Jace if he knew Al Martinez at the *Los Angeles Times*, apparently an old drinking buddy.

Jace shook his head. "I read his column sometimes. He specializes in colorful local characters?"

"That's Al."

A copyboy brought a file folder. It contained photocopies of two articles and an obituary listing. Jace recognized one of the articles as the clipping he'd seen in Hollywood. Van Bever picked up the other one.

"Yeah, here it is. A six-year-old foster child—no name here, though. The firemen found her in shock on the front lawn, her hair singed off. She didn't know what happened or how she got there." He scanned the other article. "You're right, she's not mentioned in the earlier piece." He took off his cap, smoothed his hair again, replaced the cap. "I probably didn't find out about her until after we went to press."

He passed the photocopies across the desk to Jace; the second article was mostly about how Harris Powers' classmates were coping with his death.

"You have any more info than what's here?" Jace asked.

"That's it. Hell, page twenty-six—I'm surprised it got two days' coverage, to tell you the truth. But the son was only twelve, and mourning children tug at the heartstrings, et cetera."

"You remember anything else about the girl?"

The editor started to shake his head, then stopped. "Yeah, actually, I do. The ambulance was leaving just as I pulled up, and one of the firefighters said, 'Funny thing. You'd think, after that kind of trauma, she'd be crying for her mother, wouldn't you? But she never even asked about the family."

Jace thought about that all during his drive back to Los Angeles.

Little kids start fires all the time, playing with matches. But how many of them squirt lighter fluid all over the furniture first?

20

Jace turned onto his street a little after eight on Friday evening; Elliott, passing in the other direction, acknowledge him with a nod but didn't slow. Risha was standing on the porch, obviously surprised to see Jace drive up.

"I didn't expect you so early," she said, kissing him hello as he got out of the car. "I'm not ready yet."

"Glad to see you, too." Jace reached into the back and retrieved his bags. "Not ready for what?"

They walked into the house.

"You'll find out . . ." she said slyly. "Meanwhile, stay out of the bedroom."

Jace dropped his bags at the foot of the stairs. "For how long? I was hoping for a hot shower and a cold lager."

Risha put an arm around his waist and led him into the study. "At least an hour. I'll get you a Harp, but I should tell you, there's Dom Pérignon in your future, so don't fill up on beer. Oh, Elliott said that arrived for you this morning," she said, pointing to a package on the desk.

Jace looked at the return address: UCLA Medical Center Library. He put the thick envelope into a desk drawer, unopened, embarrassed to have Risha see he was reading research on impotence.

"So where was Elliott off to?" he asked her.

She shrugged, smiling. "I dunno. I told him to take the weekend off. Thought it'd be nice for us to be alone." She went into the kitchen, calling through the door, "You want a glass?"

"Naw, save it for the champagne."

Risha came back and handed Jace a cold bottle of Harp. "Elliott put your phone messages on the sideboard. Can you amuse yourself for an hour?"

Jace was a little put out that he'd been gone all week and Risha hadn't even asked how his case was going. "Yeah, I guess."

"Good. Don't come up." She kissed him again—but this time she lingered more, used her tongue. "It'll be worth the wait," she promised as she left.

There were three messages for Jace: one from Liz, one from Phil Bloom . . . and one from Crysse Tanner. He drank off half his Harp, then dialed the Hollywood number.

"This is Jace Levy. I got a message you called?"

"Oh, yes," Crysse purred. "Actually, I wonder if you'd mind coming over here? I'd like to discuss something with you."

Jace figured she probably wanted to know what happened to the magazine article he'd supposedly been writing, but he was about ready to confront her anyway. "Sure. When's good for you?"

"I'm free right now."

Risha had told him to amuse himself for an hour. In little more than that, he could have this case wrapped up. "It'll take me about thirty minutes."

"I'll chill some wine." She paused. "You'll be alone this time, won't you?"

Crysse's pale yellow silk lounging gown was so ethereal that Jace could easily see her nipples through it.

As soon as she opened the door, he was nearly over-
come by the urge to cup her breasts; he fantasized
about lowering his lips to one erect nipple when he
reined himself in sharply. The bitch was an extortionist, an arsonist, and a murderer—not to mention an airhead—and he was here on business . . . besides, he
couldn't get it up anyway.

"Ooh, that was fast!" Crysse gushed. "I'm not ready
yet."

Second time Jace had heard that from a woman in the
last hour. "You look ready to me."

The blonde giggled. "Not me, silly—the munchies.
Why don't you pour us some wine while I finish up
here."

She took a bottle of Chablis out of the freezer and
handed it to Jace, adding a corkscrew and two glasses
before she turned back to whatever she was making in
the kitchen. Jace poured the wine, set one glass down on
the counter next to her and held the other in his hand
without tasting it. He scanned the floor warily.

"What are you looking for?" she asked.

"Your snake. I don't want to step on him."

"Her. Greta's in the bathroom. She's been agitated
lately, so I'm letting her have an aromatherapy soak in a
nice warm tub." Crysse frowned slightly, which made
her lips pout even more deliciously. "I hope she's not
getting premonitions of something. You know, animals
can sense stuff humans can't—like earthquakes and
other catechisms."

Jace smiled. "Cataclysms?"

"Oh yes, all kinds! Comets, too! You don't believe
me?" She came out of the kitchen with her glass in one
hand, a platter in the other. "Let's sit on the couch."

Jace sat, Crysse put the platter on the glass coffee
table in front of him, then sat so close, she was nearly on
his lap.

"I hope you like these—they're tofu delights."

Jace looked dismayed, which didn't require any acting. "Oh, gee, I'm sorry. I'm allergic to tofu."

"You're kidding! I didn't think anyone could be allergic to soybean—that's what they give people who are allergic to everything else! Listen, I can recommend this great nutrition guru—you go through these cleansing rituals with high colonics, then—"

"I was surprised to hear from you, Crysse. I don't remember giving you my phone number."

"Oh, you didn't give it to me—you gave it to Belinda Bastanchury the other day," Crysse said cheerily. "She called and told me you were up in Bakersfield, asking all about me."

Jace nodded vaguely and took a sip of wine, wanting to see where she was taking this. Crysse turned out to be surprisingly patient; she ate a tofu delight, nibbling with small white teeth, and drank some wine before the silence convinced her that he wasn't going to elaborate.

She licked her lips a bit too suggestively for it to be unconscious. "I figured if you were that interested in me, maybe we ought to get together again . . . without your photographer."

She traced the outline of Jace's ear with a warm fingertip. He was finding her quite a turn-on, and was actually grateful not to have the additional distraction of an erection to deal with.

"I'm not a writer," he told her bluntly, "I'm a private investigator. You've been blackmailing my client, and now you're going to stop."

"Don't be silly." She placed a hand on his inner thigh; it felt hot through his jeans. "Why should I stop?"

"Because you won't like the alternative. I know about the fire you set at Chester Lane Children's Home—and I can prove that you murdered the Powers family by burning their house down. There's no statute of limitations on murder."

Crysse slid her hand lightly over his balls, then whispered with hot, moist breath into his ear, "I'm sure we can work something out." She unbuckled his belt. "Have you ever fucked someone who's studied Tantric Yoga?"

Jace moved her hands away, then buckled his belt.

Crysse raised an eyebrow. "Not your type? Tell me what you want, baby."

"I want you to stop blackmailing my client. Permanently. I want all the tapes, and any copies you've made."

"What tapes? Who's your client?"

She ran one finger under his collar. Jace twitched. If he could have gotten hard, he would have fucked her blind. He remembered what Patrick Olds had said about Crysse being a woman you just had to nail.

"Reese Hamilton. But I also know about Robert Brandon . . . and the rest," he bluffed. "And I'll know if you hit up any of them again. Find a new way to make a living, or you'll spend your prime at Sybil Brand." Jace stood. "Give me the tapes now, Christina."

She stood, too, put her arms around Jace's neck. He shrugged her off, feeling simultaneously virtuous and stupid.

She put up her hands. "OK, OK. But look, we can still work something out. There's good money in this. I'll give you thirty percent—and you don't have to do a thing for it. Cash, Jace—thousands of dollars, every month." She smiled seductively again. "I'll give you a thousand tonight to start—and more after my next pickup. I can't double-cross you, or you'd turn me in. You haven't got anything to lose."

Jace put out his hand. "The tapes."

Crysse looked a little desperate. "Fifteen hundred tonight, but that's all the cash I have right now. I can get more on Monday. C'mon—this is a good deal. You want more than thirty percent? I'll give you forty . . ."

"The tapes."

"I don't have any tapes of Reese Hamilton; I just told him I did. OK, look, I'll split it with you, fifty-fifty!

C'mon—five thousand a month for doing nothing! I do all the contacts, all the pickups—all you have to do is take your share and keep your mouth shut."

"I want all the evidence."

"OK, you hold on to the evidence, but don't stop me, please! I don't have any other way to make money," Crysse whined.

"Give it to me," Jace said, agreeing to nothing.

Crysse went over to the TV and opened the cabinet underneath. She rummaged through the videotapes for a minute, then pulled out a Beta case.

"It's gone! I had a videotape in here of Robert Brandon, and it's gone!" She pulled out all her tapes—all obviously VHS—and searched frantically for the missing Beta.

"Give me the rest of them," Jace said, pleased that she'd not realized he'd broken in for the Brandon video.

"There aren't any others—that's the only one I had! I just told Hamilton and Perry I had tapes—honest! Look, they'll never know—they'll keep paying me to keep quiet, and you'll get half—"

Jace went over to Crysse, grabbed her, and kissed her. She responded eagerly, sucking his tongue down her throat, pressing her lucious body against his. Jace felt a surge, a twitch at his cock; he knew she'd give great head. He pulled out of the kiss reluctantly and walked to the door.

"You contact any of them again, you're history," he reminded her as he left.

Jace never noticed that a bearded man in a tan VW followed him home.

"I thought about putting a mirror over the bed, but it occurred to me that it'd be kind of pointless," Risha said with a smile. "So, what do you think?"

Jace didn't know how to react, instinctively aware that laughter would not be an appropriate response.

Their bedroom had been transformed into a Hollywood version of an *Arabian Nights* fantasy: Oriental carpets overlapped underfoot; multicolored silks were draped against the walls, under the ceiling, and around the bed—which was now on the floor, covered with printed velvets, attended by a bottle of champagne in a bucket of ice; the lighting speckled gold and red from brass cutout lampshades; musk incense burned on the dresser (now draped with a fringed-velvet shawl), assaulting Jace's delicate olfactory sense, while the sound of unseen wind chimes came from somewhere in the opulence. The door to the candlelit bathroom was open, revealing perfumed water in a two-person Jacuzzi, which had replaced their old bathtub. Risha was dressed in a diaphanous bronze harem outfit with nothing on underneath, her dark auburn hair in a style straight out of *I Dream of Jeannie*.

"Well, you certainly put a lot of work into this," Jace said carefully, doing his best to keep a straight face.

"We've been at it all week," Risha said proudly. "Elliott did all the draping in the daytime while the workmen installed the Jacuzzi. I slept on a futon in the darkroom while they were here. I was afraid it wouldn't all be ready in time—the lamps didn't arrive until six tonight!"

Jace looked at the new lamps again—nice mood lighting, maybe, but not otherwise functional. "Gonna be a little hard to read in bed," he pointed out.

Risha's face fell. "That's the first thing you thought of doing in here?"

She looked like she was about to burst into tears, and Jace recognized too late that he'd said the wrong thing.

"Oh, Rish—I was kidding. It's all very . . . sexy. Very . . . romantic." He put his arms around her. "You're very sexy."

And then she was crying and Jace didn't know why. Could she have PMS, even though she didn't menstruate?

"Risha, come on, honey—don't cry! I haven't seen you all week, let's not—"

"It's not my fault you weren't here!" she sobbed into his chest. "And when you called, all you could talk about was your case and that damned Betamax! I wanted to do something special for you; it wasn't easy, getting this all together and ready by the time you—"

"I know, Rish." He patted her back. "You did a wonderful job on it. It is special, and I love you for doing it—"

"You don't! All you care about is your work! And having a reading light!"

She pushed away from him and stomped out, returning a minute later with the lamp that used to be on his side of the bed.

"Fine! Have it your way. Go to bed with this!" She shoved the lamp at him, then grabbed her robe and stormed off downstairs.

Jace heard the darkroom door slam shut. He sighed, then followed.

"Risha?" he called, knocking on the door. "Honey, come out. Don't let this spoil our weekend." There was a long silence. Jace tried the door, but it was locked. "Rish, you're being silly. C'mon—the bedroom looks terrific, and I want to make love to you there. Tonight. Right now. Rish?"

"Go away. I'm working."

Women.

Jace took his suitcase upstairs and dumped his clothes into the hamper. He took a quick shower (thank God she hadn't replaced it with a sauna!), shaved, and put on his silk boxers and robe in case Risha came to her senses. He went back downstairs and rolled a joint, but Risha was still closeted, so he returned to the bedroom to wait. He piled up the ornate pillows at the head of the bed, against one silk-draped wall, and plugged in his old reading lamp. He got out the new Jeanne Kalogridis novel and lit up the joint. Well, at least he'd closed his case.

Welcome home.

Jace thought Risha had built a fire without checking to see if the flue was open. Given her earlier mood, it seemed unlikely she would be fooling with the fireplace at 2 A.M., but the smell was getting stronger by the second. He put down his book and went out to the landing.

Black smoke filled the living room and billowed up the stairs. Jace could hear fire crackling, but not from the fireplace. It was coming from the rear of the house—in the direction of the darkroom! He took the stairs three at a time, unshod and clad only in his silk boxers.

"Risha!" he yelled frantically. "RISHA!"

The fire was fully engaged in the study—the couch and desk chair were aflame and two of the wooden bookcases had begun to catch; oppressive dark smoke poured off the shelves as hundreds of books smoldered and caught fire. Burning embers of paper floated toward the ceiling and carried fire to the drapes. The rolling case which had held all of Risha's photos was the dark center of a tower of flames spewing acrid black smoke to the ceiling.

Jace felt incredible heat as he frantically scanned the obscured room for Risha, unaware that much of his body hair singed off. Finally, reasonably certain she wasn't inside, he pulled the wooden door shut, trying to delay the fire's sweep into the hall. He charged through the smoke, barely able to see as he entered the kitchen's far door on the way toward the darkroom and Elliott's quarters.

"Risha! My God—where are you? RISHA!"

He passed through the kitchen, which was smoky but not yet burning, yelling her name, panicked that she hadn't responded. The noise was incredible: crackling and whooshing and the crashing of furniture—and perhaps, also, the study ceiling.

"Ri-sha-a!"

Then he heard her. "Jace!"

Her voice was coming from the back hallway! He rushed out of the kitchen and found her a few feet from the darkroom door.

"We've got to get out of here!" he yelled into her ear, as much from fear as to be heard over the chaos. "Back to the kitchen door!"

He turned toward the kitchen, then stopped abruptly. Risha couldn't have passed him, yet there she was, between him and kitchen, holding out her arms to him.

"Jace!" she screamed as smoke poured from under the door to the study behind her.

He stepped toward her, but was halted by a hand on his shoulder. He whipped his head around: Risha was still behind him! Was he hallucinating from the smoke? The woman behind him was tangible—he took her hand, pulling her toward the kitchen, toward the apparition . . .

. . . who grabbed his other hand, and felt just as real.

The swinging door between the kitchen and the study began to blister, and the smoke in the kitchen thickened. Only one of these women could be Risha, and Jace had to get her out. If they didn't get to the back door soon, escape in that direction would no longer be an option. He heard sirens far off.

He turned to the Risha behind him. "Make your fangs come out," he instructed her.

She hesitated, confusion on her face.

"Now!" he commanded. "Show me your fangs!"

She opened her mouth and her fangs extended.

"You're the right one. Come on!" He pulled her toward the kitchen.

"Don't leave me, Jace!" the other one yelled. "She's an impostor—look!"

Then she, too, opened her mouth and extended her fangs.

"Jesus," Jace muttered, "what the fuck is going on here?" He pulled both Rishas into the kitchen. "If we don't get out of here now, I'm never going to find out. Both of you—outside!"

He dropped their hands and yanked at the back door. It was locked. As he fumbled with the dead bolt, the door to the study gave way and flames shot out into the kitchen. One of the Rishas screamed. Jace turned. Both women were locked in combat, brandishing fangs, but one also had a large butcher knife in her hand.

Her right hand.

Risha was left-handed. Jace grabbed the one with the knife and pulled her off of the real Risha.

"Get out!" he screamed to his mate.

The woman he held slashed back at him with the knife, cutting open his side from armpit to hip. He released her as he fell in pain.

"Jace!" the real Risha screamed from the door as the impostor jumped on Jace, her knife raised over his face.

The smoke was so thick, Jace could see only about two feet off the floor. He twisted, knocking his assailant off-balance long enough to grab her wrist and disarm her, breaking the wrist. The sirens were getting closer.

He called out, "If you're still in here, Rish—go outside! I'll be OK!"

The impostor was still fighting, trying to claw Jace's eyes with her good hand, screaming with pain and anger. Then, right before his eyes, she changed.

The long dark auburn hair turned blond and retracted to a short length; the pale, almost colorless eyes turned a cold, bright blue; freckles speckled the suddenly upturned nose over pouty, snarling lips: Crysse Tanner!

Jace lost a beat, stunned, and Crysse leapt on him, her mouth abruptly filled with far too many razor-sharp teeth, better suited to a great white shark than the lithe, young woman attacking him. As he dodged her jaws, Crysse shifted again, her skin darkening as she became Hannah Williams, the nails on her good hand becoming talons which slashed at Jace, cutting open his brow.

Blood streamed into Jace's face, blinding his right eye as he fought for purchase against . . . Harris Powers, his youthful male body stronger than Hannah's had been. A delicate woman's hand still dangled from the broken wrist, but the talons of the other hand had been replaced by a massive fist, much larger than proportional to the body, which smashed into Jace's face.

Jace reeled for a moment from the blow, and when he regained his equilibrium, he was under someone he couldn't really make out because of the smoke and blood, but he could have sworn that the man assaulting him had three hands . . . two fully functioning. Jace pulled up his knee and got his leg between their bodies; planting his foot on the man's midsection, he shoved as hard as he could, and flung the three-armed William Tanner across the kitchen, toward the flaming study.

Jace was on his feet by the time the shapechanger regained its balance, the clothing on its back smoking. Screaming wordlessly, it launched itself at Jace again, shifting in midair. The head was grotesque, purple and lumpy, with huge, bulging eyes and voracious shark's mouth. The smoking cloth across its back split as the spine humped and poked out into dark, brontosaurus-like appendages, and the arms became as thick as Smithfield hams . . . and as short, which was a big mistake, as they were too awkward to keep Jace at bay.

Jace knew he had one thing over this monster, and as the fire engines screamed up to the front of the house, he used it: He sank his fangs into the creature's neck and pumped it full of venom. In moments, the shapechanger went limp. Whatever it was, it was no longer conscious. Jace threw its body into the inferno of the study, then ran out the back door.

"Jace! I thought you were dead!" Risha threw her arms around him, raining kisses all over his damaged face.

"Not that easy to kill me now, honey," he reminded her with a weary smile. "I have you to thank for that. Risha, I love you."

"Is anyone else inside?" a fireman yelled as they jumped off their trucks.

Jace shook his head.

"No one at all. Don't risk your lives in there."

21

"So William Tanner really didn't kill his wife, just as he claimed?" Risha asked.

She threw another half-burned book into the trash barrel, which sat in the middle of the charred study. A box near the doorway held the few dozen smoky volumes that the flames had spared, a tiny fraction of the library's contents only a few days earlier. Most of the house's damage had been confined to the ground floor rear—the study, the kitchen, and the south wall of the darkroom—though the smoke and water damage had been much more extensive. Jace, Risha, and Elliott were staying at the Century Plaza, coming home at night to sift through the ashes for anything salvagable.

"It had to have been Crysse—or whatever she was," Jace amended awkwardly, "so the reason witnesses saw William shoot Hannah was that . . . 'it' was wearing his . . . appearance. Shit, I don't even know what words to use to describe this case, much less come up with any proof that Tanner doesn't belong in prison. It galls me that I can't do anything about that."

"Shape-shifter," Elliott said absently, holding the charred corner of one of Risha's photographs—all that was left of the print. Sadly, he dropped it in the trash.

"What?"

" 'It' was a shape-shifter. The legend's been around since Homer, at least. Mostly shape-shifters were gods or sorcerers, but sometimes the odd hero would be born with the talent or acquire a talisman."

"Apparently, the odd actress, too," Jace observed. "Where'd you learn that?" he asked Elliott.

The older man shrugged. "Read it somewhere sometime."

Risha scratched her nose with the back of her hand, leaving a sooty streak that Jace found endearing. "What did you tell Reese Hamilton and Robert Brandon? You didn't explain that they were being blackmailed by an alien, did you?" she asked him.

"Oh, sure," Jace laughed, "right after I told them they'd fucked one! Besides, we don't know that Crysse was an alien; she could just have been some kind of weird aberration, a mutation or something—or had a talisman, like Elliott said. I mean, we're not exactly human, are we, even though we were both born on this planet. Anyway, I told Hamilton that the case was closed, and the extortionist would never bother him again. Brandon, I didn't even talk to—hell, he fired me; I don't owe him anything. He'll eventually figure out that the extortion has stopped. Meanwhile, let him sweat."

"We've still got his video," Elliott pointed out. He pried open a desk drawer with a screwdriver and pulled out a stack of papers that were unharmed, save for an inch of discoloration on the edge that had been against the front of the drawer.

"And the Betamax," Risha added. "We can see Brandon's 'screen tests.' "

"What do you want to do with this?" Elliott asked Jace, holding out a thick manila envelope, smoke-stained on the top edge. "It arrived for you the other day."

"I'll take it," Jace said quickly, shoving the still-unopened packet of reprints on impotence research under his stack of personal items. "Yeah, let's watch the Brandon video when we get back to the hotel."

"Maybe even send it back to him?" Risha suggested.

"Or blackmail him with it." Jace grinned. "Five grand a month is better pay than sleuthing, and our hotel ain't cheap." He wiped soot off his hands with a cloth that deposited as much as it removed. "I'm hungry. You wanna go feed?" he asked Risha.

"I could eat. And I'd really like to smell something that isn't burned. I'll just take a quick shower—"

"Make it a long one; I'll join you. Elliot, it's late. Why don't you go on back to the hotel, get some sleep?"

The older man shook his head. "I want to pack up the darkroom first."

Risha took a half-melted stapler out of Elliott's hand and pushed him toward the door. "It's not going anywhere. You can do it tomorrow. It'll be easier for you by daylight anyway."

Risha arched up to Jace's mouth, moaning. She'd already come twice, but Jace knew he could take her over the top again. He sucked lightly on her clitoris and she gasped. When he pushed fingers deep inside her, she squeezed them tightly, wetly, crying his name in pleasure/pain/ecstasy/orgasm. He would have joined her climax at that moment, had he been capable, but nevertheless took great pleasure in a very hot fuck. While she spasmed against him, he decided that as long as he could still turn a woman inside out like this, maybe his sex life wasn't as dead as he'd feared.

"Now I really am hungry," Risha said, smiling and stretching, catlike. "God, Jace, that was so-o-o good!"

"Mmm. Worked up an appetite myself. Where do you want to go?"

"Hollywood."

"Again? Jeez, we eat there all the time," Jace mock-whined.

"I want to pick up Greta," Risha explained, getting up and extending a hand to Jace.

"Greta? Is that a feeder?"

"No, dear—don't you remember? Crysse Tanner's boa constrictor?"

Jace stood. "You must be kidding!"

"I am not," she told him, walking into the bathroom and turning on the shower. "We can't just leave it in her apartment to starve!"

Jace couldn't believe that they were about to kill a human, but Risha was concerned about a dumb snake. He got into the shower with her and she put her arms around him, holding him close.

"All right," he sighed, giving in, "but don't expect me to feed it."

The next night, while Risha was out shooting photos for her *City of Angels* deadline, Jace stayed in their hotel suite reading the research material from the med library, the snake curled up next to him on the couch. He'd already eliminated all testosterone treatments as inappropriate for his specific condition, and reluctantly added implants—or any other methods requiring surgery—to his closed options. If a presurgical blood test didn't reveal his vampirism, healing instantly from an incision would certainly alert any doctor that the patient wasn't fully human. That hadn't left Jace much in the way of treatment for impotence, and he was almost sure that he was fighting a losing battle when he found it.

The article in a 1991 *Journal of Urology*, about a double-blind trial in Italy, held such promise for men suffering from impotence that Jace later wondered why it hadn't been splashed in headlines around the world. He read the three pages carefully several times, looking for a reason why it wouldn't work for him, why it couldn't be the miracle it appeared to be. ". . . increasing diameter, rigidity, and arterial flow of the penis. . . . long-term therapeutic agent for organic impotence . . ."

And the drug had already been approved by the FDA, albeit for a different purpose—it was available now!

Jace picked up the phone.

Half an hour later, Phil Bloom called from the lobby. "Come down. I don't want to come up because Robyn's waiting in the car."

When Jace saw his old friend's empty hands, his face fell. "You didn't bring it?"

"Man, I came hauling over here at 11 P.M.—pissing the hell out of my extremely pregnant wife, I might add—to bring you something you obviously have no need for—do you think I'd forget it?" He pulled a box out of his pocket. "Here's your Minoxidil. There are directions and three different kinds of applicators inside."

"I owe you, Phil, thanks!"

"If you're not going to explain why you suddenly need to start growing more hair in the middle of the night, you at least owe me sixty bucks, Levy."

Jace handed him three twenties. "I'll win it back at poker anyway."

"Not if Elliott's playing, too," Phil retorted. As he turned toward the door, he added, "The bottle has the name of my doctor if you want a refill."

Jace couldn't wait to find out if topically applied Rogaine did the same thing for vampires as it did for Italians.

Two hours later, he heard Risha open the door to their suite. He grinned in anticipation.

He was ready for her.

About the Author

SHERRY GOTTLIEB was a bookseller for nearly two decades—she owned A Change of Hobbit in Santa Monica, California, the oldest and largest speculative-fiction bookstore in the world. She is the author of *Hell No, We Won't Go! Resisting the Draft During the Vietnam War* (1991), which was a nominee for the PEN West USA Literary Award for nonfiction. Her first novel, *Love Bite* (1994), which also features Jace and Risha, was ostensibly the basis for the awful 1995 TV movie *Deadly Love* starring Susan Dey.

She lives in southern California.

www.wordservices.com